*Marilyn,*

*Enjoy!*

# Losing Cadence

Laura Lovett

*Laura*

*LOSING CADENCE*

*Copyright © 2016 Laura Lovett*

*Author Photographer: Rose Moyer,*
*www.littlelaughs.com*

*Cover Designer: Corey Brennan, ELEVATE Design,*
*www.elevate.design*

*Editor: Sheryl Khanna*

*iUniverse books may be ordered through booksellers or by contacting:*

*iUniverse*
*1663 Liberty Drive*
*Bloomington, IN 47403*
*www.iuniverse.com*
*1-800-Authors (1-800-288-4677)*

*Cover stock image provided by © iStock by Getty Images.*

*ISBN: 978-1-4917-8851-6 (sc)*
*ISBN: 978-1-4917-8852-3 (hc)*
*ISBN: 978-1-4917-8853-0 (e)*

*Library of Congress Control Number: 2016901496*

*Print information available on the last page.*

*iUniverse rev. date: 03/14/2016*

# Dedication

THIS NOVEL IS DEDICATED TO my husband, Scott, who has been my rock through the journey of life, family, career and somehow fitting a novel in there along the way.

# Acknowledgements

I WOULD LIKE TO THANK my Editor, Publicist and friend, Sheryl Khanna, whose enthusiasm and encouragement brought this novel back to life after several years of dormancy. Her edits have enriched my story and added further depth to my characters. I feel it was serendipitous that my path crossed with Sheryl's, for without her editorial and communications talents my book would not have taken on the life it has.

I would also like to thank my early readers, who gave me both encouragement and the constructive feedback and edits I needed to improve the many drafts of *Losing Cadence*. These readers include Robin Phillips, Cassy Weber, Denene Derksen, Kathleen Hambley, Sharon Barrett, Tarah Borkristl, Indra Singh, Melodie Becker, Shauna Sinclair, Scott Lovett, Susan Ponting, Terri Gilson and several others.

A special thank you is also in order for Corey Brennan of Elevate Graphic Design for the gift of the cover art. His artistic talent never ceases to amaze me.

Finally, I would like to thank my late father, John Barry Hambley, for inspiring my love of reading and writing, and passing on the creative genes that have made this story possible.

# Chapter One

"WE'RE HOME, MY LOVE." THE husky voice seemed distant, yet vaguely familiar. I heard only faint sounds amidst the dark fog that swirled around in my mind. I didn't know where I was, as my eyes remained clamped shut. My body felt limp and desperately weak. I tried to pull my heavy eyelids apart, but to no avail. I willed my mouth to open, to utter a sound. Nothing. My tongue was heavy in my mouth. Everything was black. I'm going to be sick, I thought.

"My love, the love of my life, my Cadence," uttered a deep male voice in my ear. "I'm going to carry you, my love." I felt warm arms around me, lifting me out into the rain. I shivered fiercely from the bitter cold. Was it night? There was no light through my closed eyelids. I tried again to open my mouth, to ask where I was, but the words would not form. Who was he?

My nausea materialized into violent vomiting. I could feel the man's strong arms holding me up, bracing me. My body heaved and convulsed, and I felt as though I was breaking into pieces. "It's okay, darling, you'll feel better soon," said the deep voice over and over as I heaved for what felt like an eternity. Then everything went black again.

*****

I woke up slowly, sensing that I was tucked into a soft bed. This time my eyes were able to open a fraction. Shapes swam before my eyes, the images vague and blurry. I could see white all around me: white bed, white walls, white door. I tried to move, but my body refused to cooperate. I knew, somewhere in the back of my mind, that I was heavily drugged.

The white around me gave the sensation of being outside in a snow storm. A memory flashed back to me from childhood, of making snow angels in the deep, pillowy layers of freshly fallen snow. My eyes slowly scanned the blurry room and narrowed in on something that was not white, it was black. A camera mounted in the corner of the room, high up near the ceiling, its lens focusing down on me, on my every movement. A watchful eye staring into a room of white, focusing on a drugged woman who couldn't move. Where on earth was I? Then the door slowly opened.

"Hello, Miss Weaverly," whispered a woman's voice with a slight accent that sounded Spanish. "Welcome home. I saw that you were waking up, so I came to check on you. How are you feeling?" I couldn't make out her features, but could see that she was wearing white and her hair was dark.

"H…h…he…" I tried to make out a word, hello or help, which turned out to be of little consequence as I couldn't speak.

"Don't try to speak. Just get some sleep and you'll feel much better tomorrow." She came beside my bed and I felt a glass touch my lips. The stream of smooth, cool water cascaded down my parched throat. The mere act of drinking water exhausted me, so I fell back asleep. I dreamed about playing my flute on a hilltop and standing on the deck of my childhood home, making beautiful songs through my instrument as the birds sang along with me.

The next dream that floated into my mind was about my family. I dreamed about my mom, dad, sister and brother, all around the dinner table. Outside it was snowing heavily, a blizzard of white. I ran out onto the deck and looked up into the white abyss of the sky. I felt the snow falling on my face, caressing me gently with thick flakes of cool white cotton. This dream continued until I crossed the border between sleep and wakefulness, and opened my eyes to see two green ones starting back at me intensely. My body began to shake with fear.

"Cadence, my love, we're finally together. This is the happiest day of my life," he said quietly, only inches away from my ear. He was so close that I could smell the warm scent of mint on his breath. "You look so beautiful, Cadence, so peaceful, and now you're finally *home*."

The recognition came slowly, but once it fully hit, I froze in terror. This must be a dream. I opened my mouth to scream, but only a fearful whisper came out. "R…R…Rich…ard?"

"Yes, my love?"

"Wh…Wh…Why?" I tried to ask my question. Why on earth was I here? Was this a dream? This couldn't be real. I had dated Richard in high school for a few months. This didn't make *any* sense. It had been ten years since I had seen or heard of him!

"Shhh, my love, we'll have plenty of time to talk later. I want you to get some more rest now. You had a long night and were very ill. I'm just going to sit here and watch over you while you sleep. Oh, how I love you, more than *anything* in the world. I've waited so long for this moment!" He heaved a long, fulfilled sigh as his large, warm hand stroked my hair, my face. He traced the line of my lips. I wanted to bite, to scream, but my body fell back into the comfort of sleep, dreams and denial.

# Chapter Two

"WHAT IS YOUR MOST IMPORTANT future goal?" This was a difficult question to ask a group of seventeen- and eighteen-year-olds. We all sat with pens in hand, staring at the question we were completing for the yearbook committee. I couldn't think of an answer off the top of my head. Graduation was coming and, like most grade twelve girls, my main focus was on prom night. Although I had started planning my career, the distant future was the last thing on my mind as I anticipated prom night and dreamed about what it would be like to go away to college.

"Cadence, isn't this ridiculous?" whispered my best friend, Danielle. "Why does the yearbook committee ask these questions? The answers are going to be beside our pictures forever! What if we don't know what our goals are? Once we start college we can worry about all that. Now's the time to let loose, have fun and enjoy the last time in our lives without major responsibilities." Danielle didn't like talking about her future career, because she didn't have a clue what it might be. For her, it was an anxiety-provoking topic of conversation. Danielle's parents were frustrated by her lack of a career decision, with any conversation on the topic ending in a screaming match and tears. Danielle's main focus was on having fun, and doing well enough academically so that she could attend a decent college and get away from her parents.

"Yep," I said. "But it'll be funny to see these in the future, you know, see what happened to all of our friends and to actually find out if any of us meet our goals or if we end up doing something totally different," I whispered back, with a smile.

We were from a mid-size high school in Mountain View, Montana. Mountain View was a small, quiet city nestled among rolling hills and framed by the nearby mountains. Those of us going out of state to college were excited about leaving Montana, at least for a while, and experiencing a new state. I was thrilled to be going to The Julliard School to pursue my flute playing. New York would be an amazing place to live for a few years and so different from my sleepy hometown. I had played the flute for as long as I could remember, since age seven to be exact. I was truly passionate about my instrument and excelled at it, winning many state music competitions. I practiced for hours every day, but never thought I would achieve this level of success. I won a scholarship to attend The Julliard School, and was bursting with excitement ever since I found out. Getting away from my parents, who were annoying these days, would be wonderful but scary. I loved them, but they always questioned where I was going and who I was with. It would be good to get away and be free.

I started writing. The limit was two sentences given the space constraints of the typical high school yearbook. I wrote that my goal was to: *Record at least five CDs, be a well-known soloist and live on an acreage in Montana. I also want to have a happy family, with at least three children.* I smiled to myself, envisioning a house in the countryside with large windows overlooking the mountains, and beautiful rolling hills with deer wandering around my property. I imagined my kids playing in a lush green yard and a husband, although *not* my current boyfriend.

Richard and I had been dating for a couple of months, and would definitely be going our separate ways before he went back to Harvard and I went to Julliard. It was all for the best, I kept telling myself. We got along well and had some good times, but I could *not* see him as a long-term boyfriend. His intensity and peculiarity, which had originally intrigued me, were now becoming unnerving. He was so serious and focused, and always seemed to be thinking and analyzing. And when he stared at me, it was as if he was trying to read my every thought, which unsettled me. He had no idea that I felt this way, and was intent on us having a long-distance relationship.

Richard was three years older than me. He was the only child of an extremely wealthy family, having moved to Mountain View from Boston five years ago. He described his parents, Alexander and Constance White, as different and reclusive. They only had acquaintances and were extremely private people, which explained why Richard had no close friends. When I asked Richard about his home life as a kid, he would shake his head and say, "Don't go there, Cadence." Being naturally curious, I tried to ask him in different ways about what his parents were like, and about his friends, but he always cut me off and changed the subject. I felt like I didn't know much about Richard at all. In contrast, I was very open about my childhood and answered all his questions about my life. He was keenly interested in everything about me, but it felt awkward as it was so one-sided.

When Richard was sixteen, his father died suddenly from a brain aneurism. His mother, reeling from the loss, returned to her hometown of Mountain View to grieve, bringing her reluctant son with her. Heartbreakingly, just after Richard graduated from high school, his mother was diagnosed with breast cancer and prescribed a course of chemotherapy. He postponed going to college to look after her. The following year his mother seemed to be on the mend, so he made the decision to enter the Harvard School of Business, following in his father's footsteps. But misfortune struck again, and midway through the year he found out that the cancer had spread to his mother's brain, and that her prognosis was grim. He finished out the semester and rushed back to be with her.

Although he wouldn't talk about his relationship with his mother, it was clear that Richard was fiercely loyal and compelled to be with her when she needed him the most. During these months she became progressively worse and began losing her memory. She opted to have live-in home care, and although Richard considered returning to Harvard, he dismissed the idea and chose to stay home and support his mother.

What had drawn me to this quiet, intense guy was the compassion he demonstrated. I found his kindness and dedication to his mother sweet, and was intrigued by the idea of getting to know him. Richard was passionate and unique. Maybe it was his drive, or his intense focus on everything he did. It was difficult to pinpoint, but the energy was strong when he was around.

Richard was a very good-looking guy. He was six foot two, and had been quite athletic growing up. He never played team sports, preferring solitary pursuits like long-distance running and swimming. He was competitive and won many races. Since the age of sixteen he was dedicated to waking up at 5:00 a.m. so he could work out for two hours before school, a habit which he stuck to even now. He had also attained a black belt in karate, which he had practiced religiously in the evenings when he was in high school. Richard had impeccable posture and emanated a very high level of energy, which added to the intensity of his personality. He was very careful about what he ate, being unusually regimented about his health for a guy his age. He never ate junk food, saying that he needed to feed his brain and body in a way that would allow him to attain all of his goals. I found this very anal and extreme.

In addition to his very fit body, Richard had thick, blond hair and gorgeous deep green eyes, and was not without his share of admiring glances from other women when we went on dates. Richard was also incredibly smart, an "A" student, excelling in his first year at the Harvard School of Business. I remembered reading his high school yearbook goal from three years earlier, which was to: *Achieve billionaire status by the time I'm thirty-five.*

In addition to being handsome, Richard was definitely the most driven person I knew, and at twenty-one already had his life mapped out. On one of our earlier dates he explained how he wanted a family. "Cadence, they will be raised in an incredible house, even bigger than where I grew up. I want to give them all their heart's desires. And whoever I marry will be the happiest woman alive," he said, as he stared intensely into my eyes. "My love and passion will never taper off in my marriage, like what seems to happen in most. I will be with my wife forever," he stated. The tone of his voice made me uneasy, so I changed the subject to something lighter. My mindset was definitely not that far ahead into the future, and he acted like he was much older than he really was.

In fact, these types of awkward conversations continued to happen, almost to the point where Richard was becoming obsessive about planning his future. I recalled my older sister, Sandra, telling me about a new man in her life who had begun texting her every few minutes, up to a hundred times a day. "He's outta here," she confided in me, hazel eyes flashing, just before breaking it off with him via text. "I'm so *not* into obsessive behavior." I was beginning to feel Richard was obsessive in his own ways too.

Did I think Richard would be as successful as he dreamed of? Yes. But I couldn't see myself as part of his perfectly executed world. It was not that he didn't treat me well, he treated me wonderfully. He was the utmost gentleman with impeccable manners, to the point of seeming old-fashioned. But while these things unsettled me, I liked that he was very romantic, doing the types of things you'd only read about in books: surprise dates, romantic sunset picnics, fresh flowers and chocolates, the list went on.

We met in the strangest of circumstances. I was practicing for my Julliard audition, feeling the stress and pressure I'd placed on myself to get accepted. I practiced my heart out every spare minute I had. Some days, when the spring weather warranted, I'd walk into the hills near my family's acreage and practice outside. One day I walked particularly far, about twenty minutes into the surrounding hills. I had my pieces memorized and began to play. I closed my eyes, felt the breeze lifting my long, auburn hair, and lost myself in the world of tones, intervals and phrases.

When I opened my eyes, several minutes later, I saw a man sitting in the distance on the slope of a nearby hill. I was startled. Our eyes met and he stared intently at me for what felt like forever. I stopped playing and stood there awkwardly, wondering who he was. "That was beautiful!" he shouted. I was embarrassed about being watched in an area where there was seldom another soul, but at the same time I was flattered and intrigued.

"Thanks," I shouted back, and immediately began to disassemble my flute. As I carefully pulled out the head joint, I noticed him stand up and ease into a walk, which turned into a quicker stride as he saw that I was packing up. Within a minute he reached me. I'd hastily cleaned and put away my flute by that time.

"That was exceptional! I'm Richard, Richard White," he smiled as he reached for my hand. His handshake was firm and confident, and I couldn't help but notice how soft, yet large and strong, his hand was. He stood at least eight inches taller than me.

"My name's Cadence," I said awkwardly. Although I had a couple of boyfriends in high school, I still succumbed to shyness around guys I didn't know.

"That name suits you. You have a finality about you, like a cadence at the end of a song. I used to play piano and remember the sheer force of a cadence denoting the final bar. The end."

I stared back, a little confused at this odd, first-time comparison of me to finality. "What do you mean?" I asked, noticing how perfect his teeth were; they were gleaming white, framed by full lips. He was hot and possessed all of the characteristics that made the "top ten list" used by high school girls everywhere when assessing a guy for dating potential. I fleetingly wondered what it would be like to kiss him.

"Well, it just feels like I've been walking aimlessly all morning and when I heard your first note, I *knew* that I'd found what I was looking for," he calmly stated. Seeing my apprehension at this strange explanation, he continued with, "I was searching for some peace and quiet after a challenging night. My mother has cancer and it has spread to her brain. I cannot imagine losing her, yet the situation continues to worsen," his voice trailed off. His green eyes were glassy and I could tell that he was nervous about divulging his sad, personal situation to me so quickly.

"I'm *so* sorry to hear that. Your poor mother and poor you. Your family must be going through so much." I spoke awkwardly, trying to find the proper amount of empathy and compassion to convey my sympathy in a genuine way to a virtual stranger.

"Well, I don't really have any other family. I'm an only child. We have relatives scattered in a few different states, but have not been in contact with them for years. My parents have always been very private people who didn't want family involved in their affairs. I was close to my grandparents though, but they've all passed away." He looked up at the sky, then back down at me. He talks like a robot, I thought, so formal compared to other guys I knew. His eyes, though, were the deepest color of green I'd ever seen, and drew me away from my mental criticisms. They were the same dark hunter green as the trees around us. They looked sharply down at me. I was suddenly conscious of how I was dressed. I was wearing faded jeans and a simple light blue, V-neck T-shirt. My hair was gathered at the top with a clip. I didn't have any makeup on at the time, but luckily I was blessed with dark eyelashes, so mascara wasn't a must.

"It must be really tough… I can't imagine what you must be going through," I murmured.

"I already lost my father. Almost four years ago now, which was why we moved back here," Richard explained. "My mother grew up here and wanted to move back, even though she no longer has family here. She's a private person who likes the familiar solitude of being near the mountains. I was *not* happy about moving here, though. I didn't want to leave my high school in Boston, not that I really cared about any of the other students as they weren't very bright. I guess I just prefer a big city, which is more stimulating than being out here. Not that I have anything against Montana, it is beautiful here. I just had no interest in making friends with these people, so pretty much kept to myself my last year of high school." He looked down at me, head cocked, with fresh interest. "Everything happens for a reason, or so they say," he mused.

I was shocked that he so casually and confidently spoke about not making a single friend. And he seemed judgmental and somewhat arrogant, yet was also intriguing. My curiosity was definitely piqued.

"So you went to Mountain View High?" I'd never seen or heard of him. I was definitely going to check Sandra's yearbook when I got home and see if I could find his photo.

"Yes, but I'd rather not think of it, though. It was a necessary step, but I was an intentional loner. Everyone had already established their networks of friends and I had no interest in becoming a part of that crowd, so I kept to myself. Everyone here seems to have grown up together, practically since conception. How can I compete with friendship since infancy?" he asked, a playful sarcasm etching his deep voice.

"At least you only had one year left. It's actually a fun school, but I can see what you mean about everyone growing up together." I found it odd that he hadn't made *any* friends, though. People were generally welcoming to newcomers if they made any type of effort. Clearly Richard had no interest in having a social life, which I couldn't relate to. I was still drawn to him out of interest and curiosity, though, and also because he was hot. The butterflies felt the same as other crushes I'd had in the past. He was very attractive; his amazing looks definitely making up for his odd behavior.

He changed the topic. "How long have you been playing?"

"Almost eleven years," I answered. I was humble about my musical ability, not wanting to mention the many competitions I had won and where I was going to college. Besides, too much information too soon was not my strategy to catch a guy's interest. Playing hard to get was the way to go in my books, wisdom passed on from my mom, I knew, but just the same, she sometimes had a valid point.

"Wow. You're remarkable, Cadence. I can sense that this is not just a hobby, but a true passion. I bet you're going to make a career of it. A successful one," he stated with conviction. I sensed that he spoke honestly. He didn't seem to be trying to butter me up, but truly understood my passion.

"Thanks. Yes, I want to become a professional; a soloist or maybe play in an orchestra, or both."

"Fantastic. I *know* you will succeed, Cadence," he smiled. "Can I walk you home?"

"Sure," I said, glad for his offer.

As we walked, we found a lot to talk about during the twenty minutes it took to reach my house. The walk culminated in him asking me on a date for the coming weekend. Part of me thought he was too strange, but the other part was excited as he was very attractive. My girlfriends would be so jealous and fascinated to hear about this guy who was so out of the ordinary and so extremely handsome. An image of going to prom with such a hot guy entered my mind, making my heart race with excitement. After saying good-bye, I hurried into my house, wondering where my sister kept her old yearbooks.

# Chapter Three

THE FEELING OF BEING TOUCHED awakened me. This time my eyes were easier to open, and I felt less drugged. It was the woman again, her black hair pulled back into a long, shiny ponytail. She wore a white, short-sleeved blouse and a long, dark-blue skirt, with a white apron. She was fairly attractive, and looked very clean. I could smell a soapy fragrance around her. She had placed a tray beside the bed on a stand of some sort, and was carefully laying a napkin across my lap.

"Good morning, Miss Weaverly," she said, in a Spanish accent. She reminded me of the friendly chambermaid who cleaned our hotel room daily when Christian and I were in Mexico on vacation last year. I felt tears sting my eyes as I thought of Christian. "Did you sleep well?" She had dark eyes and a friendly, although somewhat sad, face.

"Yes. Where am I and who are you?" Now that words could form, my questions came out quick and bold. She looked nervous.

"My name is Maria and I work here, for you and Mr. White. I serve and clean, and do whatever is needed," she carefully explained.

"Help me!" I said with fervor. "I've been *kidnapped*. I did *not* come here freely. I was drugged and taken from my apartment in San Francisco. Where am I?" I felt tears well up in my eyes. The urgency of my voice made Maria step back, a worried look marring her pretty, dark features.

"You seem confused. I'll go get Mr. White," she said, as she began to step around the bed towards the door. I flung myself out of the bed, not realizing that my legs were still wobbly, stumbled and landed heavily on the floor. She rushed back towards me and knelt down. "Are you hurt? Please don't do that. Mr. White said you might try to run, but that you don't mean to. I know you're not well. Please...don't be upset." She was quivering, nervous about my reaction. My leg throbbed from the fall, but I was more concerned about my life. This could only be a nightmare. I couldn't be in Richard White's house. Nothing made sense. I was only a kid when we'd dated!

"Please, Maria. I'm okay, I'm *not* crazy! Why am I here?" I asked as I grabbed her arm, more forcefully than intended. She pulled away and stood up quickly, then ran towards the door.

"He will be here *very* soon," she promised, as she closed the door solidly behind her. The tears were running freely down my cheeks as I crawled towards the door and slowly stood up to turn the knob. It would not open, it was locked. I felt an icy feeling in my gut as the severity of my situation became more apparent. I pounded on the door over and over again until my hands ached. Minutes later the knob turned.

The door slowly opened. When he saw that I was in the way, Richard gently stuck his head through the crack and said, "Cadence, my love, I know you're not feeling well. Please, don't do this. I love you. Now move away from the door so I can come in," he said, in a calm voice. I moved aside so he could enter, and stood up to confront him. My head barely came to his shoulder, and I felt off balance.

"What's going on, Richard? I don't know how I got here, but I want to go home," I begged, as tears ran down my face. I stared up at him, shaking violently, my eyes pleading that he release me from this insanity. It was like going back in time, staring at my old boyfriend, now ten years older; he looked more mature and stressed, yet equally as handsome.

He looked down at me calmly and lovingly. He was acting like we were a married couple having a fight, like he was frustrated but loved me no matter what. This was ridiculous! Insane! "Cadence, this *is* your home. This is the home I built for us. It has everything you will ever need or want. Our life is here, and I have so much love to offer you. I promise I will make you happy," he whispered, his deep voice earnest as he bent down to embrace me. My knee instinctively shot up and hit him square in the groin. He let out a howl and turned around, hands clutched between his legs as he tried to regain his composure.

"You crazy bastard! What's going on? I don't want to *live* here. I have a life, a fiancé I love. I have my family and a job. I haven't seen you in *ten years*. We were kids, Richard, *kids!* Let me out of here!" I screamed, and then fell to the floor sobbing. He was still turned away. I knelt by his legs, switching from anger to begging. It reminded me of the helplessness of being a little girl, kneeling beside my dad when he was leaving for a business trip, begging him not to go. But in this case, all I wanted was to leave and never see this man again. "Please, Richard," I begged, "let me go. You don't even know me anymore! I *won't* make you happy." He still didn't turn around. Instead, his broad back began to shake.

"I love you!" he yelled. "You are *mine*, Cadence. You *will* love me. It exists inside of you and just has to be unleashed. I *knew* you would be upset. It will take you a while to adjust, maybe even months. I *knew* what was best for us, for you. I did it for the love that we built together; it will grow and be nourished here. I will love you like no other man could ever love a woman. Just remember that, Cadence. The love you will experience in the years to come will overwhelm you. You will live with such passion and intensity that you will wonder why a life without me was ever an option." He slowly turned around and bent down to embrace me. I was too weak to fight, and sobbing too hard to speak. All that would come out was a whisper.

"Please, take me home. I won't tell anyone. Please…"

"I *love* you. And you…you will grow to understand your love for me."

"Bullshit!" I screamed, with renewed intensity. "I'm not your partner and I'm not your bloody *possession*."

He didn't reply; instead he kissed me on the top of my head and said that I needed to rest. I knew then that this situation was more insane and dangerous than my worst nightmares. He scooped me up with ease and walked over to the bed, placing me down carefully and tucking me in. Another kiss on the head and he turned and left, with yet another sickening declaration of love. I cried uncontrollably, face pressed into the pillow, praying to God to help me. After what seemed like hours, I fell back asleep, exhausted from sobbing.

# Chapter Four

My first date with Richard was a private, romantic dinner at the lovely Mountain Peaks Lodge on the outskirts of town. It was the most expensive restaurant in town, so young couples rarely went there on dates. It was the type of place my parents would go to celebrate their anniversary.

Richard had planned a four course meal along with a game of questions to try and guess facts about each other. Some of the questions went deeper than I expected, like: "What is your biggest fear in life?" "What is a regret you have so far in your life?" and "What three things do you think of when you describe your soulmate?" I fumbled for the right answers, not wanting to reveal everything about myself, yet also being honest. I could tell he had thought about his answers and was curious about my every word.

"Cadence, you amaze me," he said, while staring at me as we ate crème brûlée for dessert.

"Why is that?" I asked, shyly.

"You are so pure and optimistic, like a clean slate that has yet to be written on by the cynical ink of the world," he explained.

"That's very poetic, Richard. I think the world is exciting. I know there's lots of nastiness and things to worry about, but I think most people are good. The good definitely outweighs the bad."

"Hmm. I wish that were the case," he said. "You think so highly of the human race, yet, from what I've seen, very few people are decent.

But that's what intrigues me about you, Cadence. You're so innocent and pure. I wish I could keep you like this forever," he said wistfully.

I didn't know what to say. I felt like I couldn't begin to understand this guy sitting across from me at this candlelit table, the light catching his radiant green eyes as they stared intensely into mine. I knew then that this was not just a high school flirtation from his perspective, but something that went much deeper. His intensity and views of the world made me nervous, but it was also exciting sitting across from this good looking and very intelligent guy. I was flattered that he was so interested in me. He made me feel special, like I was older and more experienced than I really was. But despite the date being unique and interesting, I couldn't help but feel that Richard White was very odd. It wasn't only the unusual comments he made about life and the world, but the intensity with which he did so. It was also the way he stared at me, sometimes not saying a word. He was very much a loner, not mentioning any friends from college. I decided to put aside his strange behavior for now, writing it off as being unique and intellectual; he was definitely more interesting and intriguing than guys my own age, plus he was *very* attractive.

It was at the end of our second date, which finished with a moonlit walk, when he kissed me for the first time. We were standing awkwardly near the fence of my parents' property, far enough away that we were shrouded in darkness, unscathed by the lights shining from my house. "I had a truly memorable evening, Cadence," he stated.

"I did too, Richard." He then leaned down and I stood on my tiptoes to kiss him. His lips were full and sweet. The kiss was not deep, but sensual. It lasted for only a couple of seconds before we parted, and then he hugged me tightly. A few seconds later he scooped my hand into his and walked me to my door like a true gentleman.

Throughout the next month Richard was romantic and considerate, and planned the most amazing dates. One of these was a helicopter ride over Montana's spectacular mountain scenery, where we were dropped off for a picnic beside a secluded lake. Richard had prepared a gourmet picnic with some of my favorite foods: smoked salmon and chocolate caramel brownies.

"I wish we could stay here forever, Cadence," he said, as he held my hand and stared at the water. "Just build a home here and not have to deal with anyone else. Have food flown in, watch the sun rise and set together…"

"It's beautiful and I can't thank you enough for bringing me here, Richard," I'd quickly interrupted to avoid the subject of living here. It was all too far-fetched to think about. I felt a mix of excitement and awe, along with an anxious feeling of something not being quite right.

My girlfriends were envious, always asking for details and curious to meet Richard. He loved to go on picnics, as they meant total privacy; he didn't like running into people and having to make small talk. Most weekends, when the weather was nice, he would take me for surprise picnics in the countryside, and open baskets full of homemade sandwiches and desserts, which he prepared himself. But despite his good looks, intelligence and charm, something made me begin to question whether I should continue our relationship. I couldn't put my finger on it, but it had to do with his odd behavior and ideas. He seemed to have a very detailed plan for his life, and was arrogantly sure of the millions that he would make and subsequently turn into billions. I was also increasingly bothered by the intensity of his gaze and the uneasy feeling it gave me.

As the weeks went on he acted more and more bizarre. His mood would change suddenly and he'd become very quiet and withdrawn, almost as if in another world; then he'd act like nothing happened. I chalked up most of his behavior to the fact that his mother was very ill and the stress was taking its toll on him. When I asked if I could meet his mother, my request was met with a cursory refusal. "Mother is too ill for visitors right now," he explained, "and besides, she has always been a very private person." He implied that regardless of whether she was sick, I simply wasn't welcome, which struck me as very strange. I wondered if she wasn't interested in meeting me or if Richard didn't want us to meet? Either way, it was for the best, as the furthest thing from my mind was taking on a serious relationship. My main focus was on going away to college and succeeding in a very challenging program at The Julliard School. Yet there was definitely chemistry between us, and I enjoyed the excitement of having a new boyfriend, for the time being.

About two months into dating, Richard really shocked me. We were sitting on a hillside near where we'd met. We were kissing and his hand slid up my shirt. Soon things intensified and he pulled my shirt off so all that was left was my mauve-colored bra. I unbuttoned his shirt and pulled it off as we continued to kiss, feeling the warmth of his muscular chest against me. Our kissing became more passionate, and we were both breathing heavily as he unfastened my bra and pulled me tight to him. I didn't want to go all the way, as I was still a virgin and scared of becoming pregnant.

Ever since my older sister had missed a period in her sophomore year and confided her terror in me, I had been extremely worried about an accidental pregnancy. Even after Sandra found out she wasn't pregnant, I remained firm in my vow to avoid that type of scare. But before I could pull away, he abruptly stopped and stood up, walking briskly away for about twenty paces. I opened my mouth to ask what was wrong but was speechless. I couldn't believe it; a guy walking away in the middle of *making out*! Plus, he didn't know I was going to stop things. I was confused and felt rejected. My heart was racing as I sat there, and my cheeks were burning with embarrassment. He stood still, with his back to me for a few minutes. I fumbled to pull on my bra and shirt. My heart rate slightly decreased by the time he turned around and walked back. He stood directly in front of me staring down into my eyes, cleared his throat and began an emotional explanation.

"Cadence, I respect you more than *anything*. If I had not stood up, I would have been unable to stop and we would have made love right here, and I couldn't do that to you. Our first time has to be *perfect* and I have to be sure that you're ready to commit your love to me."

I must have looked stunned, as I was certainly taken off guard by the whole incident. He continued, "I'm falling in love with you, Cadence." I trembled with shock. We had only been dating for two months. "I know this sounds like a cliché, but I've never felt this way about *anyone*. This feeling is uncontrollable. I want you more than I have ever wanted anyone or anything," he slowly explained, trying to find the right words to capture his strong feelings.

"Richard...I really like you too, but we hardly know each other. Let's not move too fast," I responded.

"You're right. I want to make you comfortable. I *need* to make you happy. So whatever pace you prefer is *fine* with me. I just had to walk away or it would have gone too far, too soon."

"I appreciate that, Richard," I said, and slowly stood up so I could face him squarely. I felt a mix of attraction and concern as I stared up at him. Before we knew it we were kissing once again, but this time we remained standing, and although we both wanted more, he was careful not to move beyond soft, prolonged kisses.

# Chapter Five

I WOKE UP SLOWLY FROM a nightmare. I dreamed that I'd been abducted and trapped in a strange place. The fact that this was not merely a dream struck me painfully. This time when I woke up, Richard was sitting in the corner of the room, studying me intently. A smile crept over his face, a look of anticipation, almost like a child ready to show his parents something he'd made at preschool.

"Cadence, I'm so glad you're awake; you slept for ten hours. You needed your rest, though. I know I need to be patient, but I'm excited to begin our life together!"

I felt the tears welling up, and forced myself not to cry again; I became angry instead. "Richard," I mimicked sarcastically, "I'm so glad you kidnapped me. I know I need to be patient, and try not to press felony charges immediately. I think I'll wait a day!" I glared at him and continued, "You must be on drugs to think you can get away with this." Rather than becoming angry, he was on the bed in an instant, arms firmly embracing me, hands stroking my long, auburn hair.

"Sweetheart, don't be upset! I love you *so* much. You will grow to love this place, and to understand your love for me. I know this is a shock and it will just take time to adjust," he logically explained, as if talking to a little child.

My body instinctively stiffened at his touch. I stared up into his eyes and pleaded, "Please, *please* let me go. Love works two ways, and I *know* I don't love you. I'm in love with my fiancé. Please…I'll do *anything* if you let me go. I just want to go home, Richard," I sobbed. I could see the pain etched all over his face like crystals of frost glazing a window on a cold, winter morning. But he just shook his head and continued to console me, explaining that this was what he expected and there was nothing to be worried about.

What the hell had I been thrown into? How long had I been here? Was it two days? Three? I could still remember the last evening in my San Francisco apartment, before everything went black.

I loved San Francisco and lived in the trendy Mission District on a lovely, tree-lined street. My second floor apartment was bright and airy. The main living area was decorated in pale blue tones with photos of my favorite musicians. My bedroom had many photos of Christian, my friends and family. Beyond that I had a small kitchen and bathroom.

I was practicing in my living room at about eight in the evening, exhausted from a late concert the night before. I'd recently won a position in the San Francisco Symphony, which was almost unheard of for a flautist my age. The positions came up so rarely that it was an unforeseen gift, combining luck and talent, which led me to achieve the honor of playing flute for such a fantastic orchestra.

When I finished practicing, I talked on the phone with my fiancé, Christian. We were going over some of our wedding plans, and brainstorming about some options for our honeymoon. We talked every day, and although it didn't come close to being together, it helped fill the void a little to hear his voice. Many days we would also FaceTime or Skype so we could see one another, but sometimes I found that tougher as I wanted so badly to touch him.

Christian was a cellist who played for the New York Philharmonic. We were very much in love, and facing the struggle that confronts most couples who play professionally for a living, which was trying to get jobs in the same city. Our plan was to get married the following year, and in the meantime spend as many weekends together as possible. During that time we were hoping that a position might open up in either of our orchestras, but we would also consider auditions in other cities. If nothing came up in a year, one of us would quit our position to move to the other's city and focus on a soloist or teaching career. A longer term dream was to move back to Montana, and start a music school there, while still focusing on our careers as soloists. We both loved the outdoors and agreed that Montana would be more ideal than San Francisco or New York for raising our family.

After talking with Christian that night, I fell asleep on the sofa. My intention was to rest there for a few minutes before moving to my bedroom. The move never happened, as I was out like a light as soon as my head hit the soft cushions. The next thing I remember was waking up to someone covering my mouth with a large, sweaty hand. I remember a short struggle, the tiny hot sting of a needle, and the intense fear that ripped through my veins just before the drug did. Those were my last terrifying memories before my first realization of being here with Richard.

My curiosity got the best of me, and I engaged Richard in conversation again. "Was that you, Richard? Did you pull me from my apartment or send somebody to abduct me?" I demanded.

"Darling, why go there? The details don't matter. We don't want to relive that experience, especially not now that we are finally here to begin our life together. What's most important is our love for each other," he explained.

"What do you mean *life together?*" I screamed. "Richard, I'm engaged. I love my fiancé, Christian, and I have a career I've worked so hard for. Remember how much you encouraged me to play professionally? Now I have my dream job and I can't risk losing it." Although aware that Richard most likely didn't give a damn about my career, I forged ahead anyway, grasping at straws and willing my voice not to become angry. "Please, *please* let me go!"

"Darling Cadence, *please* don't get all wound up. God, I've missed your beautiful, pale blue eyes," he sighed. "I know you have feelings for that man but they will fade in time, and your anger and resentment towards me will pass. Soon you will feel what I'm feeling. Your true emotions are merely buried beneath the surface," he explained.

"But, Richard, I don't—"

"God, you're so beautiful!" he interrupted, suppressing my arguments. "Your blue eyes are so crystal clear and your lips, your soft lovely lips. You grow lovelier every minute!" Richard exclaimed, almost like seeing me for the first time. He was psychotic, I realized with a sickening feeling. I had to escape, but first I had to know where the hell I was, and what I was up against. Richard didn't seem violent, but who knows what he would do if provoked.

I missed Christian immensely. I imagined his soft brown eyes twinkling as he played his cello so lovingly, and his curly brown hair smelling fresh and feeling soft in my hands. Surely he would be searching for me by now, along with my family, who would all be very worried. It was only a matter of time before I'd be found. Hopefully Richard left some sort of evidence in my apartment that would lead investigators to this place.

Be logical and get a grip, I thought to myself. I remembered seeing kidnapping victims on the news, and wildly searched my memory for any tips and advice they had given, like: *Play along with it for a bit and maybe you can learn more about your surroundings.* "Where are we, Richard?" I asked, yet again, trying to remain calm.

He smiled down at me, relieved that I was not yelling or crying. "We're home, in *our* home, Cadence. Would you like a tour?"

"Yes," I simply replied.

"I'll have Maria come up with some food and help you freshen up, and then I'll give you the grand tour. This is the day I have been waiting for, my love." Richard slowly stood, and kissed me on the cheek, before leaving the room and closing the door. I felt sick again, but all I could do was dry heave into the bowl placed strategically on a chair beside the bed. A minute later the door opened and Maria entered, looking apprehensive.

"Hello, Miss Weaverly. I brought you something to eat, and let me show you the bathroom." She walked to the other side of the room and opened a white door, which I hadn't even noticed before in my panicked state. I rose from the bed and followed her into a very large, opulent bathroom. The counters were a beautiful white marble, and in the corner sat a huge, whirlpool tub overlooking a beautiful garden. There was a shower off to the side, and two large sinks with mirrors everywhere. Maria asked whether I preferred a bath or shower, and I chose a shower as I didn't have the patience for a bath. My goal was to wash this ordeal from my body and find out where I was and how to get help. Maria said she would be outside the door waiting for me, and to call if I needed anything. I stripped out of my nightgown (well, not *my* nightgown), which I noticed was made of pale blue silk. Looking at myself in the mirror, I noted the bruises on my arms and stomach from the struggle that I could barely remember. My long hair was matted in clumps that fell down towards my breasts. My eyes were red and puffy from crying, and as I looked back at my horror-stricken face, my vision quickly blurred as the tears welled up again.

Once in the shower the hot water soothed my nerves. I lathered my body with a fresh, fruity soap that smelled like plump, sweet peaches. I immediately remembered that this was the soap I used as a teenager. A distant memory entered my consciousness in which Richard and I were rolling around in a pasture kissing. He stopped and pressed his nose against my neck, breathing in deeply. "The smell of your skin is so sensuously sweet, Cadence, so smooth and soft." I replied that it was my peach soap and nothing fancy. It was unnerving to see the familiar light orange bar of soap carefully laid out for me.

The same situation confronted me with the shampoo, but this time it was the salon shampoo I had been using over the past few years. It made me feel very uneasy, yet comforted in an odd way to have some of the amenities I used at home. I massaged a handful of the shampoo into my hair, and worked up a rich, frothy lather like the foamy top of a cappuccino. I followed that with my favorite salon conditioner. Damn it, this was weird. How did Richard know what to buy? It couldn't be a coincidence that he had all three of these toiletries for my use. I wondered how long had he been spying on me, as a shudder ran through my weakened body.

I stepped out of the shower, and wrapped myself in a large, fluffy white towel. Now feeling calmer, I faced myself once more in the mirror. This time my image was blurry due to the steam. I whispered to myself, "You *will* escape and you *will* go home. Just keep calm and find a way out." I had learned about the importance of positive self-talk in my introduction to psychology class in high school. I struggled to remember enough of the course to categorize Richard's mental illness. I thought to myself, *He's crazy, and you rocking the boat could be very dangerous.* I noticed a soft, white robe hanging on a hook, and cocooned myself in it, seeing my name embroidered on the front in pale blue (my favorite color). I stepped out of the bathroom, noticing that the bowl on the chair beside the bed had been discreetly removed. I turned to face Maria, who looked concerned.

"I was worried as you took quite a while, Miss Weaverly. Is everything okay?"

"Oh, yes. Other than the fact that I've been abducted," I sarcastically stated, not able to resist the remark. She ignored my statement and opened a door to a large walk-in closet filled with any woman's dream wardrobe, with everything from designer dresses, skirts, pants, and shirts to luxurious loungewear, and rows upon rows of expensive shoes. Maria explained that all the items were in my size and to choose a comfortable outfit for dinner that evening. I shook my head in disbelief when I saw a dress that I'd tried on in New York and nearly bought for a New Year's Eve party, if it hadn't been triple the price I would normally spend on a dress. It was a dark blue evening gown that flowed elegantly to the ground. I could still remember looking in the mirror at the store that snowy afternoon. "Unbelievable…how did he know about this dress?" I said to myself, but loud enough for Maria to hear.

"He loves you very much, Miss Weaverly. He wants to please you and hopes you find the wardrobe to your liking." I gave no response to that, other than a continued look of shock at how closely the clothing matched my tastes: elegant, comfortable and simple. I grabbed a pair of my favorite brand of jeans, and a soft mauve-colored shirt. Maria proceeded to point out my underwear drawer. There were about ten different bra and panty sets, including a mauve set. Clearly, Richard had remembered my taste in underwear. He knew my preference for simple, comfortable lingerie that was subtly sexy. To think that I rarely thought of Richard over the past ten years, and yet he remembered so much about me. It was clearly a deep-rooted obsession.

Even though we'd never slept together, he'd definitely seen my panties during our three-month relationship. There were many times when we'd fool around, but whenever we were close to going all the way, Richard would exert his willpower. "It's not *if*, but *when*, Cadence," he would explain, breathing heavily but stubbornly not taking my virginity, even though I'd started on birth control pills just in case. There was no doubt I was physically attracted to Richard, who was such a tender and passionate kisser that he took my breath and restraint completely away. But when reality struck after each date, and his oddities continued, I was relieved not to have had sex with him. I feared that this step would make him feel he had to propose, as he seemed very intent, in his old-fashioned way, on sex and marriage going hand in hand.

Maria scurried out of the room to find Richard once I was dressed. She instructed me to wait in one of the armchairs near the door. Both were large, soft white leather armchairs. Everything was white. Sparkling clean, new looking, and white as the winter snow. Moments later the door slowly opened and in walked Richard. I had forgotten how tall he stood at six foot two. He was still broad shouldered and strikingly handsome, with his deep green eyes and thick blond hair that I remembered from so long ago. His face was more chiseled than I remembered, and he was sporting a healthy looking tan. It was obvious that he still lifted weights regularly and took great care in his appearance.

"You look lovely, Cadence," he exclaimed. He knelt beside me and took my hands into his large, soft hands; they were warm and I felt oddly comforted and terrified at the same time. He acted as if we were married, or at the very least in a very serious relationship. There was no shyness or testing the waters, but a comfortable sense of intimacy that he displayed without hesitation.

"Thanks," I whispered, trying to hold back the tears and focus on my escape.

"There's no need to thank me. I'm so blessed to finally have you home, Cadence. I know it has been a shock, but each day will get easier. Look into my eyes and you will see my love for you," he poetically asserted, as his green eyes stared deeply into mine with a clearly passionate look.

"Why am I here, Richard?" I whispered shakily.

"So that we can be together for the rest of our lives! These last ten years apart felt like an eternity. Not an hour went by when I didn't think of you, but I needed that time to build my wealth so that I could provide for us and our family." I quivered again, stunned at the mention of "our family." Every time I felt that I had my fear under control, it inched towards hysteria and sheer terror.

"Richard, please..." I choked.

"I'm sorry, I'm jumping the gun. I'm just so excited, Cadence, that I can't stop thinking about it...you're mine now. We'll be together for the rest of our lives. I'll never tire of your beautiful face, your exquisite body, your magical talent. *Never*," he said, while stroking my cold hands. "Don't be nervous. I can feel you trembling. I would *never* hurt you. All I've ever wanted is to love and protect you, Cadence, and give you a life you could've only ever dreamed of."

I put my head down and watched the tears fall onto my new jeans. Each tear formed a small, dark spot on the blue fabric. He embraced me and all I could feel was his soft cashmere sweater. The scent of his cologne subtly filled the air around us. It was the same cologne he wore when we dated; clean and masculine, sexy but not overpowering. Many women would love that scent, I thought, but it made me nauseous. "Don't cry, Cadence. It breaks my heart to see you upset. I knew it would be like this for a while, but please understand that there is *nothing* to fear. I would *never* hurt you." He paused briefly, and added in a colder tone, "And I would *kill* anyone who tried." I stared up at him fearfully, but then his tone suddenly changed, and with renewed joviality, he took my arm. "Why don't I give you that tour now? I'm sure you will love your new home."

"Please, Richard, I want to go home," I whimpered, unable to control the trembling in my voice.

He smiled a slow lazy grin, which stopped just short of reaching his eyes, and said, "You *are* home."

Despite my earlier resolve, I was helpless against a new flood of tears.

# Chapter Six

DURING OUR THIRD MONTH OF dating I was seriously contemplating breaking up with Richard; however, I thought I should put it off until after graduation for two reasons. First, I was scared to hurt him and wanted to put off a really uncomfortable conversation. Second, I had to admit that I wanted a hot guy to be my grad date, and Richard was it. After grad I would break up with him for sure. That was the end of a chapter of my life anyway, and seemed like the best time to end our relationship. I would simply tell him that a long-distance relationship wouldn't work. I envisioned him reacting with intense sadness, given that he was so emotional and into this relationship. Breaking up was not part of his plan, and he liked having a plan in place for everything. I would say the line about us remaining friends, but it would likely never happen. I felt sick to my stomach as I imagined the outcome of this unfortunate, but necessary, conversation. But in my heart I knew it must be done, sooner rather than later.

Richard's mother insisted that he no longer put off his education to be with her, so he was doing a couple of distance education courses until returning to school full-time in September. One warm day about two weeks before graduation, Richard and I were sitting on my deck. He had his laptop out and was working on a paper for one of his courses, while I was studying for my math final. I observed Richard carefully, as focusing on math was much less interesting. Richard was concentrating intently as he typed. His light colored eyebrows were furrowed, and he had a serious expression on his face. He was well built, and his exercise and weight lifting showed in his muscular arms and broad chest. I thought how great he looked with his thick, blond hair and his perfectly straight, white teeth. He dressed impeccably, always in a perfectly ironed Polo or Tommy Hilfiger shirt, and khaki pants or shorts.

He looked up at me, smiling instantly. His eyes gave it away every time; he'd actually fallen in love with me. I had hoped it was just lust or infatuation, but deep inside I knew that he really had strong feelings for me. Could I imagine us married? *No.* While I was very attracted to Richard physically, I had a strange sense around him and at times he made me very uncomfortable. Sometimes he would not stop staring at me, which I found most unnerving. Other times he treated me like I was the only confidante he had, and that nobody else could be trusted; he had not known me for long enough to put that kind of faith in me. And he acted like he knew everything about me, yet he was only just getting to know me.

I was hopeful that he would get over me quickly, especially with so many women attracted to him at university. I had coaxed him into telling me that many women had hit on him during his first year of studies, but Richard stressed that none of them were worth his time. He told me that he didn't have the desire to date, or sleep with, any of these women as they were "wrong on so many levels." He went on to explain his "theory of indifference to the common woman" to me, which I had a hard time following. Basically, Richard felt that most women were inferior to him intellectually, and he couldn't be physically attracted to any of them, as physical attraction implied a desire to procreate and he simply couldn't risk that with someone inferior. It all sounded egotistical and extreme to me.

What was the harm in dating to find out more about what you liked or didn't like? Richard was definitely not your typical twenty-something-year-old guy. He was very picky about what he wanted, and the few girls he'd dated were never quite good enough to make it past the first couple of dates.

It was about six weeks into our relationship when I knew I'd met his "criteria." We were sitting in a park eating ice cream cones when Richard explained, "Cadence, you're perfect...beautiful, smart, talented, fun, and motivated."

"Richard, that's sweet to say, but I'm far from perfect! There are other girls who are much more beautiful and interesting than me," I said, tasting the salty sweet of my salted caramel cone.

"Are you questioning my judgment?" he teased, between licks of his vanilla cone. "I'm as picky as they come, and to me you're *perfect*," he said, planting a kiss on my lips. "Mmmm, sweet," he sighed, as I met his lips in another kiss.

I pulled away and responded, "Perfect is unrealistic, Richard."

"Ah, Cadence, that's another thing I adore about you, your humility. I feel so connected to you. You're so real and you understand me like nobody ever has. You're my soul mate," he said firmly, kissing me with more passion. I returned his kiss, but driven by hormones rather than the feeling that I'd met my soul mate.

Richard never opened up to me about his childhood, despite my continued attempts. However, he did share that his father had been very successful in business, building many small companies into large, profitable enterprises, and then selling them. Richard wanted to follow in his father's footsteps, but become "one hundred thousand times more successful," as he put it. As for his mother, Richard felt terrible guilt about leaving her to return to university. He had already taken off the entire last year, and according to the doctors, his mother might live another six months. She urged Richard to go back to university, and not waste his time staying with her. She was very unemotional and detached, Richard explained, and had never really bonded with him.

He explained that his mother was "beyond understanding," and that he'd rather talk about anything but her. "I'm devoted but detached, that's the best way of putting it, Cadence. I'll be there for my mother but I cannot begin to tell you what it was like growing up with her and my father," he said, with a level of sadness I had never heard from him before. I felt sorry for him, yet he made it clear that he didn't want to talk about the past but instead focus on the future.

"I...*love* you, Cadence," Richard said softly, catching me off guard as we were sitting on the porch swing in my backyard one sunny afternoon in early June. I'd suspected that he'd fallen in love with me, but hadn't expected him to say so this soon. My stomach felt like it would come out of my throat. His eyes were wide, waiting for some sort of response.

"I...like you too, Richard. But it's just too soon for me," I clumsily explained. "I mean, I'm so young and..."

"I understand, Cadence, all in time. I don't expect you to say it this soon. I just wanted you to know how I feel. I've felt this way since the day we met. Even before we met I imagined your aura, your soul in my world," he explained, as he squeezed my hand. My heart was thumping in my chest. I felt nauseous. He must have seen my face turn white. Should I tell him my true feelings and end this now? I immediately chickened out, too scared to hurt him. He circled his arms around me gently, and I felt his hand stroke my hair, as I scolded myself for being a total wimp and dragging this out, especially when I knew better.

Just then my mom walked onto the deck, my savior! "Richard, would you like to join us for dinner? You're certainly welcome," said my mom, her auburn hair tied back in a short ponytail. My mom had beautiful brown eyes, which had a joyful twinkle. She was about five foot six, just like me, and very energetic. She was a choir teacher at my high school, and also taught voice lessons privately. She had a beautiful voice, which had inspired my musical passion. My mom liked Richard, although she didn't want me to get too involved before leaving for college. She knew my main focus would need to be on my music, at least until my degree was well underway and I was accustomed to living so far from home. "Cadence, there'll be so many boys who find you attractive…you'll definitely have your pick. Never, *ever* settle, my dear. Enjoy your twenties and don't even think of marriage until you have your education and some work experience behind you," she'd assert, and I agreed with her.

We got along fairly well, other than the typical mother-daughter arguments over curfew, clothes and other minor issues. My mom never failed to cheer me on at my music competitions, and always arrived early to get a place in the first row. At my last national flute competition in Chicago she came with me and was getting ready to leave the hotel room while I was practicing. "Mom, it is two hours early!" I said, as she put on her shoes.

"I know, but I can't risk losing my prime cheering spot, Cadence!" She replied excitedly.

"Your talent is a rare gift and I'm grateful every day. You amaze me and I can't wait to see how far your talent takes you." The memory made me smile lovingly at my mom before Richard interrupted my thoughts.

"I wouldn't want to impose," said Richard, "even though I'm sure the meal will be amazing, Mrs. Weaverly. Thanks for thinking of me, but I should get back home to my mother."

"You're most welcome, and I understand how much your mother needs you. She is lucky to have such a wonderful son. Shall I send home some rhubarb pie for the two of you?" my mom asked cheerfully. "And how many times must I tell you, Richard, call me Shirley."

"That would be great, Shirley," Richard replied awkwardly. I didn't try to convince him to stay, even though I knew I could have in a second. It was obvious that he would do almost anything to please me, and while this was a nice thought, it was a little unsettling too.

While my mom went back into the house to wrap up the pie, Richard bent down to kiss me. His lips were full and warm, and I felt the intense desire in his kiss, but he abruptly pulled away as he heard my mom walking back from the kitchen. His desire was so strong that I found myself turned on but torn between wanting him and wanting to escape his powerful intensity. "I *love* you, Cadence. I'll call you tonight," Richard promised.

# Chapter Seven

My body convulsed as I sobbed for what felt like an hour. The entire time Richard stroked my hair, wiped away my tears with soft tissues and kissed my cheeks, my hands and my forehead. I pleaded over and over with him to let me go, but he remained determined that this was my home and that was that. The terror numbed me after a while, and the tears stopped flowing. I was able to allow a few clear thoughts to process in my mind. My main goal was escape, and I needed to do whatever it took to leave this place or at least call the police. Sobbing would not aid my mission, and it might frustrate and anger Richard. He was clearly deranged, and the last thing I wanted was to unbalance him further. What would be wisest, I calculated, would be to go along with things for now, tour the place and gain a sense of where the telephones and exits were. I finally built up the nerve to speak without sobbing. "Richard?"

He looked pleased to hear me say his name. "Yes, my love?"

"Where am I?"

"In *our* home, darling, *our* beautiful home I built especially for *us*. Are you ready for the tour?" he asked eagerly, a large smile spreading across his unnerving yet handsome face.

"Okay," I replied meekly. We stood up and he held my hand as he led me out of the room and into a large, white hallway. The floors were a glistening, dark walnut hardwood, and there were several doors on either side ahead of us. I could tell immediately that it was a large, impeccably clean and organized home, reflecting Richard's personality.

"I'm so excited, Cadence. I've been waiting so long to show you our home. Let me take you downstairs first," he explained. Past about seven doors, four on one side of the hallway and three on the other, the hallway opened up into a loft area with a white, wooden railing overlooking a large, opulent living room. An elegant curved staircase led a winding course down into this room. The first thing I noticed was a huge fireplace, with a large watercolor hanging above it. Familiarity struck as I recognized the painting as the hills near my family's acreage. The greens and blues were intense, much like they are in the summertime near my childhood home. Richard led me closer. "Look closely, Cadence. I commissioned a very prominent local artist to paint this. I flew him to the location for a week so that he could accurately capture the intricacies and mood of our meeting place," explained Richard proudly. I felt sick to my stomach as I couldn't believe what I was seeing. As I looked closer, I noticed myself as a small figure playing my flute. Nearby was another figure watching intently…Richard. It was a very beautiful painting, stunning to the eye, but eerie to see this scene captured on canvas. "What do you think?" asked Richard eagerly.

"It's…it's…um…" I was having trouble getting words out to capture the combination of awe, violation and fear I was feeling. "It's beautiful (it really was)…you shouldn't have, though…" I tried to explain. Of course he *shouldn't* have; we weren't together anymore and I was engaged to someone else. How could someone pursue a relationship so intensely after ten years of not seeing one another? His insane mental condition was becoming clearer to me, and I swallowed around the lump of fear growing in my throat.

I scanned the rest of the large living room where there were three immense white leather sofas, with an elegant glass coffee table in the middle. Placed on it was a large vase of what must have been fifty or more red roses, their color bleeding against the sterile white of the room. When I breathed in I could smell their perfume. "For you, my love. When they begin to die, another set will replace them; there will not be a day in your life without fresh roses, Cadence." I shuddered as I remembered the red roses that he'd given me for my prom so many years ago.

There was a panel of very large windows looking onto an immense yard. I spotted a large rectangular swimming pool, hot tub and large patio area. I didn't know what time it was, nor did I have a clue where we were. "I know you love swimming. Remember when we used to go swimming in the lake, and how we couldn't get enough of one another's lips? I'll never forget those wonderful days. And I know you've been swimming more often recently, so I had the pool installed last year for you," Richard explained.

"How did you know I've been swimming?" I asked sharply, feeling violated. There was a fitness center I'd been a member of for the past two years, and it had an indoor pool that I tried to use at least twice a week.

"I know a *lot* about you, Cadence. I wanted to know you and understand you as much as I could while we were apart. I didn't want to bring a stranger back into my life. I feel like I've always been a part of your life, even while we were separated," he explained. "I had a private investigator inform me of your daily activities, and watched you myself whenever I had the chance."

"How *dare* you spy on me?" I cried, my voice rough with anger. Richard looked taken aback, but remained calm and collected.

"Is it spying to be interested in the life of your soul mate?" Richard asked, sounding confused.

"I'm *not* your soul mate! I can't believe you had me watched, and spied on me yourself. How could you do that to me, Richard?" I turned away from him angrily, the emotions welling inside of me like a large tsunami. Hot tears swiftly spilled down both cheeks. How could I produce such torrents of tears? Just when I thought my tear ducts were dry, more would flow.

"Cadence, I *love* you. I knew you'd be angry, and I expected these outbursts, but once you adjust and realize you love me, things will fall into place," he comforted, putting his long, muscular arms snugly around me from behind. What else could I say? There was no reasoning. I was so vulnerable here. I must control my emotions, I repeated to myself, and focus on finding an escape.

Next Richard led me into a large dining room, with a long oak table that could easily seat twenty people. The wooden chairs had soft, plush, white cushions. Why did he choose so much white for his home? "So much white…" I inadvertently muttered to myself, but this immediately caught Richard's attention.

"Yes, white is so pure, so beautiful…like our love has always been. I wanted a place that signified a fresh, clean start for us, and what better color to exemplify it than the crispest white my designers could find," he proudly explained. I shuddered but kept my mouth shut.

I looked up at the high ceiling and there hung a large, elegant chandelier. Richard explained, "This is where we'll have dinner. The chef already knows all of your favorite foods. I hired a fantastic chef after testing three others who were not up to par. Only the best for you, my love." I was beginning to get the picture…this was to be our home for many years to come.

"And this is the kitchen," Richard said, walking me into a gigantic room, with stainless steel appliances and white granite counter tops throughout. At the far end, at one of three islands, a small, Japanese man in a crisp white chef's uniform was chopping vegetables. Richard led me to him. "Yamoto, this is my fiancée, Cadence Weaverly."

"Very honored to meet you and welcome," Yamoto said softly, bowing before me. His smile was warm, truly kind and welcoming. Alarms bells were going off in my head and I felt like screaming: *Help me! I'm being held against my will. I was abducted. Call the police!* But I used my better judgment. Richard had probably convinced him that I was mentally unstable, and prone to delusional and emotional outbursts. I was sure I'd have my work cut out to convince anyone here to help me.

"Nice to meet you, too," I responded, trying to smile in return, even though I was sure he could tell I'd been crying. I continued to wonder exactly what Richard had told him and Maria about me.

The kitchen table was near the windows looking onto the pool. There was a sliding glass door to the patio just to the right of the table. Outside I noticed a gardener pruning some large bushes at the far side of the yard. Richard noticed everything I took in. "That's Fritz, our gardener. I know you don't enjoy gardening, but you love fresh flowers," he stated. He was right. Although I enjoyed gardens, I didn't have a particular knack or desire to take care of one.

He slid open one of the glass doors and led us onto the immense patio. It was very bright outside, especially after having been indoors for days. It took a few moments for my sore eyes to adjust.

The patio looked new. To the left was a large, sunken hot tub that looked like it could easily fit twelve people. To the right was a patio set, with cushions and an umbrella all in white. Thick, colorful flowers surrounded the patio. The pool was rectangular and large enough to do laps. Several white lounge chairs sat around it, beckoning for relaxation and sunbathing. Past the patio there was a helicopter on a private landing pad. Beyond that I could see a tall hedge bordering a high wall with nothing but blue sky above.

Fritz hesitantly put down his pruning shears and made his way to us. He was a tall, lanky man with thick, brown hair, bushy eyebrows and a wiry moustache. He spoke with a thick German accent when Richard introduced me, again as his fiancée.

"Very pleased to meet you, Miss Weaverly," he stated, his dark blue eyes carefully examining my response.

"Same to you, sir," I replied. He seemed like a man of few words, and it was difficult to determine whether he was genuinely kind or empathetic. "I'll just get back to work now, sir," he stated, turning around abruptly.

"I'm sure you'll enjoy the pool and hot tub, Cadence. I know you love being outdoors. That's why I chose such a large yard. It'll be great for our children, too. Plenty of room for swing sets, playhouses and whatever else we need." Richard gently took my hand and led me back inside, past the kitchen. I felt queasy at the mention of "our" children.

We walked through another hall, with a few more doors. He didn't show me what was behind each, which heightened my curiosity. I noted that I hadn't seen a telephone yet. We came to a set of French doors, through which I could see an office furnished with a large, wooden desk and white leather furniture. Richard seemed like he was not planning to stop, but I slowed to a halt in front of it. "Is this your office, Richard?"

"Yes, but there's nothing interesting in there."

"But I want to see *all* of the house," I choked out. He looked a little caught off guard.

"Well, there are some utility and storage rooms that we needn't waste time on, but sure, you can see my office," he smiled, taking my hand as he opened one of the glass doors. The room smelled of new leather. I immediately spotted the phone on the large desk. There were also several framed photos of me on the desk. There was also one of Richard with me on prom night, standing under a large tree in my yard. I was wearing a light blue gown, with spaghetti straps, smiling intently at the camera. Next to that was my graduation photo, my auburn hair flowing in curls. On the other end was a photo of me with my flute that had been published a year ago in the entertainment section of the

37

San Francisco Chronicle. Shock mixed with fury continued to flow through me.

"Richard, how did you get this picture?"

"My dear, I got it from the photographer who photographed you for the article. I thought you looked so beautiful in that picture when I saw it in the paper, I just *had* to have the file so I could enlarge it," he explained. Before I could say more, he bent down and kissed me briefly on the lips. I was taken aback and disgusted, turning away quickly.

"Please don't do that. I'm engaged to Christian."

"No, *you are not*, my love, you are engaged to *me!*"

# Chapter Eight

"You're soooo lucky, Cadence!" exclaimed Danielle, as I closed the door behind the flower delivery boy. Tucked under my arm were two dozen long stemmed red roses. We both walked into the kitchen and I placed them on the table, pulling out an enclosure card that read: *To Cadence on your special day. Love always, Richard.*

"I know…it was very sweet of him to send these," I said, trimming the stems and arranging them in a glass vase, their perfume filling the room.

The day of our prom had finally arrived, and we were very excited about partying the night away. Danielle and I had both booked hair, makeup and nail appointments, having planned for weeks that we would spend the entire day together preparing for this night.

"I can't believe you're going to break up with him, Cadence! He's soooo good-looking and romantic. I'd kill to have a boyfriend like Richard," she chirped. She'd only met Richard a couple of times, and each time he acted completely normal and very charming, and made a special effort to get to know Danielle and her boyfriend, Dale. He knew how important Danielle was to me, and wanted to thoroughly impress her, which he certainly did. I was frustrated that I couldn't get Danielle to understand why I'd made the decision to break up with Richard.

"Danny, I told you that I'm not ready for a long-term commitment, and definitely not a long-distance relationship. I know he's good-looking and really nice, but he's just not for me. I feel like I don't even know him. He's so closed-off when it comes to his family and anything about his past. I haven't even met his mom. I know she's sick, but isn't it weird not to have met her by now? And the weirdest thing is that he doesn't have any friends and I've never even been to his house.

"That is weird," Danielle agreed.

"And he's freaked me out a bit lately by the weird things he says. It's like he's mapping out our lives together. Last week he was talking about his dream home for us. He's just too intense for me and wants a much stronger commitment than I can give him." I could tell that Danielle was trying to understand, but still thought I was off my rocker.

"I know, I know. The long-distance thing would be pretty tough. He's gonna be so devastated, though. It's so obvious that he's in love with you, Cadence. Are you still thinking of ending it sometime in the next couple of weeks? Maybe you should've gotten it over with already?"

"I know, I'm a chicken and a coward. I should've done it by now, but I'm so nervous about hurting him, and adding to the pain he's already going through with his mom being sick. But I'm *not* going to procrastinate any more, once prom is over I'll end things. But I wanted to have a date for prom, and he's so good looking and charming," I said, feeling ashamed that I'd dragged things out this long. "Is that wrong, Danny?"

"No, Cadence. Prom is once in a lifetime and you've put up with Richard's weirdness so you deserve to have him as your date. The girls will be so jealous when they see him in a tux. But I'll hold you to breaking up after, Cadence," Danielle said, with a wink. "It's not fair to drag it out much longer if you know he's not for you."

"Definitely! I still can't believe that he feels so strongly so soon. I mean, it's only been three months. To put "love always" on a card seems a bit much, don't you think?" I asked my best friend.

"Yeah, he does act like you two have been together a lot longer than you have. What does he expect, to get married soon? I mean, you're only eighteen. Most guys are terrified of long-term commitment and all they think about is sex. Richard is definitely out of the ordinary," Danielle said, shaking her head in wonder.

"Out of the ordinary is right. He doesn't do anything normal guys do. He doesn't watch sports, and says his time is much better spent trading stocks. He's so focused on money and brags about how much he has and will have," I explained. "Anyway, enough about Richard… tonight is going to be so much fun!"

We continued the discussion over lunch, and then headed to our various appointments. By five o'clock we arrived back at my house, changed into our dresses and came down to my living room for some photos. Danielle's parents were both there, as well as my parents and my younger brother, Patrick. My older sister, Sandra, was away working in Los Angeles for the summer, where she was completing a biology degree at UCLA.

"You look beautiful!" exclaimed my dad, his blue eyes clearly admiring me. "I can't believe that you've grown up so fast, Cadie," he said, putting his arm around my equally proud mom, who was beaming happily.

"And you, Danny, look gorgeous too!" said Danielle's mom gleefully. "I really like both of your hairdos, and those colors are the best choices you could have made!" I was wearing a light blue, floor-length gown with spaghetti straps that my mom had made for me. It brought out my blue eyes. Along with it I had borrowed my mom's diamond earrings and necklace. My hair was placed in an elegant updo, with a few stray curls hanging down over each ear. Danielle's dress was dark burgundy, which went well with her blond hair that was also in a stylish updo. We couldn't stop smiling as the cameras clicked individual and group photos. Everyone was dressed up to go to the dinner portion of the evening, except my younger brother, who opted for a night with his friends. He was fifteen, and even though he was proud of me, he didn't want to make the sacrifice of spending a night without his friends. I understood, as I'd felt the same way about Sandra's graduation dinner a couple of years earlier. However, as a people pleaser I still went to her dinner as I didn't like to disappoint anyone; case in point for me dragging out the imminent break-up with Richard.

"Ding dong," chimed the doorbell. My dad answered it, and there stood Richard and Dale, both looking very handsome in their tuxedos. Richard came over and admired me, smiling broadly. He took my right hand and gently planted a kiss on my palm and entwined our fingers.

"You look *stunning*, Cadence," he said, in a transfixed voice while gazing down at me. He gave me a red rose corsage, which he gently slipped on my wrist.

"Thanks, Richard, so do you," I said. He honestly did look amazing. I only wished he wasn't so strange, as it certainly wasn't his physical attractiveness that was the problem.

We all walked out onto the front lawn for more photos. It felt awkward standing there as a couple, knowing our relationship was nearly over. I tried not to think about that fact, and my accompanying guilt, and instead focused on the excitement of the evening.

"You two look lovely together," said my mom, while my dad agreed as he snapped numerous photos. Danielle and I exchanged an awkward glance, while Richard squeezed my hand even tighter.

The four of us had rented a limousine, which then pulled up to the house. Richard wanted to cover the cost, but I insisted we split it; I didn't want to feel even more guilt about spending his money right before breaking things off. The limo was white and shiny, and Danielle yelped with excitement as we climbed inside.

"Let's crack open the champagne," exclaimed Dale, who liked to start drinking early in the evening. He clumsily poured four glasses, luckily only spilling a bit on the floor rather than our dresses. Richard was holding my hand tightly, and must have kissed me at least five times, prompting Dale to say, "Get a room you two!" I instinctively pulled away at that suggestion.

We all toasted the end of high school, and drank the bubbly liquid during the ride to the hotel, except for Richard, who didn't drink much. "Alcohol slows my thinking," he told me once when I asked him about it.

The dinner was excellent, and the speeches entertaining, although a little long. I played my flute, along with a pianist, to accompany a classmate who sang about our new lives and our dreams taking flight. Everyone loved it, and I received many compliments.

When the dance began, my dad took my hand for the first song. He looked handsome in his suit, his greying hair neatly combed. He told me how proud he was of me going to Julliard and how much he'd miss me. I had tears in my eyes as we slowly moved around the dance floor. Richard was dancing nearby with my mom, and I could see her laughing as he likely made witty comments. He looked very handsome with his broad shoulders and charming confidence. Was I about to make a big mistake? No, I was convinced I was doing the right thing.

Shortly thereafter, all of the parents began to leave, and we started dancing in groups to faster music. Whenever a slow song came on Richard seemed relieved to be alone with me, with his arms possessively around me. "I'm so happy, Cadence. This all feels so right. I wish this whole night could just be you and me. I can't stop staring at you," he whispered in my ear, gently nibbling it before he pulled away to look down into my eyes again. I felt my stomach drop, not wanting him to start up again with his claims of love. "Cadence, why don't we skip the after-party? Everyone is so immature in high school anyway. We can be alone together, just the two of us. I have a reservation for a suite at the nicest hotel in the city…we can make it an *unforgettable* night," he whispered.

I quickly lifted my head so I could whisper back into his ear. "I don't want to skip the after-party. It's important for me to spend it with my friends, Richard. It'll be fun." I could tell by his body language that he was disappointed with my answer, but wouldn't push it further. I felt uneasy and wished that I'd broken up with Richard sooner rather than allowing his feelings to continue to intensify. I shuddered at the idea of the hotel room.

At around 11:00 p.m., we all began to leave the dance and make our way to various after-parties. Because we weren't able to drink legally, we'd planned these parties at houses rather than bars. The one we were attending was at our friend Steve's house, which was very large with plenty of room for the fifty people he'd invited, and only a short walk from the hotel where the dinner and dance took place. We could hear the loud music from a block away, as we walked through the warm night with Danielle and Dale behind us.

When we arrived Steve looked like he'd already consumed several drinks. Danielle and I had dropped our liquor off there earlier that day, which consisted of vodka with 7 Up and lime juice, for Vodka Slimes. Dale began to mix four very strong Vodka Slimes.

"None for me, thanks, Dale," said Richard.

"What? Man, you *really* don't drink! It's gonna be quite the party, are you *sure* you don't want one?" Dale asked.

"No, I prefer to maintain control. Plus, I'll be better able to look after Cadence if I'm sober," he explained.

I immediately pulled Richard to the corner of the kitchen. "I don't need you to *babysit* me, Richard. I'll be totally fine," I whispered, annoyed at having him act like a chaperone during the most important party of my high school life.

"I just want to make sure you don't overdo it, Cadence. I didn't mean to offend you," he whispered back. However, he remained steadfast in his desire not to drink. I decided I would drink for the two of us, and downed several Vodka Slimes with Danielle. I didn't usually drink to excess, but tonight it helped me forget about the looming break-up and focus on having a good time. Soon Danielle and I were both giggling hysterically, and dancing non-stop with our friends. Richard seemed clearly out of place, watching the party from the sidelines. Danielle and I went to pour yet another drink, but Richard intercepted me. "Cadence, you're going to be sick if you have any more. Please stop," he pleaded, with a worried look.

"Don't tell me what to do, Richard!" I said angrily, while pouring two more drinks. Richard flinched with the sharpness of my remark, as I'd never spoken to him that way before.

"Cadence, you're going to be sick! I just want what's best for you," he said loudly, trying to be heard over the deafening sound of the rock music.

"You're acting like a parent!" I retorted. This was our first argument, and definitely our last, I thought angrily.

He looked very hurt, and said, "Fine, maybe I should leave for a while. I'll come back a little later to take you home safely." He turned and quickly walked out the back door. Danielle looked surprised.

"He *is* kinda strange, Cadence. I'm glad Dale is partying along with me rather than acting like that! C'mon, let's go dance." She dragged me to the dance area in the living room, but all I could think about was the argument with Richard and how awkward the situation was becoming. After two more songs, I pulled Danielle out onto the patio for a few minutes to vent.

"Danny, I can't believe he left, and he was so condescending about our drinking. It's not like we do this often…its *prom*. What a jerk!" I said angrily, swaying from the alcohol.

"I know, what a *freak*. I think you're right about breaking up with him. I say do it tomorrow," Danielle advised, hiccupping at the end of each sentence. We'd had *way* too much to drink and I knew we shouldn't have another sip if we wanted to avoid puking our guts out.

"I'll do it soon. He's just way too weird and this has got to end," I slurred. We turned and walked back into the house. Unbeknownst to me, Richard had been sitting in the dark, on the other side of the deck, silently listening in on our conversation.

# Chapter Nine

"CLOSE YOUR EYES, CADENCE," DIRECTED Richard, as we continued the house tour. He held my hand and opened a door, guiding me into a room. "Now open them!" he exclaimed.

I opened my eyes to see that we were in a large room with several skylights and dark, shiny hardwood floors. It was a music room, as indicated by the grand piano, music stand, and shelves full of music books. The room was bright and spacious, and had four rows of seats for a potential audience. I immediately noticed my flute case sitting on a shelf. Before I could question this, I looked up and saw my various degrees and awards hanging on the walls. He'd brought my personal items from my apartment...I felt robbed! "My things are here..." I stammered, overcome again by emotion.

"I knew you'd love this room! It will be yours to spend as much time practicing in as you like. I wanted to make sure you had all of your music and of course your flute. Actually, I had a lot of your things brought here, in case you wanted them," he said matter-of-factly. He put his arms around me, but I backed away as the feelings of violation intensified. In my mind I imagined going back to my apartment, once this nightmare was over, and seeing all of my belongings as they were the night I was abducted. Now all I could think about was a stranger rifling through, and taking, my personal stuff.

"How could you take my things? Where are the rest of them?" I demanded, through a film of tears.

"Everything you could ever want is here, Cadence. Don't get upset again...there's no reason to cry. I wanted you to feel at *home*. Don't you think this room is beautiful?" he asked eagerly, trying to change the subject.

"It's nice, but…how could you?" I continued to cry softly as he led me around the room, ignoring my tears while proudly pointing out various details. I ended up sitting on one of the cushioned white chairs meant for my audience, hunching over with exhaustion, anger, violation and a whole gamut of other emotions. He sat down in the chair next to me, stroking my back and uttering loving words of comfort.

"You need to rest. Dinner will be in a couple of hours, and I've planned a very romantic one for us. I want you to be rested and to stop crying. Could you *please* do that, my love?" I could tell he was becoming frustrated, but still trying to remain patient with me. He was right as I was very tired and felt like I was going to collapse with exhaustion from the sheer trauma and emotion of everything. My mind was constantly trying to figure out the best way to escape, but I knew that now wasn't the time to take action. I needed to be more alert and have a better sense of this immense house and its inhabitants.

"Okay, please take me back to my room," I responded weakly.

"Your *temporary* room, my love; I would never let you stay in such a simple, plain room for long. I have the master bedroom all ready for us, but will wait until we're married to show it to you," he said excitedly. I cringed at the thought of sleeping in the same room, let alone the *same bed*. If I let myself, I'd become hysterical, so I forced myself to remain calm, breathe deeply, and focus on my goal to escape.

On the way back to my room we passed a large, state of the art gym. It contained a series of machines, as well as free weights. "You'll find me in here every morning," he explained, "followed by a run or a swim, depending on my mood." Clearly Richard's routine hadn't changed, which explained why his physique looked even more muscular than ten years ago.

He led me back to my room. Once inside, he walked me to the bed, where I sat down. I turned my face when he tried to kiss my lips, leaving his lips to land on my ear instead. "I love you, Cadence. Maria will be up in a couple of hours to help you get ready for dinner. Now get some rest, my love." He got up and walked to the door, turning again to give me a loving smile.

I somehow fell asleep and woke up to the sound of running water. Once I realized where I was, I felt instant fear and panic set in. Maria walked out of the bathroom and said, "Your bubble bath is ready, Miss Weaverly. It will help calm your nerves. And Mr. White said to let you know that dinner will be in an hour. He has chosen a dress for you to wear this evening; it is on the hook in the bathroom, along with your underthings. The shoes are sitting near your closet. It's a lovely ensemble," she explained carefully, alert to the fact that I could become agitated at any moment. "And, please just press the silver button near your bed if you need anything. There is also one in the bathroom, beside the bathtub. I will come at once to see what you need." I just stared at her. She looked to be in her mid-to-late thirties and was a small woman with lots of energy. Her dark eyes were pretty, I noticed, as they darted anxiously to and from mine.

"I know you think I'm insane, Maria, but *truly* I'm not. I just want you to know that whatever you've heard is *not* true. Just Google me, and you'll see the story about my disappearance," I explained quickly, as she moved hastily towards the door.

"Please, Miss Weaverly, I'm just doing my job. I know you're not well, but…" she stuttered.

"Just Google me! I'm a professional musician. I play in the San Francisco Symphony …I'm *not* insane!" Even though Maria was clearly under Richard's spell, I felt that I had to let somebody here know what was happening.

On that thought, the door closed.

I was frustrated and took some deep breaths to try and calm myself down. Part of me felt like bolting the next time the door opened, but it seemed futile not knowing where I was. Plus, everyone here was clearly brainwashed into believing that I was mentally unstable, which meant they'd all try to stop me and alert Richard.

I walked around the room, now noticing more of its details. There was one window with white wooden blinds. I walked over to it and drew the blinds open. White metal bars crisscrossed over the window, imprisoning me. But I could still see the view below, overlooking the backyard. It was sunny outside and Fritz, the gardener, was on his knees in a brightly colored flowerbed.

I went into the bathroom and closed the door. Unfortunately, there was no lock. Since I'd already taken a shower, I decided the awaiting bath would help relax my frazzled nerves. I stripped down and stepped into the warm, bubbly water. The bubbles were that familiar peach scent. I couldn't relax, but felt mildly soothed laying there. Just then the doorknob turned. I froze as Richard entered my private space. He looked very concerned, but smiled when he stared down at me in the bubbles.

"Richard, please, don't just barge in here!" I exclaimed nervously, ensuring the bubbles were fully covering my breasts.

"Cadence, I just wanted to come in for a moment. I didn't intend to scare you. God, you look lovely! I would give anything to climb in there with you right now," he said, as fear raced through my veins.

"No!" I exclaimed, sinking further into the water and quickly grabbing a wash cloth to cover my breasts. Luckily it was a very deep tub with lots of bubbles, and now all he could see was my head.

"Don't worry, Cadence. Not until we're married and then we can bathe together all the time," he said. "Anyways, I'm here because I heard your conversation with Maria. There's no need to say such things to our staff, Cadence," he lectured. "They wouldn't understand our situation or my deep love for you. Instead, they've been told exactly what you thought…that you are mentally unstable. In time, once I can trust in your love, we'll hire new staff who aren't told any lies. It pains me to have to tell people that *you*, my brilliant, talented Cadence, are mentally unstable. But if you continue saying such things to our staff, I will have to maintain my story that much longer," he declared.

I quivered in fear and disgust. "Richard, how *dare* you listen in on my conversations and keep me here like a prisoner! How could you possibly think abducting someone is okay?"

"I *love* you, Cadence," he exclaimed, in a louder tone of voice than I'd ever heard him speak. "*Never* use the word abduction again! I know this is for the best, and one day you'll understand. Do not have such conversations with Maria or any other members of our staff again!" He was angry and I realized I'd crossed a line. I'd have to be more careful in the future.

I lay crying in the bath as he closed the door and left me alone. "Why me, God? Why me?" I sobbed, as the door slowly opened again.

"I'm sorry I upset you, Cadence. I didn't mean to use that harsh tone," Richard calmly explained. He then slid down to the floor beside the door and hugged his knees, looking very sad. "Hearing you speak nastily about me reminded me of the first time you caused me horrible pain. It was the night of your prom. I stood in the dark backyard of the after-party and overheard you speak to Danielle about leaving me. It literally felt like my heart was being pierced by a knife. The pain was so real and intense, yet my love for you became even stronger that night. I knew then that I would have you no matter what. All my energy went into making you mine. It's as though you've burrowed into my heart these last ten years, Cadence, and there's no way to separate us physically or mentally," he said, with a tinge of sadness in his voice.

I stared at him, speechless and mystified. His pain was so real and I could tell that he truly believed that we must be together. I shuddered under the bubbles, clenching my fist and curling my toes in fear of what was to come.

His tone immediately changed as he stood up. "I'm looking forward to our dinner tonight," he said softly, walking over to me and crouching by the tub. He gently inched forward and tried to kiss my lips, but I turned away again. He then stood abruptly and left.

*****

My bath was not relaxing in the least, knowing that Richard might walk in again. I hurriedly finished bathing, climbed out and quickly wrapped myself in a large, fluffy white towel that smelled of lavender. I dried myself and stared in the mirror. My eyes were still red and puffy. Just then I wondered if I was still being watched, perhaps by a camera in the bathroom. I scanned the large walls and ceiling, but didn't see one, thank God! I did notice a garment bag, along with a silver-colored bra and panties hanging on two hooks behind me. These carefully selected undergarments fit perfectly when I slipped them on. Next I unzipped the garment bag to find the dress he wanted me to wear that evening, like a piece of meat on display.

I gasped as I saw the light blue fabric appear. "Oh, my God," I whispered, as I pulled my graduation dress out of the garment bag. I fumbled around for a tag, just to see if it was indeed mine. There was no tag, and I knew instantly that it was mine as my initials were embroidered where a tag would normally sit, in the subtle blue thread my mom had used. Memories flashed back of us picking the pattern together and then selecting the fabric, of trying it on and then throwing my arms around her with excitement for the beautiful job she'd done. How the hell did he get this? It had been stored in my closet at my parents' house. They'd been violated and robbed too! The thought infuriated me. I felt like my world was an inflatable life raft that kept getting punctured from every angle and was sinking fast.

I refused to put on the dress. Instead I rewrapped the towel around myself and went out of the bathroom to the walk-in closet. When I tried to push open the door, I found that it was locked. Damn! I resented being treated like a child who couldn't even pick her own clothes. Richard knew me so well; he knew I'd resist his choice and the bastard planned ahead by eliminating any other option. I sauntered back into the bathroom, wondering whether I should put on the dress or refuse. Part of me wanted to refuse, to see how far I could push him. The other part of me thought that I should oblige him for safety's sake and follow his rules until I knew more about my surroundings and could safely escape.

I thought of what Christian would say to do; he would advise me to use extreme caution, of that I was certain. I decided that I'd rather be dressed when Richard next barged in, so I put on the damn prom dress and moved back to the bedroom. It was snugger than ten years ago, as I was about eight pounds heavier than back then, but I still managed to squeeze into it. In fact, it was probably more flattering now. It felt strange to wear it again...like going back in time. The shoes he had chosen were beside the closet door; they were not my actual prom shoes. I remembered giving those away to my friend's younger sister who wore a similar colored prom dress a couple of years after I graduated. I felt a minor sense of relief that he hadn't been able to acquire my entire outfit.

The bedroom door opened and Maria's small form entered. "Miss Weaverly, are you ready for some help with your hair and makeup?" she asked pleasantly.

"No, thanks," I said flatly. "I don't want to wear any makeup or have anything done to my hair." She looked surprised.

"But...Mr. White wants you to get dressed up for a special dinner. Your personal stylist has arrived to assist. Her name is Brigitte, and she's just outside the door. She's deaf, though, so cannot speak with you," Maria added.

"Send her in," I said immediately. The more people I could be in contact with, the better chance of a potential ally, I thought. In walked a tall, thin woman with short, red curly hair, holding a black satchel. She was quite beautiful and well dressed. Smiling warmly at me, she made a motion that I sit at the mirrored vanity. She unzipped her bag and brought out a blow-dryer and curling iron. After plugging in both, she pulled several cosmetics from the drawers and assembled these on a small tray. She pulled a smock from her bag and arranged it around my shoulders, then selected a hairbrush and stood behind me. I could hear Maria in the bathroom, probably tidying up. I had hoped she'd leave so that I could try to communicate with Brigitte.

"Are you really deaf, Brigitte?" I asked quietly, as she began to run the brush through and blow-dry my hair. No response. I caught her by surprise as I turned around to mouth the words "Help me." She looked shocked, but before I could say another word, Maria was back in the bedroom, straightening the bed covers, dusting, and doing whatever else she could to appear busy and remain nearby. I noticed her frequently glancing over at us.

I had an idea. I carefully took a black eyeliner from the makeup tray while Brigitte was occupied with pulling my hair into a French twist. I pulled off the lid and wrote on the bottom of the white smock: *Help Me!* It was all I had time to write. The letters were slightly smudged, but legible enough to read. While Maria was again in the bathroom, I caught Brigitte's attention and pointed to it. Her eyes widened, but that was her only reaction as she picked up the curling iron and wound up a stray tendril of hair near my face. I hoped that she was acting inconspicuous, but would follow up on it when she left.

Quickly finishing with the curling iron, Brigitte expertly applied my makeup within about twenty minutes. As she didn't speak, she communicated when I should open or close my eyes with gestures. I tried to lock my eyes with hers, but she merely looked away uncomfortably when I desperately stared. She then removed the smock and put the makeup back into the drawers. Would she take the smock or leave it here? She folded it into a square and put it in her satchel. She motioned to Maria that she was done and Maria walked her out the door. I heard them walk away down the hall and suddenly realized that Maria hadn't shut my door properly, so I wasn't locked in. Should I stay put or follow? Perhaps I could follow Brigitte and sneak into her car. I decided that I had to take this chance and follow her. I was not wearing shoes, so I quietly scurried down the hall after them. They headed down another staircase, which I hadn't seen on my tour. Suddenly I heard them speak to one another.

"Thank you, Brigitte, for acting like you're deaf. I know most of your clients don't ask you to do such things, but ours is a really special and difficult circumstance," I heard Maria say.

"No problem. She just seems so normal to me, but I guess psychiatric problems aren't always obvious on the surface. Anyway, I'm sure it isn't easy. Oh, yes, I wanted to show you what she wrote on her smock." They stopped as Brigitte pulled the smock out of her satchel and unfolded it for Maria to see. I ducked into one of the storage rooms we passed, which had an open door; luckily no one was inside.

I could faintly hear Maria's gasp. "I'm sorry she did this, but it's not out of the ordinary. I'm sure Mr. White would appreciate seeing it though. Follow me, his office is just over here," she said. I felt sick to my stomach. How could so many people be plotting against me like this? I didn't do anything to deserve this. I know I was cowardly and selfish for delaying breaking up with Richard ten years ago, but I was just an immature kid. I wished desperately that I could go back in time to that day on the hilltop and run away the moment I saw Richard watching me play.

I quietly made my way to the office door, getting close enough so that I could peer through the crack between the hinges and clearly hear them. I was trembling and barely breathing.

"So, how was she?" Richard asked.

"She was fine, very calm. But she wrote this on her smock with an eye pencil," explained Brigitte. I could see Richard's expression of surprise and he shook his head, looking at both Brigitte and Maria with pain in his eyes.

"It's very difficult dealing with her condition. I just know she'll get better, as she was before. I would much rather have her here than in the psychiatric hospital again, even if it means having to deal with these sorts of situations. And I know with our care that she'll improve soon. Thanks for your understanding and for keeping our situation entirely confidential, Brigitte," Richard said. I felt the heat rise inside of me and started to shake with barely contained rage.

"No problem, Mr. White. I'll keep this confidential and I look forward to more appointments with Miss Weaverly. She's quite a beautiful woman. You're a lucky man."

"I know, I most certainly am. Let me walk you to the door," he said in a charming voice. Damn! My chance of getting into her car was gone. But as I peered at the desk, another idea came to mind...the phone. I darted into the room beside the office, which was a bathroom, while the three of them exited the office and turned in the opposite direction. When they were out of sight, I hurried into Richard's office and grabbed the phone in my sweaty palm. I pressed 9-1-1 and waited for ringing, but only heard a strange buzzing sound. I hung up the receiver and tried again. I tried pressing Line 1 and Line 2, and dialing on each, but still heard the same buzzing sound. I had to get out of the office so he didn't know I was trying to call the police. My fear intensified as I darted out of the office and back down the hall. I reached the staircase and began racing up. Suddenly I heard footsteps heading down the stairs towards me. Instinctively I turned back down, running as fast as I possibly could to the bottom and out into the hall. I turned right, not knowing where I was going, just wanting to find an exit. I'm going to die if I don't get out of here, I thought.

# Chapter Ten

THE REST OF MY PROM night was, unfortunately, a blur. I had that one last drink that I shouldn't have, an obnoxious Black Sambuca shooter, with a group of friends. What was meant to be an innocent toast to the end of high school sent me over the edge. I didn't make a habit of drinking a lot, so my system was in shock from the amount of alcohol flowing through my veins. Shortly thereafter I ended up vomiting in one of the bathrooms for what seemed like an hour. I then heard Richard's voice outside the door asking if I was okay. Next I felt him lift me up into his arms and carry me out to his car. Then came the sound of my parents' concerned voices as Richard walked me inside. In the back of my mind I thought, *I shouldn't be here. I'm supposed to stay at Steve's with my friends.*

"What happened, Richard? Is she okay?" asked my mom.

"She's just had too many drinks. I tried to stop her, but it was impossible with all the drinking going on there. I don't drink, Mrs. Weaverly, and I wanted to take care of Cadence tonight, so thought it best to bring her home. I'm sorry I wasn't able to stop her from drinking," he said.

"Oh, Richard, this *isn't* your fault. Thank you for bringing her home safely."

"Yes, thanks Richard. We appreciate it. Guess we've all done it at one time or another, but it's too bad her night was cut short," my dad said, as he patted Richard on the back. Why did everyone have to like Richard so much?

"May I sit with her for a while, just to make sure she's okay?" asked Richard. I wanted to refuse, but was too nauseous to react.

"Sure, Richard. You've taken such good care of her, we don't mind you spending as much time as you want watching over her, but you must be tired," said my mom.

"No, no, I'm fine. You two shouldn't have to stay up. I had the honor of being her date, and I want to see it through and take care of her," Richard said charmingly. "Again, I'm so sorry this happened, Mr. and Mrs. Weaverly." I felt sick again, and not just from the alcohol.

That night I threw up a few more times, and remembered Richard holding back my long hair as I retched. It had come unfastened from the fancy updo and was now a stringy mess. I woke up in the morning with an intense headache, amplified by the sun peering brightly through my window. I climbed out of bed to get a Tylenol and almost tripped over Richard, who was asleep on the floor beside my bed. He woke up immediately, asking if I was okay.

"What are you doing here, Richard?"

"I was watching over you. I planned to leave, but was worried about you, and ended up falling asleep here," he explained. "How are you feeling, Cadence?"

"I'm fine, just a *really* bad headache. Richard, I... I'm sorry you had to see me like this. I didn't mean to drink—"

"No problem, sweetie. I just wanted to make sure you were okay," he said, while slowly sitting up.

"Thanks, I appreciate it." I walked out of my room and into the bathroom, where I got myself a Tylenol and swallowed it with a large glass of water. I noticed the bobby pins from my updo arranged in the shape of a heart next to the sink. My stomach dropped and I felt both ashamed and resentful that Richard had stayed the night to look after me. He always seemed to be around – and it was *my* fault for not ending this sooner. I walked back into my room and sat on my bed. He sat on the floor, using the bed to support his back.

"I *really* need a shower, Richard. I think you should probably go home now," I said.

He didn't turn around, but spoke quietly, "Cadence, you really hurt me last night. I know you didn't mean what you said, and I forgive you," his deep voice trailed off.

I sat there, stunned. What did I say that hurt him? I tried to rewind the events of the past twelve hours in my mind, but it was mostly a blur.

"I care about you *so much*, Cadence. And I thought you felt the same about me," Richard said in a quiet, pained voice. He turned around to look up at me, his green eyes filled with tears. I'd never seen him cry before, even about his mother's illness. I felt terrible, and blamed myself.

"Richard, I'm so sorry. I just..." My voice trailed off. I couldn't think of how to say it, or whether now was the best time, given that I was exhausted and my head was pounding. "I didn't mean to hurt you. I don't know what I said, but..."

He touched my hand gently. "I know you didn't mean it. I'd like to talk more about our relationship and where it's going, but now is probably not the best time. How about meeting me at our special spot later this afternoon, after you get some more rest? Maybe four o'clock?" he asked, anxiously.

"That's a good idea. I really do want to talk about things," I said, both relieved and terrified of our pending break-up conversation. "And thanks again for taking care of me. I really am sorry."

"No need to apologize anymore, Cadence. Now get some rest," he said, running his hand down my arm. He slowly walked out of my room, and gently closed the door.

He must know that this wasn't working out, I thought. Hopefully it wouldn't be much of a surprise when I told him what I needed to that afternoon.

I had a hot shower and washed my hair thoroughly. I was revolted and embarrassed when I noticed vomit stains on my beautiful dress. I lay down and my mom walked in, also looking at the stained dress draped over a chair, shaking her head.

"Darling, you know exactly what I'm going to say, but I'm going to say it anyway," she said. "You shouldn't have had so much to drink. You ended up so sick and ruined your special night. Luckily Richard was patient and kind enough to take care of you and bring you home safely. I'm so worried about you doing this sort of thing in New York, so far from home. Some men would take advantage of a situation like that. It's not safe," my mom lectured.

"Mom, I'm *so* sorry. I think I just overdid it because I've had a lot to deal with lately. I know it was stupid and dangerous, and I'm *not* going to do it again. I'm so ashamed," I said, my voice beginning to waver as tears blurred my vision. I dropped my face into my hands, embarrassed about my behavior. I respected and loved my mom so much that I hated to see her disappointed in me.

She gave me a hug. "Your dad and I understand and forgive you, but *please* don't do it again. Stop after a couple of drinks. I'm so impressed with Richard—" she went on, but I hastily cut her off.

"Mom, I told you I *don't* want a long-distance relationship. Actually, I don't want a short-distance one either. I'm going to break up with him this afternoon. He's just…too intense and controlling for me," I tried to explain. I hadn't gone into detail about my feelings for Richard with my mom. We were close, but I didn't want her to interfere and felt old enough to make my own decisions.

She looked concerned. "Are you sure you should do this today, after he helped you so much last night? Maybe you should give it a bit more time…he's a very kind young man," my mom said.

"Mom! He has you and dad wrapped around his little finger. I told you, he's weird. Weird! He's not for me, so why drag it out? I should've broken up with him weeks ago," I explained, frustrated. "There are way too many red flags!" I said, as I swiped at my tears with the sleeve of my robe.

"Well, I know you'll make the right choice. I agree that you don't need the ties of a long-distance relationship holding you back at Julliard. You'll find someone who's right for you," she smiled at me. I sensed she was disappointed though, which was very maddening. Richard was so charming and polite that he pulled the wool over everyone's eyes. I mean, he wasn't a bad person, just strange for wanting such a strong commitment after a very short time. It just didn't feel right and I was going to trust my instincts.

"Thanks, mom. I need more sleep," I said, and she kissed my forehead before leaving.

Later that day, I walked slowly towards our meeting place, breathing in the fresh, crisp air of the late afternoon. Everything was green, and I was glad summer was here. My heart was pounding and I felt sick about breaking up with Richard, despite assuring myself that it was the right decision. I was ashamed not to have done it sooner, and just hoped that he'd get over it quickly.

I saw him sitting on the hillside in the distance. I quickened my pace, trembling with anxiety. He smiled warmly as I got closer, and stood to greet me, wrapping his arms around me, then bending his head to kiss my lips, but I turned my head away abruptly. He looked a bit surprised, but anxious to tell me something. "Let's sit down," he said, handing me a beautifully wrapped gift the size of a shoebox. "This is your graduation gift. I wanted to give it to you last night, but there was no time for us to be alone. Please, open it," he said.

"Richard, you didn't have to..."

"Yes, I certainly did and I *loved* buying it, Cadence."

Should I break up with him before opening it? No, that would be rude. Either way, I was sure he'd want me to have the gift. Yet, I needed to say something and I could no longer act like nothing was the matter. "Richard, maybe we should talk first. I think our relationship—"

He cut me off, "Cadence, *please* open your gift, we can talk afterwards, sweetie," he commanded in a gentle, yet urgent voice. I sensed he knew something was wrong, but wanted to deny it for as long as possible. I decided to open the gift and began to carefully unwrap the box. The paper was patterned with blue and cream stripes, and was neatly wrapped. Once the wrapping was off, I pulled the lid off the white box inside. There was another gift in the same wrapping paper, slightly smaller than the first gift. Along with it was a note on a piece of light blue paper the size of a recipe card. It read: *Dear Cadence, I have loved you from the moment we met. You are the most beautiful, talented and kindest person I know.* Tears formed in my eyes. I felt so terrible about hurting him, yet I had to do it.

"Go on, open the next box," he whispered.

"Richard, I don't think this is going to work out—" I whispered back, handing him the box.

I was shocked when he totally ignored me, cutting me off again. "*Please*, Cadence, continue. I insist that you open it," he commanded, this time more urgently.

"But, Richard, I—"

"Open it! Please!" he ordered, with agitation.

I tore open the next layer quickly, revealing another white box with a lid. I pulled off the lid and inside was another small note with a wrapped gift. I was anxious and frustrated, not knowing what to do to lessen the hurt I was about to inflict. Part of me wanted to run away, and the other part didn't want to hurt him anymore than I had to. The note read: *I can't imagine my life without you. You are so much a part of me and my future.* I looked at him, my eyes now full of tears.

"That's the last one…open it!" he said excitedly, paying no attention to my tears and obvious distress. Another red flag, I thought, a *huge* red flag. The box was small, likely jewelry.

"I can't accept this, Richard."

"Yes, you can…now open it! I can't wait another second!"

I tore at the wrapping paper and inside was a small white box, with a final blue note stuck to the top that read: *Marry me, Cadence.* The words were carefully written in neat, blue printing to match the wrapping paper.

There was a short, stunned silence. I was crying openly now. "Richard," I said softly, "I *can't* marry you. I'm too young and this isn't working," I choked out, handing the box back to him without opening it.

Richard spoke slowly. "No, no…you *don't* mean that, Cadence. If this is because of New York, I was planning on moving there with you and—"

"No, Richard. I'm so sorry but I need to end our relationship. I don't have the same feelings as you and…I'm so, *so* sorry," I said.

"No! This isn't how it's supposed to happen. It can't happen this way, it's not part of the plan. No, Cadence…" he quietly sobbed. I didn't look at him, as it was just too painful.

"I'm *very* sorry."

"I *love you*, Cadence," he whispered. "I will *never* stop loving you." His voice then became very firm and controlled. "I could never stop loving you, even if I tried. It won't work in my life plan," he said with finality, causing me to shiver from the creepiness of his words.

He then took the small box and stood up abruptly. "Aaargh!" he howled, as he turned away from me, his hands grasping his head. It was as if nature stood still and his moment of pain and shock was forever etched in my memory. I never wanted to hurt anyone like this and felt like a horrible person. Yet I also felt unnerved by his odd statements.

He suddenly turned around and looked down at me with a strange look that combined outrage and adoration, and I felt one of his tears land on my arm in a soft, warm splash. Then he turned abruptly and sprinted away. "Richard! Richard, don't go like this!" I yelled. "I didn't want to hurt you..." but he disappeared over the hill rapidly. I didn't run after him, but sat there crying tears of shock, guilt and immense relief.

# Chapter Eleven

I WAS RUNNING AS FAST as possible, fearing for my life. All I could think about was escaping. I ran inside the kitchen and Yamoto the chef turned around in shock, watching me scurry to the sliding glass doors, pulling one of them open and running out onto the patio. I ran across the lawn and towards the high stone wall, which I clearly couldn't climb. There were no trees anywhere near the wall and I felt my terror intensify. I began to scream as loud as I possibly could, "Help me! Help! Help! Somebody help me!"

Suddenly I felt arms close around me from behind and a hand clasp tightly over my mouth, muffling my screams.

"Cadence, be quiet!" said Richard urgently. He pulled me back abruptly, but I refused to budge. I was no match for his strength however, and he quickly scooped me into his arms as I struggled with all of my energy. I kicked and tried to scream for help. He carried me inside, and I saw Yamoto looking at us. "What are you staring at? You can see she's having an attack. There's no need to worry," stated Richard, clearly angry at Yamoto's expression of shock and concern.

He marched us up the stairs and soon we were in my bedroom with the door closed. I stopped struggling, feeling exhausted and defeated. I was shaking in fear as he placed me gently on the bed. Then he stood up and began pacing around the room. I could hear his heavy breathing, and prayed that he wouldn't hurt me. After what seemed like an hour, but was probably only a few minutes, he came back to the bed and sat on the end.

"Cadence, I am *very* angry with your behavior. There was *no need to do that!*" he yelled. He lowered his voice to an angry growl and said, "I am going to be totally honest with you, Cadence. You CANNOT escape. We are very isolated here, with *no* neighbors. The phones do not work without a code and I *know* you tried already. Even if you try to escape, there is an extensive alarm system both inside and outside of the mansion that will tell me exactly where you are. And, there is no point begging the staff, as they think you are mentally ill. A man who they thought was your psychiatrist came and spoke about your mental illness, and told them exactly what to expect. They have all been carefully selected and briefed many times before you arrived. I pay them exceptionally well to work here and respect our situation. Now... how many times do I have to tell you that I LOVE YOU!" he shouted.

*Oh shit*, I thought to myself. *He's more insane than I could have ever imagined. Oh my God, help me, help me!* His detailed description of my situation made me tremble with stark fear. Who would have faked being my psychiatrist? Richard probably paid him substantially to do so. This felt like being in a high security prison for a life sentence, after being found guilty of a crime I didn't commit. Would I live out my life here? No, there was no way I could. Even if it meant risking my life, I *needed* to escape soon.

He stared down at me, and I watched as his expression of rage magically dissolved into a smile. *Insane*, I thought again. "God, you look gorgeous in that blue dress. For a moment I thought we'd have to cancel our special dinner, but I think once you calm down things will be fine."

"I...I'm not hungry," I said between sobs. "How *could you* do this to me? I don't want to live as a prisoner," I said, with what little energy I had left.

"Like I said before, Cadence, you will no longer be a prisoner once you accept the situation and show me that I can trust you. Until then, I cannot risk losing you again. I know this is painful, but it is nothing compared to the pain and agony I felt the day you rejected my proposal and tried to cut me out of your life forever. My heart was literally severed that day and the only thing that began to heal it was knowing I would have you back..." his voice trailed off, and then with a suddenly more upbeat tone he said, "Now why don't you calm down and relax for a few minutes before dinner."

"I'm not hungry," I whispered, shaking my head, shocked by his erratic and over the top explanations and emotions.

"You will be when you taste the fabulous meal. Yamoto has prepared some of your favorite foods. Now, Cadence, are you going calm down and promise not to lose your cool again? I have some sedatives as an alternative. In fact, I have various medications to help calm you down, but I would rather not have to use them. The choice is yours, but if you scream again I'll have to resort to drugs," he explained.

"No, no more drugs," I cried. I didn't want to be doped up again knowing that it would make any chance of escape impossible.

"Good, I'm glad you're coming to your senses, my love. Now why don't you freshen up and I'll come back for you shortly," he said, standing up and heading towards the door. "Love you, darling," and with that, he was gone.

I lay there thinking, absorbing what had just occurred. It was obviously going to be next to impossible to escape or convince any of the staff that I was sane. But I would *not* give up. Even the brief glance I caught of Yamoto's face gave me hope that he might be an ally. There was no way I would *ever* settle into Richard's imaginary world and master plan. My emotions were a mix of fear, anger, frustration and shock. But one thing was clear...the situation seemed to worsen with each hour.

Maria entered the room a little while later, informing me that Richard would come by to take me to dinner in fifteen minutes. I weighed my options for how to act. On the one hand, I could continue rebelling and perhaps Richard would realize that his illusionary belief that I would love him would never happen. Maybe, just maybe, he would become too frustrated to keep me, so he would let me go. But from what he'd said, and his actions, I knew in my heart that he would never willingly let me go. Plus there would be the fear of the kidnapping charges. It was clear that he'd been very successful in whatever he'd done career-wise. He would have his image to be concerned about and would not want to risk any form of media attention or jail time.

The other alternative would be to keep myself calm and collected, and try to learn as much information as I could about Richard, the mansion and its inhabitants. This information could help me escape and perhaps find an ally. If I continued losing control and crying, it would further build Richard's case that I was mentally troubled. If I remained calm and dignified, I stood a better chance. But it would be incredibly difficult. My tear ducts felt like floodgates and the things that Richard said could very easily throw me into a frenzy. I willed myself to remain as calm as possible, yet not give Richard any false illusions. There was no way I could even remotely fake liking him.

I observed myself in the mirror. Mascara had run down my cheeks like two streams of black oil. I wiped my face clean. My eyes were terribly red and swollen, but nothing could be done about that. My hair was somewhat disheveled from trying to escape from Richard's grasp, and the blue prom dress had acquired a few wrinkles. Good, I thought, perhaps that would deter some of his creepy comments about me looking so beautiful. I didn't think I was beautiful anyway, as that was a strong word to be reserved for women who made heads turn. But others said I was pretty, especially the light blue color of my eyes contrasted with my auburn hair. I sighed and turned away from the mirror.

The door opened a few minutes later. Richard stood there smiling, looking very handsome in a black tuxedo. I smelled his cologne as he entered the room. *Remain calm and collected*, I reminded myself.

"You look ravishing, Cadence."

"No, I don't," I said quietly, standing still with my head bowed so I wouldn't have to look him in the eye. He took my hands into his, which felt warm around my cold and trembling fingers. He then leaned forward to kiss me. I turned away, and caught the look of hurt in his eyes. "Richard, please don't," I begged.

"I understand, Cadence. It has been an emotional day, and I don't intend to push you faster than you feel comfortable with *tonight*," he said. I trembled, imagining what it would be like to be forced into a kiss with Richard, let alone anything more intimate.

He let go of one hand, and led me out of the room, through the hall and down the large, winding staircase. We walked past the living room and entered the dining room. The lighting was dim, and a candlelit dinner was set, with two place settings together at one end of the massive table. It looked very elegant, and for a fleeting moment I wished desperately that I could share this meal with Christian instead. Richard pulled out my seat and I sat down, noticing a bottle of wine chilling in a wine bucket beside us. Richard sat in the other seat, at the head of the table, and proceeded to pour us each a glass of wine, mine white and his red. He knew that I preferred white wine, and exactly which type, without having to ask. Further evidence of my privacy being breached, I thought.

"To happy reunions and true love forever, Cadence," Richard said, as he clinked his glass with mine before I could pull it away. We both took a sip of the wine. The white was my favorite Californian Chardonnay and tasted wonderful. I was glad to have something to calm my nerves. Richard appeared to thoroughly enjoy his red wine as well. "You probably recall that I didn't drink when we dated, but since then I've developed a taste for fine wine. But never in large quantities, as I don't like to lose control," he explained.

I tried to ignore Richard's attempts at conversation as Yamoto walked in smiling at both of us while carrying a tray of appetizers. He set it down, said, "Enjoy!" and left the room.

"I asked that he prepare your favorites, Cadence. Crab-stuffed mushroom caps and bacon-wrapped scallops," Richard explained.

"Thank you, it…um…looks delicious," I said softly. I felt like screaming, demanding to know how he knew, and telling him how horrible he was to violate my privacy, but remembered my promise to remain calm and collected. I made tight fists with my hands under the table, trying to direct my energy physically. A memory entered my mind of the last time Christian and I had dinner in San Francisco at our favorite restaurant. We ordered the scallops and took turns feeding each other. Was I being watched on that wonderfully romantic evening? I cringed.

"What are you thinking about, my love?" asked Richard, as he placed a stuffed mushroom and a scallop on my plate.

*Wouldn't you like to know!* I thought. "Nothing. I'm just tired," I said, still not making eye contact.

"I know, sweetheart. The food should give you a bit more energy. Try some!" he urged. I tried a stuffed mushroom, which was very good. I didn't realize how hungry I was, and I derived some comfort from eating these foods, which I enjoyed.

"This is very good, Richard," I said, after a few more bites. I glanced at him briefly, and he was smiling warmly.

"I'm so glad you like it, darling. God, I love you," he said. "I can't wait to touch your soft, lovely body," he said, while reaching for my hand under the table. I kept it in a tight fist, but he cupped his hand over it. "Your hand is so cold, darling. Let me warm it up," he said lovingly.

I quivered at the thought, my fists tightening further. It was extremely awkward sitting there with Richard, wishing I was anywhere else. What was there to talk about? I didn't know *anything* about him and he seemed to know *everything* about me. Richard tried to make small talk about the food and the nice weather we'd been having. I didn't say much and continued to avoid eye contact.

Maria came and cleared the appetizer plates, and topped off our wine glasses. She smiled briefly at me and then left. "Why won't you look at me, Cadence?" asked Richard. "I know it's been a rough day, but aren't you enjoying our romantic dinner?"

"There's nothing to say that hasn't already been said," I stated simply.

"Nothing to say, Cadence? Don't you remember how we used to talk for hours on walks and picnics? We would talk about everything… music, family, life, dreams. We're *soul mates*. There'll never be a day in our lives when we won't have things to say to one another," he stated.

"Those days were so long ago, Richard. We were just kids. I'm not the same person. We have nothing in common—"

"That's not true!" he interrupted, in a raised voice. "We share a lot of the same interests, likes and dislikes. You don't know what I've done since we've been apart, so how can you speak of having nothing in common?" he asked.

I didn't feel like responding. What was there to say? Should I feed into his delusions by continuing a civil conversation? Maybe I should try to hurt him, I thought, as I observed the knives at my place setting, searching for some sort of sharp weapon. But could I actually do it? I was the type of person who couldn't hurt a fly. But maybe if I had a gun…

My thoughts were suddenly interrupted by the sound of a violin. In walked a short, lean Italian looking man playing a violin very beautifully; the smooth notes were exquisitely played. Richard moved his chair closer to mine, putting his arm around me as I felt his hand close around my fist again. We sat there listening and taking sips of wine. I began to relax a bit and glanced over at Richard, whose eyes were closed, his face looking content and deeply enthralled with the music and moment. He wasn't all evil, I thought. Somewhere within his deranged being there was simply a man desperate to be loved. My anger dissolved to deep pity as I had a flashback to the last time I saw him ten years earlier. I had felt the same feeling of pity then. I, too, closed my eyes as I remembered that difficult encounter...

# Chapter Twelve

THE SUMMER HAD FLOWN BY with my job as a music camp counsellor almost finished. It had been a great job working days at the camp, and enjoying the long summer evenings with my friends or practicing. In only one week I would be flying to New York to move into the residence at The Julliard School. My parents were making the trip with me, and helping to buy some of the necessities. I was nervous about moving so far away on my own, while at the same time excited to meet new friends and live in New York.

I was in my bedroom packing, which never seemed to end, as I decided which parts of my life to bring with me and which I could live without. My mother walked in and sat on the bed. "Cadence, I still can't get over this…how fast the time is going. I wish we could delay it a few more years, but such is life. I know you'll do extremely well and are ready to live as a mature, independent woman," she sighed, smiling warmly down at me, as I sat on the floor sorting through my things.

"Mom, I wish I had more time, too. It feels so weird packing and knowing it's not just for a vacation."

"I know. But remember, you'll be back for Thanksgiving and Christmas, and you'll have your room and all your stuff to come back to. I'll keep everything the way it is, just like a museum," she said, laughing. Then her eyes took on a more serious look. "Cadence, I heard some sad news when I was at the grocery store today."

"What is it?" I swallowed hard, not really wanting to know the answer.

"Well…Mrs. White passed away yesterday evening at home." she said, solemnly. I felt tears well up in my eyes, even though I'd never met Richard's mother. After we broke up I lost all contact with him. I left him a message the day after we broke up to ask how he was doing, but he never called me back, and I thought it would give the wrong impression if I phoned him again. A week after our break up, I was out practicing one afternoon in our yard, and saw him standing in the distance. When I put my flute down he quickly walked away. I yelled his name, but he ignored me and disappeared. Who could blame him? I'd hurt him and couldn't expect any type of acknowledgment.

"That's so sad, Mom," I replied, instinctively standing up and giving her a hug. I couldn't imagine losing my mom. I felt so sorry for Richard, alone without any family or friends for support.

"Poor Richard," she said, shaking her head. "He's so young to have lost his father and his mother. They aren't having a funeral, just a private service. I heard she's to be buried tomorrow morning at the Sunset Cemetery." Her eyes met mine with a questioning look. "I was thinking…we should probably send over some flowers and perhaps a lasagna or something for Richard, since he's all alone." I knew she respected my decision to break up with Richard, even though she'd grown to like him. She probably wished we'd dated through the summer at least, so I could be there for him through his difficult time. But that wasn't my responsibility, I said to myself. Still, the guilt gnawed at me.

"You're probably right, mom. I was his only friend here, but I'm sure he wouldn't want to accept anything from me…"

"I could drop it off with a card signed from our family," she said carefully, looking into my eyes to read my response. As much as I didn't want to see Richard again, I felt that it would be cowardly and wrong to send my mom there in my place. Richard had been very kind to me and none of his behavior had warranted a refusal to extend my sympathies. Besides, it had been more than six weeks, so he was probably well over me by now.

"No, mom, I'll go. I was the one who dated him and the least I can do is extend my sympathy," I explained. I looked at my mom, wanting, as I had many times in the past six weeks, to tell her that Richard had proposed to me. It was so shocking to me that all I wanted to do was talk about it to get other people's opinions on whether it was normal to propose so quickly. At the same time, I felt a deep need to respect

Richard and keep his rejected proposal a secret. In a sense, I felt that my willingness to keep his proposal a secret was my last gift to him, the gift of respect. I didn't even tell Danielle.

"Alright. How about tomorrow afternoon? I'll throw together a nice lasagna and salad, and you can pick up an arrangement from the florist."

"Do you think he would even want flowers, mom? He's a guy..."

"I think it's a thoughtful gesture, dear. He can always take them to her grave."

"Okay, I'll get a bouquet and a sympathy card tomorrow morning." Now that I was finished my summer job, between packing and practicing, I had some time during the day to run errands.

"Cadence, I think you're doing the right thing and I'm proud of you. I know it won't be comfortable, but these situations never are and I'm sure Richard will appreciate the gesture."

*****

My palms felt sweaty on the steering wheel as I drove my mom's car towards Richard's house the following afternoon. I had only ever driven by it during the few months that we'd dated. The house was a very large brick home situated on three acres of land just a few miles down from our acreage. It had a lot of windows and looked very impressive as I turned into the long driveway. It was a sunny day, without a cloud in the sky...not a day one would picture for the burial that had taken place that morning.

I trembled as I parked in front of the house, dreading an uncomfortable encounter. I wished that he wouldn't be home, as I unbuckled my seat belt and stared down at my legs for a moment, noticing how tanned they were from spending so much time outdoors that summer. I was simply procrastinating as a million reasons why I *shouldn't* be there ran through my mind. Finally, I got up the nerve to climb out of the car, and lifted the lasagna, salad and flowers into my arms. It would have made more sense to do it in two trips, but if the situation was incredibly awkward I wanted to leave as soon as I possibly could. In seconds I was standing at the door, and rang the doorbell gently. I was surprised when the knob immediately turned in an anticipatory response.

"Hello, Cadence," Richard said, staring down at me. He was dressed in a black suit and looked as handsome as always, yet exhausted. As would be expected, his eyes were red, and I could see that he was hurting deeply.

"I'm *so* sorry about your mother, Richard," I said, seeing tears well up in his eyes as I meekly tried to extend my condolences. He turned away for a moment and it seemed as though he might just turn around and close the door in my face. Instead, he gestured for me to follow him inside.

I shook my head and said, "Actually, I just wanted to drop off a lasagna and some flowers from my family...you probably haven't eaten," I stammered, feeling as awkward as I thought I would.

He bent down and gently took the offerings from my arms, lingering for a second with his hand on mine. "Thank you very much. This is so kind of you."

"You're welcome. Again, I'm so sorry, Richard. I hope that you..."

"Please Cadence, all I need is a hug. Would you *please* come in for a minute?" I was about to say no, as I'd promised myself I wouldn't enter the house. At the same time, I felt overwhelmed with compassion for this man who'd just buried his mother only hours before, so I nodded and stepped inside.

"I'll just put these in the kitchen. While I'm there, can I get you a drink...a tea perhaps?"

"No thanks, I can only stay for a minute," I explained.

I stood there for a few awkward moments before he came back and led me into a large living room, filled with antiques, directly in front of the entrance.

"I'm leaving tomorrow, Cadence. I can't stand to be in this house another day. She lost her mind by the end and didn't know me from a stranger," he explained.

"That must have been so painful, Richard. I'm so sorry..."

"We weren't close to begin with, but still...to see your mother's coffin lowered into the ground and to have nobody to hold your hand, nobody to pass you a tissue..." his voice cracked with emotion.

I swallowed deeply. What was I to say? This wasn't my fault. I'd never made a commitment to stay with him for any set length of time. Suddenly Richard took a seat on the sofa and began to shake and buried his head in his hands and sobbed. My natural instinct was to sit beside him and put my arm around his shoulder, so I did. I felt tears welling in my eyes as I tried to relate to what he must be going through. He turned and placed both arms around me in a solid hug. I returned the hug, for it was the only response I could give. I felt the torrents of grief rake through his large body. His tears were hot as they landed on my back, soaking my blue T-shirt. He held onto me tightly, and didn't loosen his grip for a couple of minutes. Finally, he gently separated from me, and wiped his eyes and nose with a tissue. Then, he grabbed hold of both my hands before I could pull away.

"Cadence, I've missed you *so* much this summer. Just to touch you again is incredible. You make me feel alive again! I tried to forget you, but I simply can't. You're on my mind constantly. I'll do anything, *anything*, to get you back. Please tell me what I did wrong," he begged.

I was shocked. I couldn't believe he was talking like this, and immediately regretted my decision to visit. I felt nauseous and was trembling. "Richard, I don't want to talk about this. We're each going in separate directions. There's no way it could've worked and—"

"It *could've* worked, dammit! I know it could've, and I know it *will* work!" he exclaimed loudly. I pulled away from his grasp in shock. "Please, give *us* one more chance. I love you *so much!*"

"No, Richard. No…I have to leave now," I said firmly, feeling tears run down my cheeks, a torrent of different emotions overflowing, including fear, sorrow and guilt.

"I refuse to say good-bye because this *isn't* good-bye. I know you'll come to your senses and realize that we had something special, Cadence, something *really* special," he stated, with a terrifying level of confidence.

I stood and walked quickly to the door, and fumbled to put on my sandals. I was angry that he'd taken advantage of the situation to discuss our relationship, when all I wanted was to extend my sympathy. I turned around to say one last good-bye, but he was gone. The room was empty, so I said good-bye to the emptiness and quickly left. As I sped down the driveway I didn't look back at the house. My heart raced and I cried all the way home. My mom was the only one home, and tried to comfort me. "Cadence, sometimes grief makes people act in strange ways. I'm sure he was just—"

"No, mom, I think he's crazy…he's *obsessed*. I never want to see him again. I never want to hear his name again…I wish I'd never met him."

That night, and for many more, I had nightmares about trying to leave Richard's house and the door being locked, of having to wander through strange rooms trying to find Richard to let me out. The nightmares were horrible, but finally subsided once I started my new life in New York. Soon Richard became no more than a faint memory evoking merely feelings of pity.

# Chapter Thirteen

THE MUSIC, COUPLED WITH THE wine, was relaxing me. By closing my eyes I could momentarily shut out my present situation. My memory of that last encounter with Richard seemed so long ago, and I'd thought of him only rarely over the past ten years. How could a man be so deranged that he would exert this much time and effort and risk losing everything, for *me*? There were millions of women out there who'd do just about anything to have a man like Richard in love with them, especially one with this much money. It was ironic to think that I had everything I could ever need or want materially, yet felt like I had absolutely nothing so long as I was trapped with Richard.

I heard the violinist bow his last graceful note that faded away into silence through a lengthy decrescendo. My thoughts were then suddenly interrupted as I felt Richard touch my knee. I quickly opened my eyes. He was no longer in his seat, but instead was down on one knee, staring up at me intently. This couldn't be happening, I thought, as I cringed knowingly in anticipation of what was to come.

"Cadence, I've waited so long to ask you this question again. I want to ask it in a special way...in a poem I wrote for you ten years ago."

"Please, Richard, I'm already engaged—" I began, but he immediately interrupted to begin his poem:

*"You are the one I loved from first sight,*
*I think of you by day and each wakeful night.*
*Never to live another day without you,*
*We will soon be one and no longer two.*

*But from one we will create another life,*
*A perfect union of husband and wife.*
*I will love you forever so please accept this ring,*
*And forevermore my heart will sing."*

"Richard," I slowly began to respond in a whisper, "I *can't*...I'm in love with another man." I felt terrible, seeing the look of absolute hurt in his shiny, green eyes, for it felt exactly as it did the first time I refused his proposal. His face was suddenly pale...he looked so tired and sad.

"Please, Cadence," he whispered back. He then handed me the familiar tiny white box that he'd wanted me to have ten years ago. On top was the same small note that read: *Marry me, Cadence.* The words were carefully written in neat blue printing, exactly as I remembered. Had he never opened it since I last refused his proposal? I trembled.

"I just can't, Richard. You can't force someone into marriage, it has to come...naturally," I explained awkwardly, my voice quivering. He closed his eyes, inhaled deeply and then slowly exhaled. Finally, he opened his eyes, shaking his head slowly.

"Cadence, there is only one answer I can accept and that's YES," he said firmly.

I wondered how I should respond. Do I say *yes* to avoid confrontation and appease Richard, then continue planning my escape as soon as possible? Doing that would risk him marrying me in the very near future, for I felt sure that there were no invitations to be mailed, no guests to RSVP. I felt sick at the thought of a wedding with Richard instead of Christian. Never in my wildest imaginings would I have pictured being married without my family present and under such duress. I recoiled at the thought of Richard forcing himself on me before I escaped, and having to live as husband and wife. Feeding into his fantasy world would do the situation no good, other than to keep him appeased. I simply couldn't take the risk of agreeing to this false union. Would he hurt me, though? I looked down into his pleading eyes, and he reminded me for a moment of a little boy seeking approval. No, he wouldn't hurt me, he couldn't. I would continue to stand my ground. I felt a surge of fresh confidence that I could continue standing up against him and escape soon.

I began to shake my head, and said firmly, "NO, Richard, I *cannot* marry you, and you *cannot* force me." There was no more to say, no apologies to be made. He began shaking his head, and sat back down beside me. His face quickly became a deep red color, and his eyes appeared darker, filled with fury. I quivered as his hands clenched into fists, and he started to tremble.

"All right, if it's this *Christian* who's getting in our way, I'll ensure that he is no longer an obstacle," he said, calmly and in a very serious tone. I was not prepared for that type of threat, and couldn't contain my rage and fear.

"Richard! How *could you* say that? I would never, ever even *look* at you again if you did anything to Christian!"

"Well, it's *your* choice, Cadence. You *will* love and marry me or I'll make the necessary arrangements to—"

"Nooooo! Please no!" I cried, changing my tone from angry defiance to begging. I couldn't let him harm my beloved Christian, the love of my life. I pictured Christian, looking so handsome as he filled the auditorium with the sweet, exquisite tones of his cello. I remembered his proposal four months earlier...how he brought me into the empty theater at night and played a beautiful song that he'd written just for me. It was such an ethereal night, a vivid memory that would always remain clear in my mind.

"It's your choice, Cadence. I'm going to leave this room for five minutes and when I come back, I'll ask you one last time and you will say either yes or no, nothing else! I don't want any more begging or pleading, nor any arguments or negotiations. I just want an answer."

"But..."

"No. There's nothing more to say. Now think about it, Cadence, it's really a simple proposition. I can have this Christian eliminated within the next twelve hours, as I have many *connections,* and am more than willing to pay dearly for the removal of such an obstacle. I will prove it to you tomorrow by showing you the newspaper article announcing his tragic *accident,*" he said, with a callousness and lack of emotion that I found more terrifying than any volume of yelling. And with that, he briskly exited the dining room.

I sat there stunned and wondering what to do. I knew in my mind and heart that Richard was serious. Even if there was only a one percent chance that he would have Christian killed, could I risk it? But before I could contemplate further, the door to the kitchen swung open, and in walked Yamoto with a large plate full of beautifully prepared lobster.

He stopped dead in his tracks when he saw me sitting there alone, tears rolling down my face.

"I'm sorry, ma'am. I'll await Mr. White's instructions as to when the main course is required," he said nervously, while hastily turning around.

"No, please, I *need* to speak with you," I begged. "Richard won't be back for a few minutes," I added.

"I can't..."

"*Please* listen to what I have to say. I *swear* I'm telling the truth," I said earnestly, my eyes pleading with him for compassion.

"Fine," he said. "But I'll pretend I just placed this platter down if he comes back. I'll only listen for one minute," he whispered nervously. "And please whisper as this room may be bugged." I heaved a sigh of relief...finally a willing ear!

I began whispering quickly. "I'm *not* insane! He kidnapped me. Google my name, Cadence Weaverly, you'll see that I play in the San Francisco Symphony. My family lives in Montana. He just threatened to have my fiancé murdered; you *have* to warn him. His name is Christian Davidson. Just call the police, please! I *beg you*, please trust me," I emphatically explained. I could tell by the concern in Yamoto's small, black eyes that he believed me. Thank God!

"I don't know whether to believe you, Miss Weaverly, but my heart tells me you are truthful so I will do as you request, but it'll be risky," he said.

"Thank you soooo much. You won't be sorry," I said, as he gave me one last look of concern, then scurried out of the dining room with his tray of food. Finally, I had a chance of being rescued. Surely Yamoto would call the police within minutes. I still couldn't risk Christian's life, though. In the time it took the police to come here, wherever here was, Richard could easily hurt me and arrange to have Christian killed. No, I couldn't risk that. I would have to say a temporary *yes* to his proposal, and hope and pray that the police arrived to get me out of this nightmare soon.

Suddenly Richard entered the dining room, having changed moods completely. His face was no longer red, and his fists were unclenched. He looked like a different person. Richard walked over to me, and again got down on one knee. I was astonished at how quickly his moods could change. *Perhaps another trait of a psychopath*, I thought. "Cadence, this is the last time I will ask. Will you marry me?"

I gulped, and replied with a hesitant, "Yes," and was nearly knocked off my chair as he flung himself into my arms and began to kiss me passionately. I maneuvered my head quickly onto his shoulder, instead embracing him in a hug to avoid any more revolting kisses. He hugged me back, tightly, so tightly that I felt I couldn't breathe. "Please, Richard, let go, I can't breathe," I begged. He released me, and got back down onto both knees, firmly grasping my hands. He then took my left hand and carefully slid a large, sparkling diamond ring onto my ring finger. It felt heavy and awkward, and must have been at least three carats. Having a ring on that finger again reminded me of the ring Christian had placed on it many months ago. That ring was much smaller, but fit my finger more elegantly, and I felt resentful of this unwanted rock taking its place. My ring from Christian had been missing from my finger when I first woke up here, and I knew that Richard would never give it back so didn't bother asking. It really was the least of my worries, but still bothered me nonetheless. Hopefully, when the police arrested Richard, this house would be searched and my ring and other personal belongings would be returned.

"You've made me the happiest man alive, Cadence. I want you so badly that I don't know if I can hold off any longer," he exclaimed, as a look of pure joy spread over his face.

"No, Richard, let's wait until the wedding night," I uttered. "It will mean so much more if we wait until then," I assured, trying to appeal to his old-fashioned sensibilities. I had difficulty stating such blatant lies, but at least these lies were for a good reason, two good reasons actually, mine and Christian's safety.

"Alright, my love, then our wedding will be tomorrow. We'll fly out to our wedding destination first thing in the morning. Everything is arranged and waiting. I'll have the jet ready for a nine o'clock departure," he excitedly explained. Again I was stunned, but felt confident that the police would find me in plenty of time. This trip would never transpire, I said to myself. I didn't even bother asking about our wedding destination, as there was no need.

"I'm exhausted, I'd like to go to sleep now, Richard. I'm really not hungry," I said, looking at him with pleading eyes and smiling slightly to add to my cause.

He looked back with utter love and devotion, saying, "Cadence, that's fine. I'll carry you up to your final night of sleeping alone." And with that I was scooped into his strong arms and carried through the maze of halls, and up the stairs to my bedroom. He laid me gingerly on the bed, and tried to engage in another passionate kiss, which landed on my cheek thanks to my quick reaction. "You'll be such a beautiful bride, tomorrow, Cadence. Never will there have been, and never will there be, a lovelier bride," he said, his voice trailing off. Then he left, quietly shutting the door and locking it behind him.

That night I didn't sleep a wink, but prayed constantly that Yamoto had contacted the police, that I would be saved and that, most importantly, Christian would not be harmed. I tried to remain optimistic and keep my anxiety at bay by recalling my most precious memories of Christian...

# Chapter Fourteen

THE MUSIC OF THE ORCHESTRA came to an exhilarating end as we finished the last song in our rehearsal. I didn't want to waste a moment, and quickly but carefully pulled apart my flute and cleaned the three separate pieces. I wiped the outside surface with my soft, felt cloth until it gleamed, then placed it delicately in my case.

"Someone's in a hurry," chirped my friend Janine, who played the violin. She had dark red hair that hung down her back in long, soft curls. We had become good friends over the past year since I started with the San Francisco Symphony.

"Yep, I have to rush home and get ready to catch the five o'clock flight to New York. I'm soooo excited to see him!"

"I'm so happy for you Cadence. I'd do anything to find a guy as great as Christian." Janine had dated numerous men, but hadn't found Mr. Right. I knew it was only a matter of time before she found him, but she felt the pressure to settle down as she was in her early thirties and wanted a child soon.

"You will, I know it! What about that firefighter? The one your cousin was trying to set you up with?"

"Well, turns out that he rescued a woman from her burning condo and they're now dating! Can you believe it? Oh well, firefighters are a risky type to marry anyway, as their job is too dangerous. I want someone I can feel secure with and be certain to grow old with, but I guess you can ever be certain of anything," she said with a sigh.

"You're right, nothing's for sure," I agreed. "But I'm willing to bet a lot of money that it won't be long before you find someone," I said confidently. "I have to run but have a good weekend and we'll catch up on Tuesday at lunch."

"Okay, and have a ball!" Janine said genuinely. It was nice having a friend who was truly happy for me. It would have been easy for her to feel jealous that I had a boyfriend and she didn't, yet she was truly happy for me, which I appreciated.

I drove home and quickly showered, lathering myself in my favorite vanilla shower gel. Every time I flew to New York, or Christian came here, we were both giddy with excitement. We were so in love that we couldn't go more than two weeks without seeing each other. I thought about him constantly, and truly believed he was my soul mate.

Soon I was seated on the flight, and as the plane took off in a gentle incline towards the clouds I thought back to how Christian and I had met. It had been one evening two years earlier when I attended a performance by the New York Philharmonic. I tried to attend performances as much as possible, but my heavy workload in the Master's program at Julliard inhibited me from going more than a few times a year. That evening I was going with my friends, Adam and Rita, both dedicated musicians as well, who also adored a night out at the New York Philharmonic.

We had lucked out with great seats very close to the front of the auditorium. Filled with delicious sushi and sake, we sat in the comfort of our seats like three peas in a pod, anticipating the delight of listening to music, a passion we all shared.

The lights dimmed, and the curtain rose to reveal the highly regarded New York Philharmonic. Once the music began, it felt like I was in heaven. Two of my favorite works were being played that evening, and as the music soared, I delighted in following every note, every section, my ear anticipating the many twists and turns of each movement. It was when the cello began its solo, however, that a sense of beauty like nothing else I had ever experienced filled the massive auditorium. I could see the expressions on the musician's face, his overwhelming passion and focus on each and every sound emitted by his magical instrument. From where we were seated, I could make out the dark brown color of his hair, which was thick with curls. By the time he bowed the last note I felt a strong connection with him. After closing my eyes and absorbing the music, I found myself opening them to stare at this stranger. The program said that his name was Christian

Davidson and that he was new to the New York Philharmonic, having recently graduated with his Master's in Music from Rice University.

We all knew that students in our program were sometimes given backstage privileges to chat with the musicians after performances. Some of them were Julliard graduates, and were happy to share tips and information with current students about the latest job opportunities in various orchestras. It was not uncommon for a bunch of the musicians to go for drinks after a show, especially on a weekend, as was the case tonight. Adam, Rita and I had wanted to go clubbing after the performance; however, at this point all I could think about was meeting Christian.

Adam and Rita were chatting about the performance and I took advantage of a short pause in the conversation to present my request. "Do you two want to come backstage with me for a bit?"

"I thought we were going clubbing," said Rita, a confused look on her dark, radiant face. She wore her black hair short and I always enjoyed her myriad of facial expressions.

"I think it'd be fun to go for a drink with a few of the musicians," I said.

"If we go with the musicians, we'll feel obligated to stay at least a couple of hours and by that time the line ups at the clubs will be insane!" added Adam. He was also confused about my sudden change of heart.

"Guys, I *really* want to meet that cellist. He was so incredible and…"

They both laughed in unison. "Oh! Now I get it!" chirped Rita, and added, "Sure, why not. If he turns out to be as arrogant as most cellists who are *that* good are, then we can take off to the clubs."

"I don't think he'll be arrogant," I said. Somehow I felt like I knew him already, just from identifying so closely with his musical thoughts.

"You sound so sure! Remember that other cellist you liked in second year? Jean Pierre from Paris?" laughed Adam, putting his arm around me jokingly.

"How could I forget? He was such a jerk and just wanted one thing. Luckily I figured it out in time," I said as I cringed from that horrible memory. We all laughed remembering a few of the different arrogant musicians we had each fallen for at one time or another.

We made our way through the crowds and down the familiar stairways and halls leading backstage. We explained ourselves to two security guards, who let us pass when we showed our Julliard student cards. The backstage area had a large lounge with comfortable leather sofas where many of the musicians would sit and chat after performances. The place was crowded, and loud with conversation. The musicians were generally happy with the performance and it was evident, that for many, the night's festivities had only just begun.

As we looked around the room, my stomach felt queasy, like I was on a roller coaster. I immediately saw Christian standing on the other side of the room, chatting with a couple of other musicians. I was not usually one to approach a man, but for some reason tonight I was not about to abide by my unwritten rules of meeting the opposite sex and led the way towards him. I felt a surge of extra confidence from having my two close friends with me. If it was readily apparent that Christian was arrogant, or already taken, it would seem like we were all just socializing, and that I wasn't trying to meet him personally. We stood beside the small group, and when there was an appropriate pause in the conversation I took the opportunity to introduce myself, Rita and Adam. Suddenly I was so nervous that I could barely speak, but managed to somehow sound cheerful.

"Hi. I'm Cadence and this is Rita and Adam. We're studying at Julliard," I explained nervously.

A warm smile spread across Christian's face. He shook my hand firmly and then shook Rita and Adam's while saying, "Great to meet you." We proceeded to shake hands with the other two musicians as well.

"I wanted to tell you that your solo was amazing." I hoped I didn't sound like a stammering fool.

"Thanks," he said humbly and smiled. He certainly had no sense of arrogance about him whatsoever. He stared at me for a moment and I noticed the lovely brown color of his twinkling eyes. We both smiled and I felt an increasingly strong connection, not to mention butterflies in my stomach. He stood about four inches taller than me, and was of a medium build. His curly, soft brown hair was by far his most outstanding feature, and I had the urge to run my hands through it. I heard my mom's voice in my head saying: *Don't ever come on to a man, Cadence. Let the man do all the work and play hard to get.* I usually followed her advice, but in this case I was glad I made the effort to approach him. As for asking him out, I was not quite that forward and hoped that he would make the first move.

"A bunch of us are heading out for drinks. Would you guys care to join us?" he asked.

"Sure, that'd be fun," I answered, my friends nodding in agreement.

Christian and I spent the rest of the evening in deep conversation, unaware of anything else going on around us. Adam and Rita ended up having a great time with some of the other musicians, and ended up going clubbing around midnight. Instead, Christian and I found a quiet coffee shop to continue our conversation, mesmerized with one another. We discovered we had a great deal in common, and could constantly make each other laugh. He was kindhearted and generous, as evidenced by his volunteer work teaching music to underprivileged children on his days off. Like me, he'd had several relationships throughout college, but nothing serious.

"I can't believe its 4:00 a.m.," he said. "Tonight has really flown by, but I should get you home," he smiled. "When can I see you again?" he shyly added.

"How about tomorrow, I mean, um, later today?" I said, not believing I actually came across so directly. But his large grin immediately quelled my doubt.

"Fantastic! Let's go catch a cab." He led me out onto the street and hailed a cab. I didn't want this night to end and when he held my hand I felt butterflies once again. When the taxi stopped he asked the driver to wait a few minutes with the meter running. He then took down my number and walked me up the stairs to my building. "I had a great time, Christian," I said, staring into his dark eyes and returning his smile.

"I know it's only our first date, Cadence, but…" and then he pulled me into a passionate kiss. It was the best kiss I'd ever experienced, with just the right amount of fervor, yet with a gentleness showing respect and patience. I wanted more, but Christian slowly pulled away. "Thank you and see you tomorrow evening," he promised, and went down the stairs towards the taxi, looking back once as I gave one final wave before closing my door. I stood there literally jumping for joy. That night marked the beginning of what would be a wonderfully romantic relationship filled with laughter and love, cemented by the passion we both shared for music and our parallel life goals.

*****

I must have fallen asleep, as I was awakened by the announcement that my flight to New York City was landing. Soon after I was walking, then running towards Christian, who lifted me off my feet and hugged me tightly. He smelled fresh and felt warm, and kissed me passionately, oblivious to anyone around us. He had planned a romantic evening, and explained that we would stop by his place to change, then head out for dinner at our favorite restaurant.

We shared a wonderfully romantic dinner, and as we were sipping our last drops of wine, he cleared his throat and said, "Cadence, the next part of this evening is a surprise. I'm going to blindfold you when we get to the car, and no peeking until I say so," he explained, with an air of mystery. This was not unusual, as he often planned surprises for me. I obliged and accepted temporary blackness for the fifteen minute drive. Once we were parked, he came around to my door and guided me out of the car, down a sidewalk, through a door and into an elevator. I giggled at the foolishness of his plan, but was enjoying the suspense. Finally, after a few more minutes, I was seated on what felt like a plush, auditorium style seat. I heard the crinkle of paper, and a cork popping, then the pouring of liquid into a glass.

"Here, my love," he said softly, helping place my fingers gently around the stem of a champagne flute. "I want to make a toast to the..." he quickly cleared his throat, a sign I immediately recognized as Christian being nervous. "To the most wonderful two years of my life. I love you so much, Cadence," he said, in the sweetest, most sincere voice possible.

I moved my hands towards the blindfold trying to remove it so I could see his expression, but he stopped my movement. "Please, I have a surprise and don't want you to remove the blindfold until I say so."

Although I was anxious to stare into his gentle, twinkling brown eyes, I nodded my head in agreement. I sensed his head approaching, and felt his warm, soft lips meet mine in a passionate kiss. I then heard the tinkling of his glass against mine, and we both took a large gulp of the tasty, bubbly champagne.

"Now for your surprise...wait here for a couple of minutes, and don't remove the blindfold until I say so," he instructed merrily.

"But...where are we?" I asked, feeling like I knew the answer, but wanting confirmation.

"That, my dear, is a surprise to be revealed very, very soon," he laughed, quickly walking away. A lingering smell of musky cologne was left where he had sat, and I inhaled deeply, a huge smile glued to my face. I had anticipated that Christian would propose sometime this year, but never could predict exactly when...or how. I was certain he was about to ask me in some way and, given his highly creative personality, I was sure it would not be the typical down on one knee approach.

A few minutes passed during which I felt like screaming for joy, barely able to contain my excitement. I distracted myself by sipping the champagne, the sensation of the cold liquid sliding down my throat intensified by the lack of vision or hearing, as all I could hear was distant shuffling.

"Cadence, this is a song I wrote for you. It's about our love, about our past and future together. It's called *Finding Cadence*," said Christian, through a microphone. I could tell we were in a very large auditorium, likely the same one where we met, although in New York there were dozens of large theaters so I could be wrong. Suddenly music filled the air with the sound of a piano, violins, violas and a double bass. A glorious piece that was indescribably beautiful wove its way around the entire auditorium. I had to remind myself to breathe, as I sat there mesmerized, focused on every single note, every pause. When the cello made its entrance my heart melted. Tears filled my eyes at the beauty of Christian's playing. Goose bumps spread across my body as the piece came to a climax, the excitement built up to its full potential. I felt my body relax as the piece began to wind down, each theme coming to a resolution. I thanked God for how lucky I was to have found such a fantastic, talented, kind and compassionate man.

"That, my love, was for you. You can remove the blindfold now," he said, in a voice that was an odd combination of emotions, etched with both joy and anticipation. I hastily put down my glass and pulled the blindfold over my head. The lights were shining on the stage, which I looked onto from the first row of the first balcony. This was his auditorium, the one where we met! "I can't imagine many more mornings waking up without you by my side. I want to start a life together. Will you marry me, Cadence?"

"YES! Of course, Christian! I would love to be your wife!" I exclaimed, not remembering another time when I was this close to bursting with happiness. Christian jumped down from the stage, while the other musicians broke out in cheers and applause, and made his way to my balcony seat, where he held me in his arms and kissed me deeply.

"Come with me, Cadence," he said, pulling me out of the seat and up the aisle. He led us quickly to a large dressing room and locked the door behind us. "I can't resist you for another second!" he said, unzipping my dress as I pulled off his shirt to reveal his lean yet muscular torso. I planted kisses all over his chest as he lowered me down onto a sofa and had my panties off and his pants down in seconds. He kissed me all over and we had the most amazing sex I believed I would ever experience. Later, as we made our way sheepishly out of the theater, the security guard winked at us as we made our final exit onto the street.

# Chapter Fifteen

YAMOTO SAT AT HIS DESK staring at the black phone, its keys beckoning him to dial the police. It had been an hour since he had that unsettling conversation with Cadence Weaverly. He could not call the police from the kitchen, as was too risky. Instead, he needed to be in his private room. It had taken forty-five minutes to pack away the uneaten lobster dinner and put together an alternate meal for Mr. White, who didn't want to proceed with such a decadent meal on his own. He had asked for a Cobb salad instead, whistling happily as he walked out of the kitchen. He seemed strangely happy, given the circumstances.

Yamoto had promised Cadence that he would call for help. Yet now that he was left to his thoughts, he wondered if in fact she was crazy, and it would only result in him losing his job. Damn! He wished he could have a night off, as he would take the thirty-minute drive into the city and stay with his brother. Unfortunately, he was confined to this strange mansion. Although the pay was phenomenal, this place felt like a jail.

Could his employer really be holding this woman hostage? It seemed so bizarre to him. Although Mr. White was very strict and particular, he didn't seem crazy, like the type of madman who would abduct and hold a woman against her will. Yamoto recalled the psychiatrist who had told them about Cadence's condition, giving a lengthy presentation on what the staff could expect.

"She will be extremely convincing. People with schizophrenia often are. Being the paranoid type, Miss Weaverly will believe the strangest things. It is not uncommon for schizophrenics to turn against those they love, accusing them of all kinds of wrongdoing. Their mind takes control and they honestly believe that what they are feeling and saying is the *truth*. Again, they will do their utmost to convince you of their beliefs..." and on and on. Had this man really been a psychiatrist? Did Mr. White pay him to say these things to the staff? It was very difficult to tell, as it had all seemed so realistic. And, if she *was* suffering from such a severe mental illness, why in the world would Mr. White even *want* to marry her? It seemed to Yamoto that Mr. White could have any woman in the world for his wife, even the most beautiful actress in Hollywood or a supermodel. This whole thing just didn't make sense.

Yamoto recalled the extremely generous and unexpected $20,000.00 bonus Mr. White had given each of the staff for their understanding, patience, trust and confidentiality. Mr. White had explained that he didn't want anyone but him accessing the Internet in his home for privacy reasons and asked that the staff not take days off for at least the first month of Cadence's arrival, as he needed all hands on deck. He asked that they promise to find him immediately should Cadence approach any of them about being held against her will. The staff was also made aware that a comprehensive surveillance system ensured that almost every room, other than the staff's private quarters, was constantly monitored. However, they quickly learned that not every room had a camera, such as the dining room. Yamoto had heard through the staff grapevine that Mr. White didn't want a camera on them while eating, nor did he want one in their bedroom. Even though there was no camera in that massive dining room, Yamoto couldn't be sure it wasn't bugged and was now regretting his conversation with Cadence.

Yamoto closed his eyes and pictured Cadence begging and pleading for his help. She seemed so honest! He wished he could Google her and find out more about her. The look in her eyes was one of pure terror and she seemed to be a very genuine, trustworthy individual. But what if he called the police and was wrong? If he did it anonymously, then Mr. White wouldn't be able to trace it back to him, or would he? Suddenly he had an idea, he could place a quick call from his cell phone to the police and block his number. In his heart he knew that he must help Cadence. He was willing to take the risk of being wrong, but wanted to place the call so that Mr. White wouldn't know it was from him. The worst that could happen would be the police showing up and finding out it was all a hoax. Mr. White would be livid, but would not know who made the call. Even if Mr. White did find out and Yamoto was fired, he could always get work elsewhere. Although the pay wouldn't be nearly as much, even in the gourmet restaurants, it would probably be a blessing in disguise to be away from this unsettling place.

Yamoto had left his cell phone in his car, a black Honda Civic parked in the staff garage behind the house. He popped the automatic locks, leaned inside and grabbed his phone. The garage was dark as it was late in the evening and he didn't want to turn on a light. Feeling nervous, he wanted to get this over with quickly. Rather than dial 9-1-1, he decided to call the local police station, as it didn't feel like an emergency.

He shivered, staring around the dark, eerie garage. As he started to dial the number he heard the creak of the door, then the sound of footsteps heading briskly towards him. Amidst his sheer terror, he dropped his phone and turned to flee as everything went black.

* * *

I lay there, eyes wide with anticipation in my shadowy bedroom. When would the police come? Surely Yamoto would have called them hours ago. How far was this place from the nearest police station? Surely my case was well publicized and Yamoto would only need to give a brief explanation before they pieced together that it was me. Then I heard a loud bang that sounded like a gunshot, which quickly receded into nothingness as if it had never happened. I lay there frozen in fear. It could be *anything*, I tried to reassure my frantic mind. Maybe a hunter? After all, we were in the middle of nowhere.

As the long hours of the night slowly passed and no help arrived, my worst fears unfolded. Had Richard found out about my conversation with Yamoto? Was Yamoto okay? Would I be married against my will tomorrow? I felt feverish as I lay in that dark, creepy room, its whiteness shrouded in a blanket of pitch black.

# Chapter Sixteen

I MUST HAVE FALLEN ASLEEP at some point during that harrowing night, as I was awakened by Richard's deep voice in my ear. I jerked away as I felt his warm lips brush mine.

*"I'm getting married in the mornin'! Ding dong! The bells are gonna chime,"* sang Richard softly, in a cheerful voice. I wished I had never woken up, feeling helpless and dispirited. My optimism had vanished into hopelessness, and I felt doomed. The energy and drive I had to escape had been shattered by the police not arriving, and by the horrifying sound of the gunshot that rang out in the dead of the night. I kept my eyes closed, ignoring Richard. Maybe if I pretended that I was asleep he would leave me alone, but no such luck as Richard's large hand clasped around mine under the covers and his other trailed slowly up my leg.

"What's wrong, my love? Why are those beautiful baby blue eyes closed? The sky is so clear for our wedding flight. When I first saw the pale blue outside of my window this morning, I thought of your eyes and what a lucky man I am."

I made no response and my eyes remained firmly shut. What was there to say? I had told him repeatedly that I wanted to leave, that I didn't love him. I had promised I would marry him to spare Christian, thinking I would surely be free by now. Wishful thinking at the hands of a madman, I thought cynically.

"Cadence, the least you can do is give me a smile on the morning of our wedding day!" he stated, an edge of frustration creeping into his voice as his hand gently rubbed up and down my lower arm.

"Please, I'm not feeling well...leave me alone," I whispered, feeling apathetic towards everything.

He sat silently for a minute and then began to speak. "Cadence, I don't want to do this, but you've given me no choice. You agreed to marry me today, and all of the arrangements have been made. Please, I beg of you to do so without arguing. I don't want to have to resort to further persuasion, especially on our wedding day," he stated matter-of-factly, as if speaking to a misbehaving child.

With my lack of sleep and general feeling of failure, I was not about to argue. On the other hand, I certainly wasn't going to jump out of bed to eagerly begin getting ready for our sham of a wedding. Somewhere inside my soul there was still a spark of survival, a willingness to stand my ground at whatever cost. The spark came to the surface as I spoke calmly. "Richard, I thought about it all night and do *not* want to marry you. I shouldn't have said yes and only did because I felt forced and blackmailed," I said quietly. Would this risk Christian's safety? I immediately regretted my words.

"Let me show you something, Cadence," Richard said, in a calm and calculated manner, his voice changing like the flip of a light switch. He walked towards the wall that was directly across from my bed, and opened a cabinet that I had mistaken for part of the wall, as its seams blended in so well with the bright white paint. There sat a television with a remote control beside it. He grabbed the remote and flipped on the power, then entered a specific channel that I could see was a San Francisco news station. After a couple of minutes of sports highlights, a familiar female anchor came on to give the breaking news of the morning.

"A terrifying attack took place at four in the morning in the apartment of missing San Francisco musician, Cadence Weaverly. Her anguished fiancé, New York Philharmonic cellist Christian Davidson, was violently assaulted while asleep in her apartment. Neighbors called the police, but the assailant escaped. Davidson was transported to hospital by EMS, where he remains in stable condition. His injuries are not considered life-threatening. Police continue their investigation, while family and friends of both Weaverly and Davidson remain gathered in San Francisco, where they continue to work closely with investigators to locate the missing San Francisco flautist.

I sat on the edge of the bed feeling numb from what I'd just heard. Emotions raced through my body, a mixture of fear and anger, both fighting for prominence as I sat there shaking. Suddenly my mom appeared on the screen, looking distraught but trying to remain composed. Her soft, smooth voice spoke to the viewers: "Please, please STOP hurting us, whoever you are! We are begging you, PLEASE bring our daughter back! We will NEVER stop looking for you, Cadence. We love you so much and know that you are alive out there somewhere…" Then tears ran down my mom's suffering face as the female anchor came back on, informing viewers of a substantial reward offered for any information leading to my safe return.

"HOW *COULD* YOU?" I screamed at Richard, through a film of hot tears. Anger took over and pushed aside the intense fear I'd been feeling while being in the same room with this completely psychotic madman.

"Cadence, I warned you that he would be *dealt with* if you didn't obey my wishes," he calmly explained, as if doling out punishment to a child.

"I *agreed* to marry you last night, Richard! How could you have Christian harmed?" I sobbed. Poor Christian! I would give anything to have stopped him from being hurt. I loved him so much!

"Yes, Cadence, you agreed, *and then you went behind my BACK and broke your promise!*" he roared back, while standing up to pace the room.

"What do you mean?"

"You know what I mean! Would you like to hear the recording of you begging my chef to call the police and him agreeing? Given the circumstances, I think I'm actually being quite forgiving by not having had this Christian permanently eliminated last night! I had the incredible urge to have as many of his bones broken as possible, while sparing his life to appease *you*. I could have had his fingers broken and ended his pathetic little *career*. Next time there will be *no* chance for Christian to struggle," he said, confidently.

"*Don't hurt Christian anymore, Richard!*" I pleaded, while following him as he strode back and forth across the room. When there was no response from his enraged red face, I pleaded further, this time in a calmer tone, "Please, Richard, I'll do *anything* as long as you leave Christian and all of my family and friends alone."

"*Anything?* Okay then…" he said menacingly, then lunged forward and pushed me onto the bed, his heavy body pinning me down. He kissed me roughly, prying apart my lips with his tongue. I tried to kick and hit and yell but he didn't notice anything beyond his aggressive lust. I gasped for air, and felt as though I were drowning. He ground his pelvis into mine and I could feel the hardness of his erection through his pants.

I was certain he would rape me, but just as suddenly as he attacked, he pushed himself away and resumed pacing furiously. "Our first time making love ISN'T SUPPOSED TO BE LIKE THIS!" he roared, glaring at me. "I want you more than I've ever wanted *anything*, Cadence, but I'll wait and make love to you *after* we're married, as that's what I promised. And, unlike you, I keep my promises. And not another word about that man or I will not hesitate to finish him off!"

My life suddenly seemed inconsequential when I thought of losing Christian forever. Moreover, Richard had proven that he was capable of having anyone harmed to increase his control over me. I simply couldn't risk any chance of further harm to Christian, and so had to fulfill Richard's wishes. As much as I wanted to kick and scream, and to refuse his demands, doing so would sign Christian's death warrant, and risk the lives of my family. And even if he couldn't get to Christian again, he could harm my parents, siblings, friends…he truly held all the power. Even if my loved ones were under police protection, which I was hoping they now were, how long would that last? And knowing Richard, he would find a way to hurt them, as he certainly seemed to have far-reaching connections and hoards of money. I bowed my head in defeat, knowing that starting now I had to oblige Richard and feed into his fairy tale world of delusions. There may be a chance to escape down the road, but I couldn't realistically count on anyone or anything in the near future. I would never give up on the possibility of escaping, but for the time being I couldn't risk any more harm to those I loved.

With that thought in mind, I climbed off the bed, walked towards Richard and wrapped my arms around him from behind. He flinched, but then stopped in his tracks and stood still. I could feel his deep, quick breaths, and the intense heat coming from his large, muscular body.

"I'm sorry, Richard," I said, cocking my head so that my voice would reach his ear. "I know I was wrong to approach Yamoto, I was just scared. It wasn't Yamoto's fault for trying to help me," I said, suddenly hoping with all my heart that the gunshot I heard last night didn't involve Yamoto.

"I forgive you, Cadence. Yamoto is gone. He broke his contractual agreement by obliging your request and was punished accordingly," he explained, his breaths beginning to slow to a more comfortable pace.

"Please tell me you didn't hurt him, Richard? It was my fault and he…"

"Cadence, he's gone. He was not to be trusted and was dispensed with a quick and painless single bullet to the head," he explained, calmly. "By the time he realized what was happening, it was all over."

*Dispensed?* I thought incredulously. *Dispensed?* "How could you?" I whimpered, falling to my knees, weeping for the loss of innocent Yamoto and feeling incredibly sorry that I ever put him in that predicament. I had never imagined his life would be taken for trying to help me. How incredibly selfish I'd been. I would do anything to turn back time and not have approached Yamoto. Richard *truly* was a monster.

Richard got down on his knees and gathered me into his arms. I wanted to fight back, instinctively, but I was too weak and terrified to do anything but cry and passively accept his caresses and loving murmurs.

When my tears finally subsided, I got up enough courage to speak calmly to Richard, in an attempt to iron out the final details of our deal. As he stared into my eyes, and held my hands tightly, I began with what little strength I had left, "Richard, I will marry you, but you have to swear to me that you will *not* have anyone else hurt or killed. If anyone else is hurt in any way, I vow that I will do everything in my power to leave you immediately. I will risk anything, my life included, to escape from you if anything like this ever happens again." I stared intently into his eyes, trying to read his deranged thoughts in their dark green depths.

"Okay, Cadence, as long as you live with me as my wife and *never* try to escape. I expect that the vows you make to me this evening will be the oath that you live by; breaking any of them will mean that you have reneged on our agreement," he said matter-of-factly, as if negotiating a business contract.

I didn't respond immediately, but let his words sink in. How could I commit to never trying to escape again? That would mean I was defeated and had given up all hope of escape. On the other hand, the safety of my loved ones was paramount. Agreeing to Richard's terms didn't mean that I'd never find a way out, it just meant that I'd only ever risk it if I was one hundred percent certain I could escape and warn the police before Richard could harm anyone. I knew that if I tried any form of escape whatsoever, I would be taking an extremely great risk. For now, I would play my role as the leading lady in the movie of this lunatic's life. "Okay, Richard, I agree," I said quietly, as he sealed our contract with another unwanted, passionate kiss.

# Chapter Seventeen

THE NEXT HOUR WAS A blur as I got ready. I was then blindfolded and driven to Richard's private airport, which turned out to be close-by. I felt like a robot as I did exactly what I was told, all the while agonizing over the attack on Christian and Yamoto's murder.

Richard's mood was chipper and excited, while I had to exert every bit of energy I had to yield even a small reaction or weak smile. I gazed out the window, once my blindfold was removed, and stared at the mass of white fluffy clouds. My body and mind were exhausted, and I felt void of any emotion. It was as if my soul had left my body, as if it couldn't take any more anguish, and would come back once I was home where I belonged. But would I ever return home?

I clasped my hands tightly in my lap so Richard wouldn't be able to hold them, yet his large hand still crept onto my leg, gently caressing my thigh before stroking my cold fingers. I kept staring out the window so I wouldn't have to make eye contact. The soft, white leather seats were comfortably reclined, but despite being utterly exhausted I couldn't fall asleep. I felt horrible over Yamoto's death, and wished our jet would just crash and end this misery.

"Cadence, are you hungry? The food that has been prepared is very delicious and you should eat. You need your energy for our wedding," Richard said, in a concerned voice. He'd been very excited to take me on his jet, acting like a little boy proud of his new bike. When I didn't smile or make conversation, he became sullen.

"No, I'm not hungry, just tired," I said wearily, still staring out the window.

"Sweetheart, please look at me. This is our wedding day. You promised you wouldn't make things difficult," he whispered, with an edge to his voice.

I didn't know what to say. Sure, I wouldn't try to escape at this point, but I felt empty inside. I also felt nauseous and figured the bathroom would offer a temporary reprieve from this conversation. "I have to use the bathroom," I whispered back. He sighed as I stood up and walked back to the large bathroom, which was the size of four bathrooms on a regular passenger jet. It was sparkling clean and smelled like peaches. I immediately noticed a photo on the wall, which was a close-up of me playing a solo in the symphony a few months back. He had likely been in the audience, using a zoom lens to capture this photo totally unbeknownst to me. How many times had he watched me play? I felt a shiver run down my spine.

I still had a difficult time believing that I was on a private jet with Richard, whom I would very likely be married to by the end of the day. How could this be happening to me? I sat down on a small stool beside a vanity in the corner and cupped my head in my palms. I would stay here as long as possible, trying to kill as much time as I could before I'd be forced to continue a conversation with Richard. But as I should have expected, my brief solitude was interrupted by a knock on the door.

"Are you alright, darling?"

"I'm fine…please leave me alone." Sadly, there was no lock on the door.

"Sweetheart, I'm coming in," he said, and before I could respond the door opened. He looked down at me, then bent over and took my hands, gently pulling me up. "Let's go back to our seats. The meal is almost ready and I have wine poured for us," he said. I reluctantly went back to my seat, and he made a toast, "To our wedding day, the happiest day of our lives." I took a deep sip of the chilled wine, which was refreshing. I followed it quickly with another, and another. Perhaps I could simply forget this was happening and drink myself into oblivion.

"Cadence, you're drinking fast. You must like my choice of wine?"

I nodded, taking another long sip. By the time our meals arrived I had a nice buzz going, and continued drinking while only picking at my meal. I felt a wave of curiosity come over me, with a sudden urge to learn more about how this lunatic's mind worked.

"Richard, can you tell me what you expect our lives to be like?" I asked boldly. He looked surprised, yet smiled; he was probably relieved that I had finally initiated a conversation.

"Well, I plan to spend as much time together as possible: time outdoors, traveling, swimming, whatever you fancy. I have achieved a high level of success with my businesses, so I'm able to work only part of the time and can do most of my work remotely. You'll be able to practice as many hours each day as you like and never have any worries," he said confidently. "And we'll start a family as soon as possible, because I really want a child who is ours," he said. I felt even sicker to my stomach as I absorbed his words.

"Don't I get a say in any of this?" I asked, not able to stop myself from beginning an argument.

He looked surprised, but was still smiling and planted a soft kiss on my forehead. "Yes, of course you do. What do you want from our life together, Cadence?" he asked.

"Well," I said, looking directly into his eyes, "I want my career back. I want to see my family and friends. I want to know where we live," I said, the alcohol increasing my confidence. "And I'm *not* ready to have a child yet."

Richard's expression turned to stone, and he stared up at the ceiling shaking his head as he heaved a large, frustrated sigh. "*Please*, Cadence, don't say such hurtful things. You *could* have had a life with me that involved your family, friends and career, if only you had stayed with me ten years ago. You knew how much I loved you. I could've given you *everything* you ever wanted, but you *made* me do it this way!" he said furiously, his face becoming flushed. "I loved you so much. Do you know how *painful* these past ten years have been for me? How I worked day and night to build a life for us, without even a touch from you to keep me going? All the times I had to watch you from a distance, longing for you as I saw you in the arms of another man? You have hurt me more than you can *ever* imagine, yet I forgive you because I love you more than you could ever know," he said anxiously, clenching my hands tightly. "Now it's *my* turn to say what we'll do. You had your ten years, and now your life is *mine*," he said firmly. "And *nobody* else will share it, nobody *except* our children."

I gulped, feeling absolutely helpless, yet I continued, "I'm sorry I hurt you, I never meant to cause you so much pain. But *please*, Richard, let's wait to have a child! I'm still young and would rather get to know you again than rush into a family," I begged. It was one thing for me to live in this deranged situation, it was another thing entirely to bring a child into it.

"God will decide when we have a child, not you or I, Cadence," he said, in a slightly offended tone. "You won't be taking any more birth control pills, so it's out of our hands and not open to further discussion."

"How can you dictate my life like you're the parent and I'm the child? What kind of relationship will we have if I don't get any say?" I asked, feeling an urgency to convince him that my opinion mattered.

"When I'm convinced that you and I are on the same page, then you'll get a say. Until then, my dear, you'll not ruin our lives any more than you already have over the last decade."

I gave up on the conversation knowing that there was no way to have a logical, two-sided discussion and compromise with this psychopath. I closed my eyes, wishing again that the plane would crash.

# Chapter Eighteen

ALL TOO SOON THE JET landed and when we stepped outside it was very hot and humid. We were on what looked like a private airstrip, lined with dense shrubbery and palm trees. Richard explained that we were transferring to a helicopter since the small island we were going to didn't have a place to land a plane. I panicked when I saw the helicopter and automatically turned to flee. Richard grabbed my arm forcefully and whispered, "Don't even think about it, Cadence." Even if I did shout for help, I knew that Richard would quickly convince others that there wasn't a problem; then Christian would be in danger, as Richard would see this as breaking our deal. I felt utterly helpless, like a toddler being led by a parent. We walked a short way to a helicopter and climbed inside.

The helicopter lifted loudly into the air, and within seconds I could see the ocean underneath us; it was a deep greenish-blue. I loved the ocean and thought back to my last vacation with Christian, when we spent time at a beautiful five-star resort on the Mayan Riviera. We loved to sit on our fourth floor balcony and watch the sun set over the sprawling sea as we sipped wine. We couldn't get enough of the beach and aqua-colored water, frolicking like children in the waves. The thought brought a slight and fleeting smile to my lips.

"What are you thinking about, my love?" he asked, yet again interrupting my thoughts.

"Nothing," I lied. *Escape!* I wanted to say.

"It's so obvious when you're dishonest, Cadence. I can see right through you. Whatever you *were* thinking about made you smile, and

I wish that soon it will be thoughts of me that bring your beautiful lips into such a sweet smile," he said dreamily.

I didn't bother responding, but continued to stare out the window and noticed a small island in the distance, framed by a white beach.

"That's it, Cadence, *our* island…just you, me, and a few servants. We will be secluded from the world, and have ten days of just each other," he explained excitedly. I wished I'd tried to escape at the airstrip, now feeling absolutely no control over this impending situation. I already felt suffocated, and couldn't imagine how trapped I would feel having Richard with me twenty-four hours a day.

"Where are we?" I asked.

"We're in the Caribbean, on a remote island called White Island. I bought the island two years ago, having researched and visited about thirty islands in order to pick the ideal one for us."

I couldn't believe it. Before today I could have only ever dreamed of owning an island, which in any other circumstance would be amazing. A memory from ten years ago floated into my mind. Richard and I were lying on a hammock on my deck, looking at the stars and describing what each of our dream vacations would entail. I'd explained that mine would be to visit a secluded island, with hundreds of palm trees and soft, white sand that was as fine as baby powder. Unbelievably I now had this island, yet would rather be anywhere else.

"Well, aren't you going to say anything, Cadence? You used to get so excited about things, where has that spark gone?" Richard asked, sounding frustrated. *You killed it, you lunatic!* I thought angrily. I was sure he'd thought through this arrival many times, and had imagined a much more positive reaction from me.

"It's beautiful," I said, hesitantly.

"Well, now that we're landing I want to go over some details with you. There's one house on the island, which we'll go to right away to prepare for the ceremony. We'll each freshen up in separate quarters and Maria will help get you ready. I've also flown in a stylist to do your hair and makeup. Our ceremony will take place at seven o'clock in a gazebo overlooking the ocean, followed by a candlelit dinner on the beach," he quickly explained, in his usual highly organized and businesslike manner.

"You brought Maria?" I asked, the only response I could give to this elaborate, forced plan.

"Yes, of course. She flew here earlier today. I really trust her, and know that she'll be very helpful. In addition, there's a chef, a bartender and a gardener, as well as a security guard. They're all very discreet and will respect our privacy, and I'm now very confident that you will not try to solicit their help to escape," he said, with a meaningful look. I cringed inwardly, thinking again of poor Yamoto. "My dear, it will be like there is only you and me here," he continued. "We can do whatever we want, even make love on our very own beach," he exclaimed. I felt a pang of panic at the thought.

I continued to show no emotion, and wondered if I should put up another fight. How could I possibly go through with this? But I knew that if I refused he would follow through with his promise to kill Christian. I was caught in a horrible bind and knew I didn't have a choice.

As the helicopter was landing I could see the beautiful island, with lush greenery and multitudes of palm trees, surrounded by white sand beaches and the stunning blue-green sea. When the helicopter landed, we walked a short distance to a magnificent white house which had numerous windows and balconies overlooking the ocean. We climbed some stairs, and I could see the ocean very close-by. I was in awe of the size of the house, and the expansive beach that was only steps away. The large patio contained a hammock for two, a hot tub, and a swimming pool with its own small swim-up bar. "This is unbelievable," I said to myself, not realizing that Richard heard.

"I knew it!" he exclaimed, "I *knew* you would love our beach home!" He grabbed me and kissed me hard, lifting me off the ground and twirling me in a circle. *Murderer!* I thought as I tried to fight him off, but was no match for his strength. He finally let me down and led me into the house to give me a tour. It had a large sunny kitchen and a beautiful dining room, with both indoor and outdoor tables. There was a large living room as well, with dozens of red roses sitting in the middle of a coffee table in a very large crystal vase. "I'm keeping our room a surprise for later, so you can change in the other suite," he said, opening the door to a large room with a tiled floor that was beautifully decorated, yet simple and elegant. It had a Caribbean style theme, with artwork of people dancing in bright colors and fresh tropical flowers placed throughout the room. Candles were giving off subtle aromas that smelled like tropical fruit.

"Everything you need is here…other than me," he laughed, winking down at me. "I will see you when you walk down the aisle in about two hours, my love. I only wish it were sooner," he said, forcing one more kiss on me before leaving.

I stood in the empty room, absently wiping his kiss away with the back of my hand while wondering again if I was dreaming. The thought of escaping entered my mind once more, but I quickly dispelled it with the sobering notion of risking both Christian's and my family's lives if I were to do so. I would have to go through with this charade of a wedding, and pretend I was in a dream, then try to escape once I was back in the United States where I at least stood a chance.

Suddenly the door opened and Maria entered, smiling warmly. "Miss Weaverly, I have been asked to assist you. Shall I run you a bath or would you prefer a shower?"

"Thanks Maria, but I can take care of that myself."

"Okay, but let me show you where your clothing is for this evening," she said, opening a nearby walk-in closet. I immediately saw the soft white color of a wedding gown. I stepped inside the closet to examine it, curious as to what Richard had picked for me to wear. I gasped as I noticed that it was the gown I had bought for my upcoming wedding to Christian. How could he do this? Not only would he force me to marry him, but he'd do so having me wear the gown meant for my real wedding. I sank to my knees in the dark closet and cried into the soft fabric of the gown, ignoring Maria's pleas for me to use tissues and not wet the dress.

I finally got up and went to the bed feeling utterly exhausted, where I lay down for a nap. Before leaving the room, Maria warned me that I needed to shower and get ready soon, and that she would wake me up in half an hour. I was asleep instantly, and dreamed about the day I found that wedding dress. I came out of the change room wearing it, and saw the huge smiles light up my mom's and sister's faces. "That's the one!" they both exclaimed in unison, my mom wiping a tear from her cheek.

"I love it, too," I said happily. The dress was strapless, and had beautiful beading on the bodice, which flowed into a princess style skirt, with a medium length train.

"Who *is* that man staring in the window?" my mom asked the sales lady, while I turned to see a tall man wearing sunglasses and a trench coat standing on the sidewalk, gazing in at us.

"Some creep…how nosey! I will have him leave at once," the sales lady said, rushing towards the door, but before she reached him, he quickly strode away.

My mom and sister continued to compliment me on finding the ideal dress. It fit me perfectly, as luck would have it, and they agreed to sell me the sample and save the hassle of having to wait for it to be made. I took it to my apartment where it had hung in a cloth bag for only two weeks before I was abducted.

# Chapter Nineteen

"WAKE UP, MISS WEAVERLY," URGED Maria, standing at the side of my bed. I had fallen into a deep sleep, and was awoken much more quickly than I wanted. In fact, part of me wished I would never wake up. The dream that I just had entered my mind. Had that been Richard outside of the dress shop? I wondered in retrospect. *Without a doubt,* my deepest instincts told me.

"Okay, I'm awake," I mumbled, having no motivation to get out of bed.

"You have time for a quick shower, as the stylist will be here to do your hair and makeup shortly," explained Maria, somewhat anxiously. She could probably tell that I lacked the will to move.

"I don't need a stylist, Maria. I can do my own hair and makeup just fine," I said firmly.

"Not on your wedding day! Mr. White specifically requested—"

"Damn Mr. White...trying to plan my every move! I'm *not* an invalid, Maria," I said, frostily. Why was I bothering to put up a fight? What good would it do anyway?

"Please, Miss Weaverly, don't speak of Mr. White like that, he may hear you," she pleaded nervously, avoiding eye contact with me and wringing the corner of her dress between her hands.

"Okay, I'm sorry. Fine, I'll shower then." I noticed Maria heave a sigh of relief, as I rolled out of the soft bed and sauntered into the grandiose bathroom. I then entered the large, tiled shower. I wasn't surprised this time to find all the toiletries I was accustomed to. Without thinking, I shaved my bikini, legs and underarms, which hadn't been touched in days. Why bother, I wondered, as I finished out of habit.

Once I was dried off and in a robe, the stylist was waiting at the vanity in the bedroom. She looked Jamaican and had a warm, pleasant smile. "Wow, you gonna look lovely, Miss Weaverly! You a purdy lady," she said, as she began blow drying my hair. "You must be excited about yer weddin'," she said, as she styled my long hair into an updo.

I didn't know how to respond, but figured there was no point in alerting her to my many problems, the worst of them being the death of Yamoto and the injury and potential risk to the lives of my loved ones, not to mention my imminent forced wedding to this murderous lunatic. "I guess so," I said.

"Jeez, ya *guess* so! I'd give anythin' to be marryin' such a fine lookin', rich man who owns this here beautiful island," she said, shaking her head but still smiling.

I tried to smile back, and closed my eyes to try to relax myself. The time passed quickly, and soon she had applied my makeup, which looked lovely and brought my forlorn face to life. She was quite talented at her trade, and I complimented her on it.

"Why, thank ya, Miss. Tis' an easy job startin' with a face and hair as purdy as yers," she said. "And those blue eyes, the color of our ocean here." For a moment I wanted to hug her and cry out all of my fears and worries into her soft, warm shoulder, but I restrained myself.

Once the stylist left, Maria made sure that I put on some of the perfume Richard loved; the same one I had worn back when we were dating. She then helped me into the wedding dress. It fit almost as well as it had in the store, even though I'd lost several pounds from the stress of the past few days.

"Mr. White asked that you wear this diamond necklace and earrings…they were his mother's," said Maria, as she did up the clasp without waiting for my approval. Yet again, I didn't have a choice. The string of diamonds shone brilliantly and must have been very valuable. Its weight made me think of a noose around my neck, a thought which I tried to quickly shut out.

I looked in the mirror, feeling a sudden mix of emotions. This is how I dreamed I would look on my wedding day and I loved the feeling of the beautiful dress. I also felt a wave of anger that I was being forced to go through these motions. It was one thing to abduct me, another to actually force me into a wedding ceremony and expect me to be a happy, glowing bride!

"Ready, Miss Weaverly?"

"No, but I really have no choice, so let's go," I said, noticing Maria flinch at my remark.

"I'll be a witness, as will Leroy, the chef." I turned and stared at Maria, walking next to me. *Do you know what happened to Yamoto?* I wanted to ask. *Mr. White murdered him and Leroy is his replacement!* I wished beyond wishing that she knew the truth and realized what she was doing. It would take all of my focus and willpower not to cause a scene and try to run from the ceremony, but I had to keep my promise to Richard to protect Christian.

"Do you like the dress I chose to wear for your wedding?" asked Maria, catching me off guard. In my state of panic I didn't realize she wasn't wearing her customary white maid's outfit. Instead she was dressed in an elegant blue evening gown, her lovely, shiny black hair hanging in curls.

"You look beautiful, Maria. What a nice dress," I said, not usually one to miss things like this. Normally, I was very observant and liked to make people feel good.

"Thank you, Miss—"

"Please, call me Cadence," I interrupted.

"Thank you, Miss Cadence."

*****

All too soon I was standing by the patio doors. Maria handed me a fragrant bouquet of tropical flowers and said she would lead the way to the gazebo where Richard was waiting. It was across the lawn and I couldn't help but notice the brilliant sunset beginning to slowly pave the way to night. The magnificent sky was painted in bright pinks and oranges. I could hear music playing, one of my favorite pieces beckoning me to walk towards the gazebo and Richard. I tried to take a step and hesitated. I could run, run through the house screaming, or try to find a boat, even swim. *Stop it, Cadence*, I thought. There's *no way* you're getting out of this, I reminded myself. I couldn't risk the lives of those I loved most.

With that thought, I slowly walked down the aisle wishing I was on my dad's arm, as I always imagined I would be on my wedding day.

The aisle was lined with dozens of torches leading the way to the large gazebo. Inside there was an official looking man wearing black robes, who also looked Jamaican. Standing on either side of Richard were Maria and another man, who must be Leroy, the chef. He too looked Jamaican, and very kind and jovial.

I felt as though I was in a trance as I stepped into the gazebo, meeting Richard's intense stare. He looked very handsome in a light grey suit, smiling broadly down at me and mouthing the words *I love you*. I stopped beside him and he gently took my hand in his. This would be extremely romantic if only I loved him, I thought, as the candlelight flickered all around us, and the sun continued its smooth descent towards the ocean. As the music faded away, Maria discreetly took my bouquet. The Officiant welcomed us and after a brief introduction quickly proceeded to the exchanging of vows. I hadn't noticed the photographer off to the side until now, as he began snapping photos.

"Please repeat after me, Mr. White," the Officiant said. "I, Richard, take you, Cadence…"

"I, Richard, take you, Cadence…" said Richard earnestly, grasping my hands tightly, willing me to stay with him. He spoke the vows without hesitation, as if he'd rehearsed this moment many times before.

"Now please repeat after me, Cadence. I, Cadence, take you, Richard…"

"I …Cadence, t…t…take you, Rich…Richard," I said in a fragile voice, my whole body shaking. I suddenly felt faint, and started to sway, closing my eyes to maintain my balance. I felt Richard's hand grasp my waist, again willing me to stay and finish my vows. Despite my intentions, I looked up at Richard and whispered, *"Please,* don't make me…" I pleaded with my eyes, as a few tears escaped and slid down my cheeks.

He stared down at me with an irate glare, then leaned down and whispered, "Cadence, you know what will happen if you don't do this," then he delicately nibbled my ear. I immediately continued the vows, finishing my empty words mindlessly.

"I now pronounce you husband and wife. You may kiss your bride." And with that, Richard lifted me off the ground and kissed me passionately for a few seconds, before gently placing me back down. Maria and Leroy clapped and congratulated us both, then the music began and Richard took my hand and walked me out of the gazebo and towards the beach, as the sun finally disappeared. I felt that the sunset symbolized the darkness that had just surrounded my life, and wiped a few more fresh tears from my cheeks.

"You look *absolutely ravishing* my love, my...*wife!*" Richard said. I ignored him as I inhaled the scents of the tropical flowers around us, once again reminded of my last vacation with Christian. At the end of the beach was a wooden platform set up with a candlelit dinner surrounded by torches. I couldn't deny that it was absolutely beautiful... the most romantic place for a dinner I could imagine. The waves were lapping against the shore only a few feet away, and classical music was playing as a waiter stood nearby to cater to us. Maybe this wouldn't be so bad, I thought...if only I was with Christian.

Before sitting at the table, Richard walked me to the edge of the water and took my hands. "Cadence, I am the happiest man alive. I now have you back after so many years of waiting. Please look at me and kiss me like you used to when we were dating...don't make me constantly fight for your affection," he asked.

I almost felt a surge of sympathy for a moment, until I thought of how I would be held hostage for God only knew how long. "Richard, I can't just suddenly turn on my emotions. You know I didn't have a choice in any of this," I said quietly, my voice edged with fatigue and frustration.

He looked hurt and bowed his head, shaking it gently. "There will come a day when you *will* love me, but for now I need your affection at the very least. You used to find me attractive, so please try to bring back those feelings," he said, a pleading look in his green eyes. He suddenly began kissing me hungrily. His forcefulness didn't give me a chance to pull away, so I endured the kiss and tried to block out everything else. The kiss felt vaguely familiar...his same style of kiss from ten years ago.

Finally the kiss ended and he embraced me tightly. "That felt wonderful, my love. *Thank you* for not fighting me," he said. Little did he know that I was only temporarily finished fighting; I would never give up on trying to escape from the jail he'd built around me.

# Chapter Twenty

STARS COVERED THE SKY, ILLUMINATING the evening with a soft, white glow. "Would you like another glass of wine, Madame?" asked the waiter, pouring as I slowly nodded. It was my third glass of wine, which was helping to numb my anxiety.

"I'm glad you like the wine, Cadence. Are you *sure* you liked the main course? You barely touched it," Richard asked, sounding concerned.

"It was fine…I'm just really tired," I said, resigned to the fact that I was not going to get away with another night in my own bed.

"I'm sorry, darling. How about some Jamaican coffee? Or perhaps a Spanish coffee?" he asked.

"I'd prefer wine," I answered, again staring up at the stars. *I'd prefer anything but this.*

Richard kept on trying to initiate a conversation, but I simply responded with short answers. Soon the waiter brought out a wedding cake. It was a miniature replica of a traditional three-tiered wedding cake, with thick white icing and ornate flowers. I gasped as I saw the cake topper. It was the tiny bride and groom sitting on a wooden swing that my grandmother had given me before she died. I had been saving it for Christian's and my wedding cake. My eyes filled with tears as I reached forward and pulled it off the cake, cradling it gently in my hands.

"How could you take this from me?" I asked, in barely a whisper.

"*Take* it? What's yours is mine, Cadence, and what's mine is yours. I was only trying to surprise you. I know how much you loved it and would want it on your wedding cake," he said calmly, looking surprised at my reaction.

"How did you know that?" I asked.

"I know *everything* about you, Cadence. I read your e-mail about it, when you said how important it was to have it on your wedding cake," he explained in a nonchalant tone.

"What? You read my e-mails?" I asked, shaking my head. Christian and I not only talked on a daily basis, but also e-mailed and texted regularly when we were apart, and I recalled explaining the cake topper to him over e-mail only weeks ago.

"Cadence, please calm down. You've gotten yourself all worked up again. I needed to be part of your life, even if you were unaware of my presence. I needed to know what was important to you, and how you've changed over the years, so that you weren't a stranger to me. But the truth is, so much of you is just as I remember: your expressions are the same, the aura around you is the same, even your scent is the same..." he said, his voice drifting off as he stared across at me longingly.

"You're unbelievable...unbelievably obsessive and controlling," I said, taking another deep drink of my wine.

"But you love me nonetheless," he said, smiling.

"I *don't* love you," I stated quietly.

"You *do,* you just don't realize it yet."

"I don't."

"Dance with me," he suddenly demanded, with a dazzling smile. Before I could respond he was standing up and tugging at my arm, forcing me to my feet. I tried to push him away, but as usual was no match for his strength. He pulled me close to him as I struggled to get free. Tears streamed down my face as the song Christian and I had chosen for our first dance began playing. It was the classic, *Unchained Melody* by the Righteous Brothers, a favorite of ours that would never grow old; it had also been my parents' first dance. How could this be happening? Just when I thought Richard had crossed the line further into my private life, he would pull out another surprise from his insane repertoire.

His lips suddenly interrupted my thoughts, and I felt like I couldn't breathe as he kissed me hungrily. Finally, I was able to pull away. "Can we please sit?" I asked, as the song finished.

"Of course, my love."

I walked quickly back to the table and drank more of my wine. If reality wasn't going to go away, at least I could smooth its razor-sharp edges. If I was going to be forced to sleep with Richard, I was certainly not going to do so sober.

"Cadence, stop drinking so much, I don't want a repeat performance of your graduation," he said, sounding like a scolding parent.

"Richard, I'm an adult and I'm enjoying this wine," I said firmly, taking another swig.

"Let's go for a walk down the beach," he commanded, trying to change the subject.

"Okay," I said, grabbing the bottle, which was half full, to take with me.

"What *are* you doing?" he asked, reaching to take the bottle away from me.

"Richard, I *am* bringing the wine. Don't try to stop me or I won't go on the walk," I said, feeling childish as I tried to assert myself.

"Suit yourself," he said, clasping my hand firmly in his as he helped me off the platform and onto the soft, white sand. "Let's take off our shoes," he said. We both slipped off our shoes and began walking on the sand which felt like baby powder between my toes. I had never felt sand as soft as this.

"This sand is so soft," I quietly commented, not really meaning to start a conversation.

"Isn't it? I *knew* you'd love it!" We kept walking, the moon and starlight creating a soft glow along our path. It was quite dark, though, and I felt isolated as the lights of the house began to fade as we walked further down the beach. "Can I ask you a question?" he said, a little hesitantly.

"Sure," I replied, taking another swig of wine directly from the bottle. I noticed him wince at this, a look of disgust etched on his shadowy face. Like ten years ago, he still didn't drink very much and frowned upon those who did, yet he obviously thought that kidnapping and murder were perfectly okay.

"What attracted you to me ten years ago?" he asked.

I was surprised at his question, but it was relatively harmless compared to what else he could have asked. I thought about it for a few moments. At the time I found Richard very attractive, both physically and intellectually. He was also very different from the high school guys

I was accustomed to, which had instantly sparked my curiosity. Plus he was mature for his age and his intensity was magnetic, drawing me towards him and wanting to get closer. Yet that same intensity is what also pushed me away, as it quickly became overwhelming and unnerving. "You were mysterious, and well...handsome and smart," I said, trying to explain my thoughts and feelings from way back then.

"Am I still any of those things?" he asked softly, slowing down our pace.

What was I to say? I felt intoxicated and confused as to what emotions I should feel. I felt hatred towards him and strong fear, while at the same time pity. He was being so gentle, almost like a little boy crying out for love. I had a strong inclination not to hurt his feelings. "Well, yes, you're still those things," I said, thinking he was still very mysterious but now in a completely deranged sort of way. And as much as I hated to look at him, he was still very handsome. And he was smart...he had a sharp intelligence, which I had no doubt was behind his great wealth. Plus, only a brilliant mind could have orchestrated and gotten away with this whole bizarre abduction.

He stopped and looked into my eyes. "Thank you, Cadence," he whispered, then bent down and planted a gentle kiss on my cheek. I was shocked that he didn't force another passionate kiss on my lips. "Let's walk a bit further...this night is perfect," he said, squeezing my hand as we began to walk again. We were silent for a minute and then Richard asked me another question, "Cadence, have you ever made love on a beach?"

My eyes widened, shocked at the intrusiveness of his question. "That is *none* of your business!" I said, but nonetheless thought back to my vacation with Christian on the Mayan Riviera. Although the idea had crossed our minds, neither of us liked the thought of sand and crab interference, so opted for our hotel room instead.

"Please be honest with me. Did you and your boyfriend make love on the beach on the Mayan Riviera?" he asked.

"How dare you ask me such a personal question? And besides, with all of your spying you probably know the answer anyway," I said, trying to pull my hand from his.

"I wasn't there, Cadence. It would have been too painful. And I decided not to have you followed, as I couldn't bear to hear about your trip," he said sadly. Again I felt a mix of pity and anger. "I wanted so much to bring you back into my life before that trip, but I wasn't quite ready. Things had to be perfect or something could have gone wrong. But every moment you were on that vacation was very painful for me," he explained. "I couldn't sleep for the entire week and I regretted letting you go away with him."

I was at a loss for words, and couldn't believe his level of possessiveness, talking about me as if he controlled me even then. *Letting* me go away with Christian? I found myself remembering that wonderful holiday. I was glad he didn't spy on me, and thankful that the moments Christian and I shared at that beautiful resort would always be between just the two of us. "Thanks for not spying on me. My privacy is very important to me," I said, in what I hoped was an icy tone. I was feeling very light-headed from the wine. I hoped that he'd forgotten about the making love on the beach question, but my hopes were dashed when Richard said, "Anyway, the reason I asked is because I have always imagined us together for the first time under the stars," he said quietly.

I took another gulp of wine, wishing I was not hearing this. "Let's go back," I said suddenly, "I'm cold and…"

"Cadence, it's a very warm evening and we're getting close to our spot," he said, abruptly turning down my request.

"What?"

"Up ahead, you can see it faintly," he said, pointing down the beach.

As we continued a few more steps along the beach, I began to see the outline of what looked like a bed. I cringed and made another attempt to turn back. This *couldn't* be happening. "Richard, I really don't feel like…"

"Cadence, please don't ruin this moment," he said, tugging my arm to move me along faster. Finally, we were only a few feet away and stopped. A large bed was sitting on the beach; it was elegantly made up in what appeared to be white silk sheets covered in red rose petals. Surrounding the bed were four torches burning romantically.

I was consumed with an uncontrollable impulse to run. Without even a pause to entertain a second of reason, I suddenly turned around and bolted as fast as I could, willing myself to fly away from this island. I felt like a plane ready for takeoff…if only I could get more speed. "CADENCE!" he yelled, chasing after me. In only a matter of seconds

I felt his arms surround me and force me roughly to the ground. Luckily the sand was soft, as the fall was rough. Before I could wrestle away he had my wrists pinned down and was braced on top of me.

"LET ME GO!" I screamed, but my yell was cut off by his lips. He began kissing me forcefully, moving his head in unison with mine each time I tried to turn away. I felt like I was suffocating. Finally he pulled away and I gasped for air.

"You are *mine*, Cadence! I *can't* wait any longer," he whispered into my ear, while nipping my earlobe.

"NOOOO!" I yelled, struggling to get free. This was followed by more kisses, each more ferocious and hungrier than the last, his tongue eagerly exploring my mouth. This couldn't be happening, I thought, as I desperately fought to free myself. "STOP!" I gasped, as he ripped at my dress, tearing the fabric to expose my breasts.

"You are *so beautiful*," he said, planting kisses on each of my breasts, then burying his head between them and moving down to kiss my stomach. He then pulled off my dress and underwear as I kicked and thrashed in the soft, white sand.

"Please don't rape me!" I begged, as torrents of tears ran down my cheeks.

"You're my WIFE, Cadence, I'm *making love* to you," he said, suddenly scooping me up into his arms and carrying me towards the bed. "Don't fight me, Cadence. I'd like to make love to you but it's up to you how it goes," he said, the hint of a threat etched in his voice. He quickly pulled off his clothing, while maintaining a constant grip on me so I wouldn't try to escape. His large, tanned, muscular body glistened with sweat.

Somewhere in my intoxicated and petrified mind I reasoned that there was no point in fighting. His threats had proven to be real and I had no chance of getting help or escaping from this deserted, private beach on his own bloody island. He began kissing me again and this time I didn't kick or try to scream, but just cried silently and let him continue. Soon he was forcing himself into me and moaning in ecstasy. "Oh Cadence, you're finally *mine*."

# Chapter Twenty-One

I WAS AWAKENED IN THE morning by the sound of a bird chirping nearby. It was early dawn, and the waves were lapping gently on the beach. Richard was asleep beside me. I had a throbbing headache from the wine, and felt sore and bruised from his horrible violation the night before. My eyes were dry and raw from crying until very late into the night, when I was finally able to fall into a restless sleep. I dreamed about Christian, that he and I were trying to escape from this island together, but in whichever direction we ran there was a wall we couldn't climb.

As I looked at Richard and saw how deeply he was sleeping a thought came to me... I could try to suffocate him with my pillow. Perhaps by the time he realized what was happening he would be close to passing out and not strong enough to fight back? I needed to try, I thought, as I imagined him violating me over and over again in the days to come.

I slowly sat up, every movement calculated so as not to wake him. I firmly gripped both sides of my pillow, slowly inching it towards his face. He looked peaceful and boyish, his blond hair tussled and a slight smile on his lips as he breathed deeply and regularly. For a moment I was brought back to one of our picnics when he had taken a nap in much the same position. My arms stopped inching the pillow forward as I realized I couldn't go through with this. I was not a murderer, and as horrible as this man was, I thought about how thoughtful and kind he was before I broke his heart. I brought the pillow back to its place, faced away from him and silently cried in defeat.

Suddenly Richard stirred. When he softly said my name, I pretended I was still sleeping. I felt him gently stroke my hair, but continued to breathe slowly and steadily so he wouldn't know I was awake, or at least I hoped he wouldn't.

What was I going to do? I was scared, scared that I would be stuck in this *marriage* for many more days, perhaps even weeks or months. My situation was much worse now that I was his wife. The horrible possibility of becoming pregnant entered my mind and I wished desperately that I had some form of birth control. Suddenly I felt panicked and my heart began to quicken its pace. I needed to escape soon, before there was more than myself to consider. However, my escape would have to be carefully orchestrated so that Richard wouldn't have time to hurt Christian or my family; I shuddered at the thought. Richard must have felt my shudder.

"Are you awake, my love?"

No response.

"I can tell that you're awake," he said, leaning over me and planting a kiss on my cheek. "I can't believe that you are *finally* my wife, Mrs. White, Cadence White, my perfect, beautiful bride. I always imagined making love to you, but it was even more wonderful than I ever thought it could be. You have turned into an absolutely gorgeous woman, Cadence," he said, sighing deeply. "Please say something, Cadence…I know you're awake," he said impatiently, pressing up against me from behind, once again with a hard, eager erection. Not again, I nervously thought.

"Please let me sleep some more, I don't feel well," I mumbled.

"Darling, there will be plenty of time to sleep on our honeymoon, but right now I can't resist you," he said, as he began to kiss my neck. As his hand crept around to squeeze my breast, I wondered how many more times would I have to endure this?

As he began touching me, I tried to preoccupy my mind by going through my favorite symphonies. I played out each bar of music in my mind, envisioning the notes unfolding. Even though I had no control over being raped by Richard, I did have control over what I thought about while he was doing it. Within a few minutes he sensed that I had tuned out and was not at all responsive, so he stopped.

"Cadence, please *make love* to me," he whispered. "I can't stand you lying there like a rag doll. I need to please you...I need to make you feel like you make me feel," he begged.

"I ... I can't, Richard. You can control almost everything I do, but you can't make me love or want you," I said, with a blunt certainty.

There were a few seconds of silence and then he said, "It's *him*, isn't it?"

"What?"

"It's *him*! That nuisance is preoccupying your mind and emotions. You won't be able to love me until he no longer exists," Richard stated.

I turned around quickly, looking him square in the eye. "Christian has nothing to do with this! I would feel the exact same way, even if I had been single before all of this. This is about you trapping me and forcing me to marry you, then expecting me to act like we're normal lovers while you *rape* me!" I declared. "If you do *anything* else to Christian, or anyone else, I will never, ever let you touch me again...I *will* kill myself first!" I declared. I was terrified of how he might respond, given how unpredictable he was.

"I need a few minutes to think on this," he said, as if this was a business negotiation and I had made an offer he needed to consider. He stood up and walked down towards the water. He was completely naked and looked very handsome and fit, I thought; in any other circumstance I might find him attractive, but at present he was the most revolting creature on earth. He was an unpredictable and savage monster, who was extremely manipulative and conniving.

He turned and walked down the beach a short way. I noticed him shaking his head and clenching his fists. Then he suddenly screamed, "Aaaarrrggghhh!" I shuddered with fear at the deafening sound. I knew he was crazy, but it wasn't until this moment that I realized he was like a wild animal...calm and calculating one moment, then ferocious and uncontrolled the next. My life and those of my loved ones were entirely at his disposal, I thought uneasily. What if he cracked and I had no way of negotiating with him? I *had* to find a way to maintain the upper hand.

He walked briskly back to the bed, and stood facing me. I pulled a sheet around my naked body, and stared up at him fearfully. He meant business. "Cadence, I will give you *one more* chance. I expect you to give me affection as I give it to you. Even if you are not in love with me yet, I want you to do everything in your power to *fall* in love with me. I don't want to have one-way conversations, where you don't take any interest. I don't want to make love to a rag doll. I have given you everything you could ever possibly want, as well as my deep love and devotion," he said, his voice cracking with hurt and frustration. "I know this has not been easy for you, Cadence, and that you have feelings for that *man*," he said, a tone of disgust in his voice as he said "man." The love of my life was nothing more than a bothersome insect to this lunatic.

I noticed his eyes had become teary, as he was very hurt. He was like a little boy at that moment, crying out for a hug. But I stayed still, my heart racing with fear, and my mind a confused myriad of emotions.

"I don't want our relationship to be such a struggle," he went on. "So much in life is a struggle. Everyone I ever loved has left me and for so many years I was alone," he said quietly, his voice cracking again. "Please *love* me, Cadence, please *try* to love me," he said, suddenly sitting on the bed, then flopping down and hugging me tightly with only the silky sheet separating us.

He began sobbing; it reminded me of the time I had visited him after his mother died and he had cried in my arms, sobs raking through his large body. I looked down at his blond head and almost felt a maternal instinct to hug him back. How could someone be a monster one moment and a vulnerable child the next? One moment he was raping me and I would have killed him if I had a weapon, and the next moment I was fighting off the urge to hug him and stroke his soft hair, to wipe his tears away and tell him everything would be okay. He was indeed taking me on a roller coaster ride of confusing, conflicting emotions, and giving me a glimpse of how unpredictable and complex his mind was.

He continued to sob and I felt like a statue, rigid and unable to provide comfort. But perhaps I should be comforting him? If he believed Christian was getting in the way of me falling in love with him, and I continued to act this way, he may have Christian killed. My gut feeling told me that I needed to show him some sort of affection. It would be the most difficult thing I'd ever done, but would increase his trust in me and protect my loved ones. Once I was safely back in the United States, I could plan my escape. With that thought, I hesitatingly placed my hand on his head and gently stroked his soft hair. His sobs gradually subsided, and he slowly looked up at me with red, swollen eyes. Just a little boy crying out for love, I thought. That thought was the only one that would enable me to return any form of affection.

He pulled gently away and whispered, "*Thank you*, Cadence. You are all I have in this world and I *need* you."

"I know," I said, which was the sad and bizarre truth. "I'll try harder, Richard, but *please* promise me you won't hurt Christian or anyone else," I said gently, but firmly. "This is *not* their fault and if you hurt my loved ones I will never be able to love you," I said, with a certainty that made him pull away from the hug and look me in the eyes.

"Okay, I promise, so long as you try to fall in love with me and *never* leave me," he said, again spelling out the terms of our agreement like a business contract, but this time more gently.

He began kissing me and I tried my best not to pull away. He made love to me again, but this time more gently and it was actually tolerable. It took great effort to be somewhat responsive and affectionate, but I forced myself to do so as I knew it would be my ticket to freedom. When he fell asleep in my arms I let myself quietly cry. Please God, I prayed, help me to escape soon, but most importantly keep those I love safe!

I fell into an exhausted sleep and my dreams again led me to Christian. This time we were back in the dressing room, on the sofa, and he was gently taking me from behind. I felt his talented hands caressing my nipples. I softly moaned in pleasure, but was startled awake by a deeper moan in return, as I realized Richard was the one behind me!

"Oh, Cadence, I've turned you on," he whispered huskily, quickening his pace and stimulating me with his fingers as I hesitantly left my dream behind.

I was conflicted. I was very turned on by my vivid dream, yet Richard felt so *different* from Christian; his fingers were not nearly as delicate and experienced with my body. Could I pretend and appease Richard by trying to enjoy this? Before I could decide, Richard came once again.

"I can't believe it, Cadence," he said, out of breath. "It feels better each time! Just when I think it can't feel any better, *you* make it happen. But now I want to please you like you've pleased me," he said confidently.

"That'll take time, Richard. For now I'd rather take it slow," I said.

"But I heard and felt your pleasure. I know you enjoyed it!" he said, confused.

"I know, but I still need to take it slow. You hurt me by forcing yourself on me last night and I need time to recover before it feels good," I said, again trying to buy some time.

"Okay, my darling. We'll have plenty of time, that's for sure," he promised.

*Oh Christian, please come back to me in my dreams. I miss you so much!* I thought, as Richard tucked me into his arms.

# Chapter Twenty-Two

"ARE YOU HUNGRY, MY LOVE?" Richard asked, stretching luxuriously after waking up for the second time that morning. The ocean looked a light shade of aqua, as the waves gently rolled onto the glistening white sandy beach very close to where we lay.

"Yes, very," I said, feeling famished.

He turned away and reached down beside the bed, pulling up some sort of radio. He pressed a button, then said, "We're ready for breakfast, Maria."

Two seconds later came a response, "It will be there shortly, Mr. White."

"Why don't we just head back, Richard, rather than make them bring it all the way out here?" I asked, feeling awkward about the whole situation. Not only was I not accustomed to having servants, but I was in a bed, naked, on a beach with Richard. The only clothing I had was the torn wedding gown, and I grimaced at the thought of trying to hold the ripped bodice together.

"Darling, it's beautiful out here and I've arranged a special breakfast for us to enjoy before we go back. Besides, there's no rush and I know you'll like it," he said, while gently clasping my hand and stroking it with his thumb.

"But I don't have any clothes," I said shyly, as I felt anxiety building inside me again about having so little control over my situation.

Again he reached down on his side of the bed, fumbling for a moment before he pulled up a white box tied with a bright red ribbon.

"This is for you to wear on our first morning as husband and wife," he said, handing me the box. "Open it, my love."

I hesitated for a moment, then carefully pulled off the ribbon and opened the box. Inside was a white silk dressing gown, with a matching negligee. "Thank you," I said, feeling awkward, but relieved to have something to wear, even if it was merely lingerie. I pulled on the negligee and put the dressing gown on over it, as Richard stared at me.

"You are just so….absolutely….stunningly….beautiful," he whispered.

"I don't think so," I said. I was quite humble, and like most women I'd always found it easier to focus on my flaws.

"Why, Cadence? What on earth do you think is *not* beautiful about your body?" he asked, looking genuinely perplexed.

For a moment I felt anger at having to talk with Richard as if this really were a normal relationship. But if I shut down or exploded again, I feared he might consider my part of the bargain breached. I decided to bury my anger for the time being and continue the conversation as naturally as I could. "Well, I could have smaller thighs and bigger breasts," I said, hesitantly.

"Your thighs are perfect. You're curvy in just the right places, and your *breasts*…" he said animatedly, closing his eyes and grinning broadly. "Your breasts are perfect, just the right size for me to hold," he said, still closing his eyes but reaching out to cup my breast. He missed and his open hand gently touched my stomach.

I felt a tickling sensation and was always hopeless when it came to being tickled, so let out an involuntary giggle. This fueled the fire, and he opened his eyes and began tickling me more. "Stop! Stop!" I begged, trying to suppress my laughter. For the first time in days, I momentarily forgot my horrible situation and was able to relax in the moment. I could barely remember the last time I had laughed.

Richard laughed too as he continued to tickle me, but stopped for a moment to reminisce. "You haven't changed a bit. I remember our tickle fights so well. Remember the time we were kicked out of the movie theater when I began tickling you? It was a terrible movie and we left the theater still laughing."

"Yes, I remember," I said, remembering it from the early days of our relationship.

"We share so many great memories and I look forward to building many more," he said, tickling me again. I pleaded for him to stop, but he pinned me down with both my wrists in one of his hands, as he used his other hand to tickle my stomach playfully.

"Please, *please* stop!" I giggled uncontrollably, and suddenly he did, looking me in the eye. A serious look replaced his grin and he said, "Cadence, I'm so glad I can still make you laugh. I know I've made you cry so much over the past few days, but I plan to make it up to you."

I looked away from his gaze, suddenly coming back to reality and feeling guilty for laughing, despite the fact that it was involuntary. What on earth was there to laugh about, I thought bitterly. An innocent man had lost his life and I was lying beside a murderer!

"Darling, you look so serious all of a sudden. Be careful or the tickle monster will come back," he joked, moving his hand slowly towards my stomach, like a spider crawling towards its prey. He stopped briefly to stroke my inner thigh, sighing deeply as his fingers moved over my soft flesh.

Suddenly a bell rang in the distance.

"That's Maria with our breakfast. I told her to ring to warn us, just in case we were…busy," he explained, with a wink. "Do you think we have time to make love once more before she gets here?" he asked.

"No way! I would *never*…" I said anxiously.

"I'm just teasing, Cadence," Richard quickly explained. "You're so gullible. But, I would give *anything* to make love to you again this morning."

I grimaced internally, the feeling of panic surging through my body again. I then turned towards the sound of the bell, which was getting very close. Maria appeared in the distance, around a slight bend in the beach. Behind her followed Leroy, the chef who had stood up for us yesterday at our "wedding." They each carried a large tray, which they placed on a table that was set up near the bed.

"Good mornin', Mr. and Mrs. White" said Leroy cheerfully.

"Good morning," Richard responded happily.

Maria offered us her congratulations, with Leroy quickly following. They expertly set the table with white linen and china. Maria set down a fresh fruit plate, as Leroy brought out plates of steaming eggs, bacon, hash browns and muffins. Completing the breakfast was coffee and freshly squeezed orange juice. "Enjoy," they said, almost in unison, as they hastily turned to leave.

"Thank you," said Richard. I said thanks as well and then we sat down to eat. Richard insisted that we take turns feeding each other. I tried to talk him out of this as I was famished, plus I found it ridiculous, but he wouldn't relent. Regardless, I was so hungry that I still enjoyed the breakfast immensely. It was delicious and temporarily got my mind off of my predicament. While we ate Richard talked about the island, explaining its typical weather patterns and history. When we were finished eating, he eagerly forced himself upon me again.

He was in such a good mood afterwards, that I thought I'd bring up the birth control issue again. Perhaps if I talked about it calmly and rationally he would agree.

"Richard?"

"Hmm?"

"I was thinking," I said, and forced myself to stroke his arm. He smiled broadly at me. "If I become pregnant right away, we won't have very much time alone as husband and wife to get to know each other," I said hesitantly. "And, well…" I was trying to find the right words to convince him without getting him riled up again.

"Continue," he said, staring at me intensely.

"I really think we should wait for a few months, rather than rush into becoming parents." The word "parents" sounded so foreign to me in this situation. I simply couldn't let it happen, I thought anxiously.

He continued staring at me, then began speaking slowly and confidently. "I don't think you'll truly feel like we're a family *unless* we become parents. Besides, it may take us a while to become pregnant. We will leave it to fate," he said, with a ring of finality in his tone.

"You can't dictate what we do, and as a married couple we both should have a say," I said, beginning to shake slightly with anger.

"Cadence," he said, frustration brewing in his deep voice, "you have had a say in *everything* over the past ten years. It's my turn to have a say in a few key areas of our lives. I know what's right for us," he exclaimed.

My anger melted into sadness, as quickly as an ice cube submersed in boiling water. I felt tears well up in my eyes, then roll down my flushed cheeks. Richard embraced me, hugging me tightly to him as we sat on that big bed in the middle of the isolated beach.

"Sweetheart, I *know* this is difficult for you, but I also know what a great mother you'll be. You've always loved babies," he said knowingly.

"I *do* love babies," I said tearfully, "but just not yet! Please let me take birth control for a few more months. Please..." I whispered into his ear as he continued hugging me.

"No. I'm being firm about this because I love you," he stated. I felt enraged, but there was no point in discussing it further. I continued to cry as he hugged me and stroked my back and hair. Shortly afterwards some dark looking clouds appeared in the distance, and Richard said we should get back.

We walked down the beach, my hand clasped in his, the leftovers of our wedding night fading into the distance...a rumpled bed, a table for two and a ripped wedding gown.

# Chapter Twenty-Three

"You can open your eyes now," said Richard excitedly, as he led me into the master suite. I opened them and saw a spectacular room. There was a panel of windows and a balcony overlooking the beautiful aqua-colored sea. Near the windows sat a four-poster, king size bed covered in white linens and red rose petals. On the other side was a large, corner hot tub for two lined with candles. My eye caught a large, framed photograph hanging across from the bed. As I drew nearer I realized it was of Richard and me yesterday at our "wedding." I couldn't believe a photograph was already developed and framed.

In the photo we were standing together, him looking overjoyed, and me with what might have appeared as a real smile, but was very much forced. My eyes revealed a very subtle look of fear, which could easily be mistaken for timidity. It was the first time I'd seen what we looked like objectively and I could admit that, yes, to others we might look like a happy couple.

I was suddenly gripped with a very unsettling thought. What if this photo was seen by my family and friends or Christian? Would they be able to clearly see my state of fear or would it appear that I had fallen in love, run away and willingly married Richard? I thought angrily that Richard had yet another level of control over me. He had played out the perfect exotic wedding in which I could appear as the willing bride. After all, if I were held against my will why would I take the time to get dressed up and pose for newlywed photos? Outsiders to this bizarre situation may not understand the physical and psychological control Richard had over me. I suddenly felt sick to my stomach, and the patience I had commanded in myself yesterday and today was quickly fading. I wanted to escape more than ever, as I felt that each day would further solidify Richard's control over me.

"Cadence, you're in dreamland again," Richard said, impatiently. "What do you think of our bedroom?"

"It's, um, very nice…and so large," I said, trying to mask my inner panic with enthusiasm.

"I'm glad you like it, my love," he said. "Let's go for a swim and then soak in the hot tub," he said.

"Okay," I responded, relieved that he didn't want to "make love" again.

"Come here," he said, as he walked towards a large chest of drawers. "I picked out a few bikinis for you. I know you'll like them."

I looked through the drawer and immediately recalled having tried each of these on prior to my trip to Mexico. I had been with my friend, Janine, at a small San Francisco beachwear store. Trying on bikinis was always awkward and I remembered commenting on how there wasn't much privacy as the change rooms were close to the windows overlooking the street. People walked back and forth, window shopping as we tried on swimwear.

I grabbed one of the bikinis, the most modest of them all, and headed towards the bathroom to change. Richard tugged on my arm and said, "Why not change out here? Nobody can see into our room and there's no need to be shy around me."

"I would rather change in private," I said. He looked hurt.

"Okay, suit yourself…literally," he said, chuckling and shaking his head as I went into the huge bathroom and shut the door. It was my only moment of privacy in the last twenty-four hours and I felt a sense of relief to be out of his view. He was suffocating me with his constant hugs and kisses, and oppressive presence. The thought of another day on the island made me ill. But how on earth would I escape from here? More importantly, if I *were* to escape I would need to warn Christian immediately of Richard's threats.

I procrastinated for a few minutes before I heard Richard asking me to hurry. I slipped on the blue and white bikini, and wrapped myself in a white, fluffy towel. I opened the door and gasped as Richard had been standing right there, and immediately began kissing me. I pulled away, the relief of having a few minutes to myself evaporating at once.

"Even a few minutes without you makes me feel so alone," he whispered. "Let's make a pact to spend every moment together on our honeymoon. When we go back I'll have to work some of the time, so let's make up for that time apart here," he explained.

"Richard, I need *some* privacy," I said quietly.

"Okay, bathroom breaks alone, but that's all the time I can manage to be without you," he said urgently, then kissed me again.

*****

We walked down the stairs and onto the large patio. Despite the ominous clouds in the distance, it was still quite sunny out. It must have been around noon, as the sun was directly overhead. The swimming pool was rectangular, and looked clear and refreshing. At the far end was a swim-up bar with what appeared to be two stools under the clear water. Another servant, whom I had not yet met, was awaiting our drink order. He looked Jamaican and about thirty years old. Richard led the way to the bar, and we each took a stool.

"My name's Alvin. I'm most pleased and honored to meet ya, Mrs. White," he said cheerfully, with a thick Jamaican accent.

"Nice to meet you too, Alvin," I said, trying to get a read on him. Would he possibly be an ally? Don't even think that, I told myself, since the chance of escaping from this remote island was next to impossible. *And look what happened to Yamoto!*

"What can I get the two of ya to drink?" he asked, standing in front of a fully stocked bar, lined with bowls of tropical fruit.

"How about a couple of your Tropical White Delights? Cadence, I know you like coconut so you'll *love* this drink," Richard explained. He was right, coconut was a favorite of mine, so I nodded in agreement.

I watched as he filled the blender with a mix of Jamaican rum, ice, fresh coconut, pineapple, and a few other exotic fruits. He decorated the drinks with a garnish, adding tiny umbrellas and stir sticks with a small bride and groom perched on top.

"Enjoy," he said. "And just ring the bell when ya need anythin' else." He then retreated through a door in the back of the bar to give us privacy.

"Cheers to our long, happy and healthy marriage," said Richard. We clinked glasses and I enjoyed my first sip of this exotic drink.

"This is very good," I said.

"I'm so glad you like it," Richard responded. "And you'll really like what I have planned for tonight…a private dinner on our bedroom patio with fresh seafood. It will be wonderful," he said.

We spent the next two hours swimming, drinking and then sitting in the hot tub beside the pool, with two more Tropical White Delights. The storm was now very close and the sky had darkened to an ominous bluish-black color, like a nasty bruise. I was somewhat relaxed, as much as I could be given the circumstances, and didn't want to leave the warmth and comfort of the hot tub to go to our bedroom.

Richard had been kissing me as often as he could all afternoon, and began kissing me more passionately in the hot tub. He nuzzled my ear and whispered, "Let's make love right here."

I backed away. "NO! We're in *public!*" I said, embarrassed even at the thought of having sex in full view of the staff.

"Who cares, they are just our *servants*. They know when to turn away and give us privacy," Richard explained, perplexed as to why I'd care what mere servants thought.

"I care, Richard. *I* care!" I said.

He gave a long, frustrated sigh, giving up. "Okay, let's go back to our private hot tub then."

"But it's so nice in here. I don't want to get out. Can't we stay a while longer?"

"It's your choice, Cadence, but if we stay we are making love *here,*" he said, in a matter-of-fact tone. With that I climbed out of the hot tub begrudgingly and we dried off, then headed up to our room.

Richard was too impatient to wait for the hot tub to fill, so we made love on the large, four-poster bed. I was tired and sore, so fell asleep as the thunder and lightning played out its dramatic symphony overhead.

# Chapter Twenty-Four

I WOKE UP TO THE sound of running water and saw Richard across the room filling up the hot tub. The storm had passed and it looked like it was clearing up outside. "You're awake, my love," he said, smiling broadly, apparently comfortable walking around completely naked. "I'm running a bath for us. It's almost five thirty and I have our dinner planned for seven, so we need to freshen up and get ready," he explained, continuing to dictate my every waking hour.

I dreaded the thought of yet again being naked beside Richard, his hands and lips creeping every which way. "I'd actually prefer a shower."

He stared at me surprised for a moment, then his frown transformed into a smile. "Okay, we can try out the shower for two! I had double shower heads put in there," he happily explained. I sighed, feeling again suffocated, but not having the energy to argue further.

We showered and Richard kept touching me; he insisted on washing my hair and massaging my back. I was relieved when it was over and I had a few minutes to myself to do my hair and makeup. Was it possible that after many weeks, or even months of this, that I'd give up and simply live as Richard's wife, forgetting my past life? What a horrible thought, I said to myself. I thought about cults that brainwashed unwilling members into becoming utterly devoted to their cause, to the point of giving up their minds and lives for it. I quivered at the thought of *ever* accepting this situation.

My eyes welled with tears just thinking of ever forgetting Christian. I wondered how he was physically after being so brutally attacked. He must be worried sick, as it had been less than a week since my abduction. Time here seemed to be very drawn out and it felt more like several weeks since I last enjoyed my freedom, my real life. Now I had no life of my own, but was instead Richard's prized possession. I vowed that the moment we left this island I would exert all my efforts into escaping. And in the meantime, I would try to get through this with my sanity intact.

I wore my hair down and put on very little makeup. Richard had chosen a pale pink evening gown for me, which he gave me along with a small gift box. Inside was a pair of large diamond earrings and a diamond solitaire necklace, with what seemed like a two-carat heart shaped diamond hanging from it. He carefully put it around my neck. Clearly Richard had an endless supply of very expensive gifts in store for me. I was never one for a lot of jewelry and wished he would stop planning my entire wardrobe down to my accessories. I felt like a doll being dressed and undressed on a child's whim.

Maria came in when we were dressed, and set the table on our patio with white linen. She lit a candle in the middle, and turned on a nearby sound system, instantly filling the room with soft jazz background music. Richard walked me out onto the patio, pulled out my chair and we both sat down. Below the waves lapped gently onto the beach, and a warm ocean breeze caressed us. Maria brought us a bottle of wine, and Leroy soon followed with an appetizer of fresh mussels. "These are absolutely delicious, Cadence, are you sure you won't even try one?" Richard asked.

"No thanks, I've never liked the things. Maybe it's the way they look, but I just can't stomach them," I said. I opted for a fresh roll with butter instead.

"I can't believe my source got that wrong. Sorry about that," he said, matter-of-factly. I simply bowed my head to hide my reaction, which was relief that he didn't know *everything* about me.

Richard talked about how we'd spend the next eight days here. How we'd make love on various parts of the beach. And how we'd go for moonlit walks. It would be similar to the last twenty-four hours, he said happily. I nodded unexcitedly, clenching my hands into tight fists under the table, my nails digging small crescent-shaped grooves into my palms.

Leroy brought out shrimp cocktails next, followed by a seafood bisque. The main course was lobster, accompanied with hot melted butter and rice pilaf. It was delicious. Dessert was a rich coconut cake decorated with tropical flowers.

"This is delicious," I said, noticing that Richard wasn't having any dessert. "Don't you like it?" I asked, surprised as Richard usually had a ravenous appetite.

"I like it, I just don't feel very well," he said, grimacing. "My stomach is suddenly really upset and I have terrible heartburn."

My first thought was a selfish one: maybe he wouldn't feel well enough for anything sexual this evening. I then felt a small twinge of sympathy. "I'm sorry you're not feeling well. Maybe you should lie down?"

"Yes, I think I will. But I feel bad. I wanted to go on a moonlit beach walk with you, and…" he suddenly stood up and ran quickly to the bathroom.

That hit suddenly, I thought. Could it be food poisoning? I felt totally fine, albeit slightly intoxicated from the wine.

I walked inside and heard Richard moaning in the bathroom. Maria entered our bedroom and jumped when she nearly bumped into me. "Miss Cadence, where—"

"He's in the bathroom. He's sick," I interrupted.

"Oh my goodness, Mr. White *never* gets sick. Is there anything I can bring? There are some medications in your cabinet, but we have a full stock of other treatments downstairs if there is anything he needs," she explained.

For the first time in what felt like forever, I was in control. After having every aspect of my life dictated to me for the past few days, it was a relief to be left with some decision-making power. "I'll keep an eye on him and call you if I need anything," I said. Maria looked somewhat uncomfortable, being used to taking orders only from Richard.

"I'll come up and check on you in a while, and will be downstairs in the kitchen if he needs *anything* in the meantime," she said nervously.

"Okay, thanks," I said. She scurried out and I walked to the closed bathroom door, and tapped on it gently. "Richard, are you okay?" I asked. In response I heard him retching, then vomiting. I turned the knob but he had locked it.

"I'll be okay, just…" he said, between vomiting episodes.

I was worried for a second, but then asked myself *why*. Why on earth would I be worried about his welfare? Nevertheless, I did feel bad for him. The thought of escaping while he was ill came to mind, but I quickly pushed it away as he was only one of many barriers on this island to my escape. I would have to get past the staff and then find transportation off the island. Plus, he probably would be back to himself soon, giving me very little time to make a successful getaway.

I stayed outside the bathroom, pacing back and forth, my emotions sliding between empathy for Richard, and anger about this whole situation. Suddenly Richard exited the bathroom, looking extremely sick and pale, his face covered with beads of sweat. "I need to lie down," he muttered, walking slowly to the bed and dropping onto it still fully dressed.

I followed hesitantly. "Can I get you anything?" I asked.

"No, just a bucket in case I'm sick again," he said, moaning. "I'm sorry..."

"Okay, I'll go get one," I said. I thought of grabbing the waste basket in the bathroom, but it was mesh so wouldn't do. I went out of the bedroom and quickly headed downstairs towards the kitchen to find Maria.

The hallway was fairly dark, but I remembered my way to the kitchen. As I was about to open the door, someone suddenly grabbed me from behind and a hand swiftly pressed over my mouth before I could scream. Déjà vu, I thought fearfully.

# Chapter Twenty-Five

I FLAILED MY ARMS AND kicked my legs wildly, but soon realized there were two strong men dragging me out of the back of the house and there was no way I could break free. I tried to scream, but it only came out as a muffled sound as my mouth was completely covered by a sweaty, salty tasting palm. I was carried down a set of stairs, which were unfamiliar as they were at the back of the house where I'd never been.

When we reached the ground I was put back on my feet, but the hand remained firmly over my mouth. I continued to struggle fiercely, realizing that whatever chance of rescue I had from any of Richard's staff was quickly disappearing as I was dragged into the dark night.

"Stop fightin' or I'll kill ya!" whispered the man who was not holding me. He pulled out a knife and held the shiny blade near my throat. I gasped, shivering with fear, my heart thumping wildly in my chest. "And don't make another sound!" he commanded, in a thick Jamaican accent.

Why was this happening to me? Suddenly I wished desperately to be back in the safety of the bedroom with Richard.

The man with the knife led the way down a path surrounded by thick trees and bushes. I had the feeling these men were serious and it was unwise to fight any further. Surely Maria would notice I was missing soon? Or had they harmed Maria? I shuddered at the thought.

Soon the path opened up onto a stretch of moonlit beach and there sat a motorboat, tied up to a small stump, bobbing roughly in the dark water. I was led into the water and hoisted into the boat. For a split second I was tempted to jump over the other side and run for my life, but the man with the knife was on the beach untying the rope, and would certainly catch me in seconds.

I looked up and saw some lights from the house in the distance, through the trees. Too far away to be heard if I bothered yelling, I thought hopelessly. The man who had been covering my mouth took his hand away, then grabbed my other wrist and tied both of my arms behind me. I held back a scream as a terrifying thought formed in my mind. What if we sank? I wouldn't even be able to swim! My thoughts were interrupted by the sound of the motor, and off we went out onto the deep, dark sea. The water was rough, and the boat bounced up and down forcefully.

The man who had been holding me now let go and sat down across from me in the back of the boat. I looked at him and immediately recognized him as the bartender from today! Albert…Alan…no, Alvin! "Alvin?" I asked, clearly seeing he was very scared, but trying to appear tough and in control.

"Yep, that's my name, Mrs. White," he said.

"Why are you taking me away?" I asked, as calmly as I could.

He hesitated for a moment, likely wondering if he should respond or tell me to shut up. "We're takin' ya for ransom. We won't hurt ya as long as we get our money. Just don't try anythin' stupid," he said, again trying to sound tougher than he actually was.

I thought it strange that only hours ago he was serving me tropical drinks and now he was abducting me. My heart was racing and many thoughts were buzzing around rapidly in my mind. I was finally out of Richard's control, only to be taken into a seemingly worse situation.

"I won't try to escape, but *please* untie me. If we sink I'll drown," I begged.

"Can't do that, but if we start to sink I'll untie ya," he said, and I knew then that Alvin had some kernel of kindness under his hard shell.

A few minutes passed and I thought up many questions to ask. "Alvin, did you drug Richard?" I asked, hesitantly.

"That's *none* of yer business," he said, which seemed to indicate that he had. He looked away awkwardly. Clearly, he was not a professional criminal. Should that make me relieved, or even more fearful for my life? I wondered.

"How much are you expecting to get out of this?" I asked, realizing that it was again none of my business, yet I was curious about how much they pegged my worth at.

"We're askin' for five million. We've heard that Mr. White is one of the richest Americans to own our land and he's got hundreds of millions to his name. People like him take away our land and then expect us to be their servants. We can never even own and benefit from *our* land. My family is very poor and this money'll give us a new life," he explained. I felt much better knowing that he wasn't a hard core criminal.

"You're a good man to your family," I said, no longer feeling fearful of Alvin, but still concerned about the other man. "Who's he? A friend?" I asked, pointing to the driver, who still held the knife in one hand.

"His name's Sam. He's a good friend of mine. He came up with this idea. We both tried to get hired on to work for Mr. White, but only I got a job. A police check was required, and Sam's been in trouble with the cops before for drugs and burglary and other stuff. If he don't get this money and escape from Jamaica, he'll be jailed," he explained.

As the boat continued over the rough waves I began to feel seasick, but tried to focus my thoughts on the best way to use this situation to my advantage. These men were taking a huge risk trying to negotiate with Richard, who was much more powerful than they were. He would be furious and would use every means he had to have them killed. At the same time, he would be *very* worried about me, not only about my well-being, but about me escaping and the story of my abduction being leaked. What a mess, I thought. No one would ever believe that I'd been abducted from an abduction. It was all so complicated, and I felt like I was walking on a tightrope and could easily fall down on either side if I wasn't extremely careful.

I couldn't control the seasickness and vomited twice over the side of the boat. I was relieved when I finally saw some lights in the distance, and knew we were close to land. When we reached a dock Sam got out first and tied up the boat, his knife now stowed in a case tied to his belt. Alvin then helped me out of the boat, as my hands were still tied behind my back. We walked up a sandy path and entered a small parking lot with one car, a two-door, rusty white coupe, sitting there waiting for our arrival. I sat in the back and Sam drove, while Alvin sat in the passenger seat, periodically glancing back at me with a serious expression etched on his dark face.

"We shouldn't let her see where we're goin'," said Sam. "It's too risky." He then reached into the glove compartment and pulled out a dirty rag. "Blindfold her with this," he said to Alvin, handing him the dirt-streaked rag.

"It's filthy! Can't I just promise to keep my eyes closed?" I interjected.

"No, we need ya blindfolded!" Sam said, his voice rising angrily. Alvin turned around and tied the dirty rag gently around my head, tying it into a loose knot in the back. It smelled like mildew and I gagged in reaction. My hands were still tied behind me, so if I did vomit I would be forced to do so all over myself.

After a few minutes I adjusted to the sickening smell and leaned my head back to relax. I heard whispering back and forth, which was loud enough for me to hear so I listened carefully.

"Tomorrow mornin'…by then the drug will be outta his system and we'll tell him our demands," whispered Sam.

"But what if he's already feelin' better and has people after us?" asked Alvin, his tone fearful. "He can afford the best investigators and I know how much he loves this lady, he'll do *anythin'* to get her back!"

"The drug lasts at least twelve hours…he won't feel good enough to get outta bed to even give orders until then. And Leroy and Maria will both be passed out until at least mornin', thanks to yer idea," said Sam.

"It went over well…they didn't hesitate to have a drink with me. They're actually good people, so I feel bad for druggin' 'em, but with those two awake we never could've gotten her off the island," said Alvin.

"Nobody's hurt, *yet*, so as long as he cooperates this should all go over real good. Like ya say, Alv, everyone knows he worships this lady and will do anythin' to get her back. What's a few million to him?" Sam said, sounding confident about their plan.

He clearly didn't know Richard, I thought. Richard was *not* one to be told what the deal was, he was the one to set the terms and conditions. He wouldn't settle for anything less than complete control. I didn't doubt that he would do anything to get me back, as he'd already proven that. I also believed that he'd do *anything* to pay back those who took me. These two weren't going to live long enough to enjoy their millions.

Hope began to brew inside of me, as I compared my chances of escaping from Richard versus these two novices. Richard made it next to impossible for me to escape, but these two would surely leave some holes in their plan, like a piece of Swiss cheese instead of a solid block of old cheddar. I knew I had a better chance of getting away from them, albeit it was more risky to my life. If they caught me, Sam might kill me. If Richard caught me, he wouldn't kill me but hurt or kill Christian instead. As always, my first priority in any escape plan would be to warn Christian and my family. I hoped and prayed I'd find a means to do so.

*****

After about a thirty-minute drive, the car came to a halt. I was helped out of the car, still blindfolded, and brought inside some sort of building. Sam then said, "Her room is back here."

I shuffled my feet as Alvin led me into a room and then closed the door behind us. "I'll take off yer blindfold and untie yer hands now," he said. I was relieved when the filthy rag was removed from my face and at last my hands were free. I found myself in a tiny room with no windows. There was an old dirty mattress in the corner and a small lamp on the floor beside it. "You'll be stayin' here durin' our negotiations. I'm sorry it's not nicer," apologized Alvin, sounding somewhat embarrassed. "I know you're used to mansions and fancy rooms, bein' so rich," he said.

"I'm actually not rich, at least I wasn't before marrying Richard," I said. For a second I wanted to continue and tell him how I was forced to marry Richard and I was actually glad to be out of his control. But in the car I decided that I'd keep that to myself for the time being. I didn't want to add extra confusion, and I doubted if they'd believe such a far-fetched story. After all, Alvin had served us tropical drinks at a pool bar, would he believe that I was forced into such a luxurious honeymoon? It would likely be beyond his comprehension, and perhaps increase their suspicion of me. Besides, I couldn't risk it getting back to Richard, who would be very fearful that the story of my abduction could get out to the public now that I was out of his control. Richard's ultimatum was still clear in my mind, and I wasn't about to risk Christian's or my family's safety, until I was certain that I could warn them.

"Well, I'll go get ya some water. If ya have to use the bathroom, just bang on the door," he instructed. He closed and locked the door and I sat down on the mattress. I wondered if Richard had found out

I was missing yet. I shuddered to think of his retaliation against Sam and Alvin if he caught them. Another horrifying thought grabbed me. *What if he thinks Maria was a part of this? What if he thinks I escaped?* I wrapped my arms around myself and shuddered, alone in that dank and humid room.

# Chapter Twenty-Six

RICHARD WAS JOLTED AWAKE BY another tidal wave of nausea and stumbled to the bathroom, reaching the toilet without a second to spare. He heaved violently then sat on the floor, exhausted. It was as if all of his strength had been sucked away and even a simple movement took great effort. Being such a strong, physically fit man he was not at all accustomed to feeling this weak and helpless. He finally summoned enough strength to stand up and as he walked weakly towards the bed, he noticed that the clock on the night stand read 4:00 a.m. Moonlight coming through the windows illuminated the dark room enough for him to see that Cadence's side of the bed was empty. His heart began to thump madly and he broke into a cold sweat.

The worst of the sickness had left him and the surge of adrenalin enabled him to rush out of the room calling her name. "Cadence? Cadence?" he yelled, but there was no response. The house was dark and quiet. An intense fear and anger bubbled up inside of him and he practically ran right through Maria's door, which was luckily open a crack. As he flicked on the light he heard her groan. She was lying in bed, her head falling over the side and her hand dangling beside a large bowl of vomit. Her dark hair was a tangled, stringy mess and she looked very sick. "Maria! Wake up!" he ordered. Her eyes slowly opened and she tried to speak, but was sick again. As she began to retch, Richard hurried out of her room and down the hall to Leroy's quarters. The door was locked and Richard banged loudly, over and over again with increasing strength. He was contemplating kicking it in when the doorknob turned and Leroy pulled open the door. He too looked very sick.

"Where the hell is Cadence?" Richard demanded.

"I don't know," Leroy answered, looking very weak but concerned.

"All three of us, you, me and Maria, are sick. What's going on?" Richard yelled, shaking with rage.

"Mr. White, I've no idea what…"

"WHERE'S CADENCE?" Richard yelled, grabbing Leroy by the shoulders and shaking him roughly. Leroy doubled over and vomited on the wooden floor. Richard pulled away with a frustrated growl then spun around and headed back down the hall to Maria's room. Maria was now sitting up in bed, clutching her stomach with both hands.

"When did you see her last?" Richard demanded.

"L…last night," stammered Maria, shrinking away in fear, "when you were sick and I came up to check on the two of you. She was concerned about you and I told her that if there was anything she needed to come down and get me," Maria explained.

"You should have been guarding our door, Maria! You know Cadence is still unpredictable!" Richard snapped furiously, as Maria trembled with fear.

"I'm sorry…I…was just downstairs in the kitchen and planned to check often, and then I got very sick," she explained hesitantly.

"If she's escaped, I…I…" but before Richard could threaten Maria, Leroy entered the room, reeking of vomit but looking more coherent than a few moments ago.

"I thought about it and think I know who drugged us…it was Alvin," said Leroy. "He brought Maria and me a drink yesterday evening. I felt fine before the drink, but can't remember much after it," said Leroy.

"Me too," said Maria, her dark eyes wide with fright.

"I told you that drinking is not allowed on the job. I swear, if anything has happened to Cadence, I will hold you both responsible!" roared Richard. Maria and Leroy were shaking with fear as Richard paced wildly back and forth. Maria had seen Richard angry before, but never anything like this; he was like a savage beast, capable of anything, and they were stuck with him on this isolated island.

"We're *very* sorry, sir," spoke Leroy hastily, "but Alvin said there was no alcohol in our drinks."

"Yes, Mr. White, I couldn't taste any liquor in my drink; we would have *never* done so if ..." whispered Maria, now crying.

"I don't want *any* excuses. We need to focus all of our efforts on finding Cadence. I'm going to call in some help. In the meantime, I want you to start searching the island, Leroy. And Maria, find Bob right away and have him help you search as well. Also, look for Alvin," he demanded. Bob was the security guard who should have been keeping a careful watch on all the comings and goings from the house. He was stationed out front, and was supposed to do rounds every hour. If Cadence had tried to leave, surely he would have heard? "Nobody else was on the island last night, right?" Richard asked, thinking of the gardener he flew in as needed.

"Nobody else," answered Leroy.

"Okay, get going!" ordered Richard.

"Yes sir," they both said in unison, and scurried out of the room, both still looking very weak.

"And don't even think of leaving if you value your life!" Richard shouted after them. He was so furious that he had wanted to strangle them both on the spot, but used every ounce of willpower not to; he needed them at the moment, needed them *badly*. What would he do if Cadence was gone? He shuddered at the thought and within seconds was dialing Tony's number on his satellite phone.

"Hello," answered a sleepy voice.

"Tony, it's Richard White. I have an emergency and need you and your guys here immediately!"

"What happened?" said the deep husky voice, with faint sounds of movement in the background as Tony slipped on a pair of jeans. This was not the first time he was woken up in the middle of the night with an urgent request from one of his clients.

"Cadence is gone. I've been drugged and so have my maid and chef. Maria and Leroy both had a drink from Alvin, the new bartender I recently hired. Remember screening him? Anyway, they were both sick right after the drink, so we're sure they were drugged. I think Alvin has taken Cadence," he choked out.

"Oh, shit! Good thing we're close-by. I'll send Frank there ASAP and Joe and I will stay here, because if she's somehow made it here we need to be on her trail. If she's still on your island there's no need for all of us to be there since it won't take long to find her," he said, now fully awake, his mind calculating one possibility after another. Richard was glad he had them on call in nearby Jamaica.

"Thanks, Tony. I don't know what I'll do if she's gone…I'll do *anything* to get her back," said Richard, his voice cracking.

"I'm sorry this happened, boss, but we'll get your lady back for ya. We're the best in this business and she won't have gotten far," said Tony confidently. It was Tony and his guys who had successfully abducted Cadence, and they had attacked Christian as well. With the money they were making from Richard, they would do anything he wanted. He was by far their highest paying client ever.

"And if Alvin took her, I want him killed!" said Richard, with a great urgency in his voice.

"You bet, boss. I'll call you back in a few minutes. I need to get my guys up and going right away," he said.

"Okay," said Richard, not waiting for a response. He stuffed his phone in his pocket and went back to his room. He was sick once more, and then took a few moments to examine the bedroom and look for any signs of a struggle or how Cadence had left. Nothing was out of place, absolutely nothing. He looked in the closet and didn't see anything missing. "What was she wearing?" he asked himself out loud. The pink gown, he suddenly remembered. He looked through the closet and on the ground, but it was nowhere to be found. Her delicate high heeled sandals that matched the dress were sitting near the door, sparkling with miniature pink rhinestones. He knelt down and picked one up, images of the Cinderella fairy tale coming to mind. She was so beautiful, so perfect and lovely. He kissed her shoe and began sobbing uncontrollably.

After a few minutes he regained his composure and began entertaining the question that was burning in his mind. Had she escaped or was she taken? He knew she was not yet in love with him. If she had the choice, she would not have chosen to be here with him, he thought bitterly. He knew that would change with time, but it was still too soon. Too damn soon! But would she be so desperate as to try to escape from this remote island? To risk her life and those of her family and *him*, that pain in the ass, Christian? He couldn't believe that Cadence would be so stupid. She was a very intelligent woman, which was one of the many aspects of her that he loved. Plus, he'd been treating her like a queen. But if she had tried to escape, perhaps by convincing Alvin to help her, Richard would have Christian killed by noon tomorrow. And he would *definitely* get her back. She was not going to go on with her life unless she was with him, living as his wife.

His rapid thoughts were interrupted by the ringing of his phone. "Hello?" he asked, frantically.

"Boss, Frank is on his way, boarding the chopper right now," said Tony. "He should be there in about fifteen minutes. I need to ask you a few questions so we can get a fix on what's going on," he added. Tony was a large, stocky Italian man who Richard was paying royally to have on call for the first year of his marriage, when Cadence was at the greatest risk of trying to escape.

"Sure, ask away," said Richard.

"Were there any signs that she wanted to escape?" asked Tony.

"Well, you know she didn't marry me willingly. She was still in shock I think, but I don't believe she would have tried to get away from this island. I had threatened to have Christian killed if she tried to leave me and she knew I meant it," explained Richard.

"So your hunch is she was taken by Alvin?" asked Tony.

"If I had to bet on it, yes. I really don't think she would have risked trying to leave on her own. Maybe if we were back home, but not here," he said, feeling weak again. He heard the distant sounds of voices in the house, which sounded like Maria and Bob. "Listen, sounds like Maria and Bob just walked in. Let me hear what they have to say. Actually, I'll put you on speaker," said Richard, glaring at Maria and Bob as they entered the room.

Bob was a thirty-five year old Jamaican security guard who had worked in a couple of the upscale resorts in Jamaica, protecting wealthy tourists. Richard had thoroughly researched and interviewed many security guards before choosing Bob, who seemed to be exceptionally reliable, brave and intelligent. Of course, Richard's first choice would have been to have Tony or one of his men guard the place, but they weren't keen on being stuck on the tiny, isolated island, and "bored out of their skulls" as they put it. They thought it was unnecessary for them to stand guard on the island, and that they could be on call from Jamaica, only minutes away by helicopter. What a mistake, thought Richard angrily.

"Sir, I didn't see or hear *anythin'*!" explained Bob nervously. "I did my hourly rounds and everythin' looked fine. I'll go out and help search for her…I'll do everythin' I can to find her," he offered.

Richard continued to glare at him. "So you're telling me you saw and heard *nothing*? NOTHING AT ALL?" he yelled.

"No sir, nothin'!" Bob said, feeling anxious about having fallen asleep at his post that evening. Maria woke him up and he begged her not to tell Mr. White that he was asleep on-the-job. After all, his job entailed working the night shift and he was being paid very well to stay awake and guard this damned island. But who would have thought something would happen here in the middle of nowhere? He had tried desperately to stay awake, but his job was so incredibly boring! He drank two of the Cokes that Alvin brought him, but despite the caffeine, sleep had come forcefully and took him into its arms, a relaxing escape from the monotony of his job here on White Island. He swallowed, a lump having formed in his throat. There was no way Mr. White would find out that he'd fallen asleep, was there? Maybe the Cokes had been drugged, he thought, as he had fallen asleep awfully quickly after drinking them. Plus, he still felt groggy. He had never been as scared for his life as he was at that moment, with this tall, intimidating man staring down at him menacingly.

Tony's voice came through the speakerphone, "Well, if Bob's telling the truth then Cadence may still be on the island somewhere. The only way to leave is by motorboat or helicopter, both of which Bob should've heard. The island is small enough that the sound of a motor would be heard from anywhere. Unless Cadence left in a non-motorized boat, but with the rough seas she wouldn't get very far. If we don't find her on the island, at first light we'll need to search the surrounding waters," explained Tony.

Bob felt a surge of fear…if Cadence had left by helicopter or motorboat he had no excuse for not hearing it.

"Okay, we'll continue searching," said Richard. "As Tony says, we should determine if Cadence is on this island as soon as possible. And Bob, I'm *not* done with you…you'd better hope we find her on the island," he threatened matter-of-factly.

Tony's voice instructed from the satellite phone, "Keep your phone with you and I'll be in touch, boss. When Frank comes he will help search the island. Any evidence should be reported to Frank immediately."

They all split up, Richard directing each of them to a section of the island, while Richard searched the house. "Cadence!" he yelled, over and over again. He felt as though he had lost half of himself, and that he would die if he didn't find her. He ran his fingers through his thick hair, simultaneously wiping the sweat from his forehead. Why had he lost her again, only days after being reunited? They were having such a wonderful honeymoon. He didn't want to have to lock her up to ensure she stayed, but at this point he realized he had been far too lax and would never risk this again…it was just too painful.

He walked out of the back of the house, down a path that led to a stretch of beach he didn't particularly like as it wasn't as pristine as the beach at the front of the house. He had a flashlight which shone a wide beam of light in front of him as he walked. Suddenly something caught his eye on the path, something small and shiny. He bent down and picked up a diamond earring, one from the set he had given Cadence last evening. "Cadence! Cadence!" he yelled frantically, running down the path and onto the beach. "WHERE ARE YOU?"

"Noooooooo!" he cried out into the darkness. He was enveloped in the same feeling of loss that he felt when his mother had died and Cadence came by to offer her condolences. The grief had ripped him to the core when she refused to stay with him when he needed her most. As he watched her car drive away through blurry tears, he wondered if he would be able to live another day. The loneliness in the days that followed was worse than any illness he could imagine. He knew that he could not survive losing her again and fell to his knees in a state of complete panic. He pounded the sand with his fists until they throbbed in pain, but willed himself to stand and continue the search.

Suddenly he saw footprints in the sand for a few yards, which ended abruptly where the tide had stolen them away. "Oh God, please, *please* bring her back. I can't live without her!" he choked out, as he stared at the dark, rough ocean. Almost in response he heard the faint sound of a helicopter making its way through the starlit night towards White Island. He forced himself to regain his composure and then ran back up the path to meet Frank, the diamond earring clasped tightly in his hand.

# Chapter Twenty-Seven

FRANK CLIMBED OUT OF THE helicopter. His swarthy olive complexion gave testament to his Italian heritage. He looked to be in his late thirties, was short, lean and very muscular. He emanated a lot of energy, as if he were on a constant caffeine high. He had jet black, shiny hair tied into a ponytail. His dark eyes darted back and forth taking in his surroundings and then focused squarely on Richard, who looked quite different than when Frank had last seen him. Last time he was in Richard's classy office building, along with Tony and Joe, negotiating their pay, which was more generous than they could've hoped for. Richard had been dressed impeccably, clean shaven and very professional. This morning he was completely disheveled, smelled faintly of vomit, and his eyes were bloodshot and wild.

"Thank God you're here, Frank! I found this," he said, opening his large hand to reveal the glittering diamond earring. "It was on the path to the beach behind the house, and there were footprints." "Okay, lead the way to where you found it," said Frank, enjoying the adrenalin rush, but bitter that he'd been torn away from the arms of the sexy stripper he'd been with the last two nights. It had been a good time with drugs, booze, sex, and more drugs and booze. What better way to spend time in Jamaica? He certainly hadn't thought something would actually go wrong and he'd be required to work.

They hurried down the path and Richard stopped midway to the beach. "Here's where I found it."

"Okay, let's take another look around this area and see if she dropped anything else," instructed Frank, his tiny dark eyes quickly scanning the path with the help of the flashlight. After a few more minutes of searching they continued on towards the beach, where Richard pointed out the footprints. Frank pulled out a note pad and tape measure, and measured a few of them, jotting down some numbers. "Sorry to say, but some of these definitely look like hers, Mr. White," he said. "She was barefoot. She's about a size six, right?"

"Yes, she is," said Richard, his voice cracking again. He bent down and touched one of the smaller footprints, the soft sand cool to his touch. He wished that when he looked up she would suddenly be standing there. He would give anything to feel her soft legs again and to kiss each of her perfect toes.

"And there was at least one other person with her who was wearing shoes, about size nine men's," explained Frank. "The rest of the prints are too washed out to tell."

"Oh, God," said Richard. "Do you think they left by boat then?"

"Sorry to say, but yeah," said Frank, "all signs point to that." He immediately dialed Tony, and quickly explained the situation.

Richard continued to run his finger around the outline of her small footprint. Had the man who was with her taken her because she *wanted* to go, or taken her against her will? He had to believe it was the latter... she wouldn't be so stupid as to escape willingly from him. Plus, she wouldn't leave in bare feet, would she? No, she wouldn't he reasoned, as anger boiled up inside of him. He would kill the man who took her as soon as possible, and make him suffer while doing it. Nobody would take what was *his* and get away with it!

"Let's head back up, Mr. White. I need to look around the house for more evidence. Tony is arranging a search boat for Joe, and then he'll begin the land search."

"Why would Alvin take her?" asked Richard, as he walked quickly after Frank.

"If she was taken, which probably is the case, it's likely for ransom. At least that's what Tony's thinking, and I agree," explained Frank. "Nobody in their right minds would take her away if money wasn't involved...except you," he said with a smirk, trying to inject a bit of humor into the situation.

Richard didn't appreciate his attempt at humor and glared at Frank before continuing. "Of course, holding her for ransom makes the most sense. But if that is the case they will be *very* sorry they ever took something of mine!" said Richard, feeling stupid for asking the question in the first place. He was normally very analytical and should have figured out that it probably was for ransom, but this morning his mind was dealing with a multitude of different emotions, not to mention fatigue and nausea.

They soon reached the house and Frank searched it carefully, while Richard looked around the outside. The sky was beginning to lighten ever so slightly, and he knew the sun would rise in the next hour or so. Where was she? Was she wishing, even just a little, to be safely back here? Would she try to escape from her captor? He shuddered at the thought, hoping that her captor or captors had her under tight reins until Tony's men got to her. Tight but gentle reins, he hoped, for if anyone laid a finger on her he would make sure that person watched that finger being sliced off before he or she died.

His thoughts were interrupted by the ring of his satellite phone. Hopefully Tony had made some progress, he thought as he answered.

"Mr. White?" a distant voice asked.

"Yes, speaking," Richard said hesitantly.

"This is Alvin. Mrs. White is with me," explained the Jamaican voice Richard recognized as his bartender's.

"You better not hurt her," Richard said, in a deadly calm voice.

"We won't hurt her if ya do exactly as we say."

"What do you want?"

"Five million dollars in US cash. We want the money left in plastic containers at midnight on the beach in front of the Sunshine Hotel in Negril. We want it delivered and left beside the scuba shack."

"Then I want my wife left beside the same shack," said Richard, matter-of-factly.

There was a moment of hesitation on the other end and then, "Nope, we can't do that. One of our guys will pick up the money, and once he's safely back with us we'll drop Mrs. White off by a payphone so that she can call you."

Richard's heart leapt in his chest. "No, there is *no way* you are leaving her like that! I insist that she is left near the money. A fair

151

trade," he said, trying desperately to control himself from yelling into the phone.

"Listen, Mr. White, ya may be used to gettin' yer way on everythin', but it's *our* way now. We've got yer wife and we'll only bring her back on *our* terms," Alvin said confidently, although he was shaking with fear.

Frank walked onto the deck and knew immediately what was happening. He wished Richard was on a landline so he could tap it quickly and listen in, as well as record it, but there was obviously no land line on the island. "Should I take over?" whispered Frank, but Richard was by then in a state of rage.

"I WANT HER BACK AND IF YOU SO MUCH AS LAY A FINGER ON HER YOU WILL REGRET YOU EVER LIVED!" roared Richard.

"We'll call back when ya can control your temper. Good-bye," said Alvin, ending the call and breaking into a cold sweat.

Richard threw down his phone, which Frank immediately retrieved, glad that it was still in one piece. "Boss, let me handle the next call. We need to deal with this carefully and—"

"SHUT UP!" Richard yelled, grabbing Frank by the shoulders and shaking him. Frank tried to pull back, but Richard was bigger and stronger and was not about to let go. "I LOVE THAT WOMAN, AND NOBODY IS GOING TO LEAVE HER AT SOME TELEPHONE BOOTH! I CAN'T RISK LOSING HER AGAIN!"

"Calm down, boss, calm down!" said Frank, who didn't scare easily, but was becoming alarmed by Richard's erratic behavior. Richard was losing his mind and Frank knew all too well what he would do to *anyone* who stood in his way or disagreed with him.

Richard let go of Frank, who took a few quick steps back. Richard was breathing heavily, and ran both hands through his already disheveled hair. He paced back and forth for a couple of minutes and finally was able to speak in a rational voice. "Okay, Frank, you can take the next call, but there is no way in *hell* I'm going to have her left somewhere unless we know *exactly* where and when! You know she's at risk of escaping from me, and I don't want her to have the opportunity to do so. I don't want them to walk away with a *cent* until I have Cadence in my arms. That's the *only* deal I will make," he explained, a calm tone creeping back into his voice.

"I think we can get that deal, boss, provided you let me take care of the negotiations."

"Good, because Cadence cannot get away from me again. I would rather they kill her than have her slip away from me again into another life."

# Chapter Twenty-Eight

I WOKE UP TO THE sound of voices in the other room. I had been up most of the night, trying to devise an escape plan. Even if I could get to a phone and call Christian, I'd probably stand a chance, but the thought of being caught by Richard terrified me. My fear of Alvin and Sam was minute compared to my fear of Richard, his threats towards my loved ones still ringing clearly in my mind.

I quietly got off of the moldy-smelling mattress, walked over to the door and pressed my ear against it. I heard Alvin's voice, sounding quite upset. "We just can't risk it, Sam! What if the money's fake? What if it's not all there? We need some time to confirm that he lived up to his end of the bargain before returnin' the lady. As soon as he gets her back he'll try to get revenge on us, so we need time to get away! That guy can afford professional help to find us, and what point is the money if we're dead in our graves?"

*Which you surely will be*, thought Cadence.

"How about we leave her locked up here and Margo can watch over her?" Sam's voice cut in. "Once we call Margo with the okay that we're safe and in the air, we'll let that prick have the address. Margo can then get the hell out, and Mr. White won't be searchin' for a woman anyway. As long as Mrs. White doesn't see her, there's no fear of Margo being found."

"But Margo's my woman, Sam! What if the plan doesn't work out? I want her with me!"

"Alvin, she's the only other person who knows about our plan. We can't trust anyone else to watch over this lady. If we just leave her alone," he explained, his voice becoming softer, "she could somehow escape. The door isn't..." but his voice became a whisper and I couldn't make out his words. The door must be weak, I thought, realizing I might be able to kick it down and get out if nobody was on the other side to threaten or stop me.

"Okay, okay, that does make the most sense. I'll talk to Margo but she won't be happy, *that* I can tell ya. I'll call her right now and then we'd better call Mr. White back to see if he's ready to accept our deal," said Alvin.

I tried to listen to the call, but Alvin must have moved to the other side of the room as his voice was significantly quieter. Would it be worth trying to break out of this room and get past this Margo woman? Surely she'd have a weapon, but would likely use it only if absolutely necessary. I got the impression that Sam and Alvin wouldn't want to renege on their part of the deal by Richard finding an injured or dead wife. All they seemed to want was to be far, far away from Jamaica with a lot of cash. I didn't get the sense that they had anything personal against Richard or me, or wanted to harm anyone.

Their voices became louder again and I could hear Alvin quite clearly now. "I want to speak with Mr. White, not ya!" said Alvin. And then seconds later, "I won't negotiate with ya. Next time I call, Mr. White better answer...we don't want to be forced to hurt his wife," he snapped. I felt anxious, but didn't believe these men would hurt me. I waited a minute and then knocked on the wall, my signal for having to use the bathroom. Moments later the door slowly opened and a very worried looking Alvin asked what I wanted.

"I need to use the bathroom, please. And I'm thirsty and hungry," I added.

"Okay, this way," he said. I followed him through the dimly lit cabin. It smelled briny, as if it were very close to the ocean. In fact, I thought I heard the distant sound of waves crashing on a beach. All the windows seemed to have shutters, which were closed, so although it was probably light out, it gave the aura of still being night. Alvin opened the door to a very small, simple bathroom containing a rust-filled toilet and corner shower. I went inside and closed the door, which didn't have a lock.

I was disappointed that there wasn't a window, but even if there had been, would I take such a risk? Probably not, I thought. I had to be smart about this, despite my impulse to escape right away. When I came out, Alvin asked me to have a seat on the small sofa in the middle of the room. It was wicker, and the cushions were patterned with faded, pastel-colored seashells.

"Here's a glass of water, Mrs. White," said Alvin, using the same polite tone he had when he handed Richard and me tropical drinks at the swim-up bar. I drank the lukewarm water thankfully, hoping it was sterilized, as who knew where it came from. "We're goin' to phone Mr. White, and we need ya to scream when we say so; I want him to think we're threatenin' ya. If ya don't scream, we'll have to make ya scream, but I'd rather not do that. Can ya promise you'll scream when I touch yer arm?" asked Alvin.

"Yes, of course," I said. I needed to be on good terms with these two men. If they became suspicious of me, they might not leave me alone with Margo, which was beginning to look like my best and only opportunity to escape.

Alvin dialed his cell phone, with Sam standing nearby watching me cautiously. I heard the faint sound of a voice answering and then Alvin said, "Mr. White? What? I told ya I wanted to speak with Mr. White and *only* Mr. White!" Then seconds later, "Mr. White, here's the deal. We'll come by the scuba shack at the Sunshine Hotel at midnight. We expect to find the money, all of it, in plastic containers. We don't want *anyone* interruptin' us in *any* way. We'll take the money away, and then we need to count it and make sure it's real. Once we're sure, which will be before sunrise, we will call ya and give ya the address of where Mrs. White is being held, and ya can come and get her. We *won't* harm her if ya agree with this plan."

For a minute Alvin listened, shaking his head and frowning angrily. "No, we *won't* agree to that! I guess we'll have to hurt your wife then!" I heard Richard's voice yelling at Alvin to stop, but Alvin ignored it and gently tapped my arm, as he held the phone near my mouth. I shrieked, as realistically as possible, and then pleaded, "Help me Richard!"

"Cadence!" said Richard, sounding distraught, but Alvin had already pulled the phone away.

"We'll hurt her *very badly* if ya don't agree to our deal!" said Alvin, trembling with fear. I could now clearly hear Richard's voice.

"Okay, okay, I agree. BUT YOU BETTER NOT LAY A FINGER ON HER, AND IF YOU DO NOT PROVIDE US WITH HER

LOCATION BY SUNRISE I WILL HAVE YOU ALL KILLED!"
yelled Richard, absolutely hysterical. Hearing his voice through a phone
several feet away sounded almost as if he was standing here in the room
with us.

"No need for threats, Mr. White. We'll make sure she's safe and
we promise to live up to our end of the bargain," said Alvin, trying
desperately to mask the quiver that had crept into his voice.

"I WANT HER LOCKED UP, WHEREVER SHE IS, SO SHE
CANNOT GET AWAY! LEAVE THE KEY OUTSIDE FOR US. IF
SHE IS HURT OR MISSING I WILL…"

"We have a deal, Mr. White. Good-bye," said Alvin, sweating
profusely through his thin, white linen shirt.

"Good job, Alv," said Sam.

Sam turned to me, his look of extreme anxiety turning into one of
perplexity. "How come he wants you locked up?" he asked. "I mean,
why would ya try to get away knowin' yer husband will be here soon?"

I took a few seconds to formulate a response. "I think he means
that I won't know whether I'm still being held captive, and will try to
escape to find *him*," I lied, part of me wanting to tell them the truth.
But if they knew the true situation, I doubted they would leave me
alone with only Margo as my guard.

"Oh," said Alvin, appearing to believe me. "Ya said ya were
hungry…want a Jamaican patty?" he asked. I nodded and watched
him take a yellow colored patty out of the fridge. "Sorry, it'll have to be
cold as the oven ain't workin'. But it's really good…my aunt makes 'em."

"Thanks," I said, feeling starved. Despite being cold and hard, the
patty was delicious and I enjoyed every spicy bite. I washed it down
with more lukewarm water.

"Do ya think he'll live up to his part of the bargain, Mrs. White?"

I thought about how to respond, for the truth was that Richard
would do everything in his power to get revenge on these guys. He
was not accustomed to taking orders, and being the weaker party in
a negotiation. Not only had they abducted me, but they had put him
at risk of losing me again, which in his mind would be worse than
anything. I doubted Alvin and Sam would get out of this alive. "Yes, I
do. He's a man of his word," I lied. The patty I had just eaten suddenly
felt like a lead weight in my stomach as I thought about the cruelty
Richard was capable of.

"Well, ya know him best so that's good news for us," said Alvin. "Someone else will be here guardin' ya while we're gone tonight. Ya won't get to meet this person and don't bother tryin' to talk to 'em. They'll be armed, so don't try to escape. As soon as we have our money and are safely away, your husband will be able to come and rescue ya. In the meantime, ya need to stay in yer room. Here's some water and magazines. Before ya know it, the night'll be over and you'll be free," said Alvin, trying to give me some comfort in the fact that my knight in shining armor would soon be there. I cringed at the thought of being carried away, once again, in Richard's arms.

# Chapter Twenty-Nine

THE HOURS PASSED BY SLOWLY. I was lying on my stomach on the mattress, flipping through a recent People magazine. It felt good to be reading about the world that continued on during my captivity. Other than the brief news clip Richard had shown me a few days ago, I hadn't had access to newspapers or television in over a week. I wondered if Richard was planning on keeping me in the dark forever about the real world, or if he was only doing so for the time being because he wanted all of my attention focused on him.

I glanced over a few photos from a recent wedding of two movie stars I hadn't heard of, which brought back bitter thoughts of the forced wedding Richard had orchestrated. I gasped, though, when I turned the page to see a photo of myself staring back at me. "Where is Cadence?" read the bold title. My graduation photo from Julliard grinned back at me. I never thought I'd be in a magazine, let alone featured as a lost person.

I saw photos of my distraught family and of Christian and I intermixed with the description of my "highly unusual" disappearance. I noticed a caption that read, "Family offers reward of $500,000 for information leading to the whereabouts of Cadence Weaverly." Apparently my family and Christian were raising money to find me, and were hopeful that I was still alive. It said that Christian had organized a concert by the New York Philharmonic to raise funds towards increasing the reward. There was also a photo of Christian, his eyes bloodshot and dark hair disheveled, with a description that read,

"Fiancé vows to never give up the search for his beloved." Tears welled in my eyes and slid down my cheeks as I read those words.

"I'll get out of this mess," I whispered to the picture of Christian, a tear hitting his shoulder and dampening the shiny paper. "I love you *so much* and I'll do everything in my power to escape and come back to you."

I read the article from start to finish. It felt surreal to read about myself in a People magazine, and while it saddened me deeply, it also motivated me to continue fighting to escape. My thoughts were interrupted by the sound of a high-pitched woman's voice in the cabin.

"Please let me come with ya! She won't be able to escape anyway!"

Shhh, Margo, *whisper!*" demanded Alvin, in a hushed voice.

"I'm scared…if ya love me ya *won't* leave me here!" she said, quieter but still shrill enough for me to hear. I carefully stood up and pressed my ear against the door.

"I promised Cadence would be here. If ya don't guard her, she might escape. Mr. White will *kill* Sam and me if we don't live up to our end of the bargain!"

"So ya'd rather *me* dead? *I'm* the one left behind and in the most danger!" she said, in a shaky voice that was clearly accompanied by tears.

"Of course not! That's why I'll call and let ya know when we leave the Sunshine Hotel with the money. Then ya can drive to the airport and we can all get away as planned…nobody would suspect ya anyway!"

"But what if she tries to get away? Then what?"

"She won't and if she does try to leave, ya have the gun to threaten her with. But she's a nice calm lady who just wants her husband to come and rescue her, so ya have *no* worries, honey. And before ya know it, you'll be flyin' to meet me and we'll have a new life together. No more slavin' away for American tourists. No more worryin' about tryin' to afford our own place one day. We'll never have to worry about money again!"

"Fine, but I don't like it. I have a bad feelin' about this," she said in a calmer, quieter voice. "What if ya don't call?"

"I'll call and let ya know what's goin' on as soon as we're on the road with the money, just after midnight. If ya don't hear from me by 12:15 a.m., leave, as it probably means somethin' went wrong. But this place is far enough away that you'll have half an hour to get away before anyone reaches the cabin. But I swear that nothin' will go wrong. Just stick to the plan."

"Okay, but ya'd better not forget to call! I'm gonna be worried sick, Alvin!"

"I will. Now we have to get goin' soon and take care of a few things in the next couple of hours before we pick up the money. You'll be fine, just fine," he promised.

"Be safe, I *can't* lose ya Alvin!"

"I will. Ya know I will."

The voices disappeared from the cabin and I was left in silence. I heard a vehicle start and drive away. When would be the ideal time to escape? Would Margo actually use the gun to keep me here? Would she shoot me if I ran? These thoughts buzzed around in my mind, each one taking the stage momentarily before the next one replaced it.

I didn't know the time but suspected it was between nine and ten o'clock. I felt that my window of opportunity was fast approaching. The ideal time would be when Alvin and Sam were far away, and the chances of them turning back were low. If I waited much past midnight I risked being caught while trying to escape, especially if Richard forced Sam or Alvin to reveal my whereabouts. I needed to get as far away as possible by midnight.

After carefully thinking through each scenario I decided on a plan. I said a prayer, took a deep breath and knocked on the door. "Hello?"

Silence.

"Margo, I know you're there and I *really* need to talk with you." *Please, God, someone answer!*

Silence.

"Margo, I *need* to warn you about Richard White. You are in great danger and I don't want you to get hurt." I spoke loudly and clearly, my mouth pressed to the wooden door. There was no response.

"I promise I won't try to run away. I just don't want to see either of us hurt. Please, trust me!"

Nothing.

"Please, *please*, just let me out to speak with you! I know you have a gun and you can hold it towards me so I won't try to escape. I just want to speak with you!"

"I can't let ya out, Mrs. White," a voice finally replied. I heaved a sigh of relief. Finally, I was getting through!

"Then I'll have to break the door down, which I don't want to do," I replied.

"Ya can't do that!" Margo said in a shrill voice.

"Margo, it's a very weak door, so I *know* I can. It might hurt, but I'll do it anyway," I explained matter-of-factly.

"I have a gun!" said Margo. "I don't want to hurt ya, but will if ya try to escape!" she said, sounding terrified.

"I know you have a gun. I heard your whole conversation with Alvin. But remember, if you shoot me Alvin will be killed and you will be too. You'd be better off to leave this place rather than hurt me. I don't want to get in your way...I *want* you to escape safely, with the money. Trust me. I just want you to understand my situation, which isn't what it seems!" I said.

There were a couple of minutes of silence. I could only imagine how confused Margo must be. Then a response. "How do I know you're not lyin'? Why would I believe you'd want us to get away with *yer* money? Do ya think I'm *stupid*, lady?"

"It's Richard's money, not mine. Trust me, our marriage is *not* what you think!"

"Whatever! Ya's a rich man's wife, Mrs. White, and don't try tellin' me otherwise!"

"No," I said, tears entering my voice. "He abducted me and forced me to marry him. I know it sounds unbelievable, but it's true."

Ya really *do* think I'm stupid, Mrs. White," she said nervously, laughing from the other side of the door.

"My name's not Mrs. White, it's Cadence Weaverly," I said.

"Alvin saw ya get married, so why're you lyin'?" she asked, frustration apparent in her nervous voice.

"Read page forty-two of this magazine," I said, sliding the People magazine under the door.

I heard the ruffling of pages and then silence.

A few minutes passed. "This could be anyone, just 'cause you have the same name don't mean nothin'," said Margo.

"Margo, there are photos of me, so isn't that enough proof?"

"I don't know what ya look like," she said, increasingly nervous.

"Then let me out so you can see."

"Okay, but I have a gun and if ya try to run I'll use it," she said, slowly unlocking the door.

I cautiously opened it, and standing on the other side of the room was a beautiful Jamaican woman with long hair in dozens of tiny braids. She held a gun pointed towards me in one hand, and the magazine clenched in the other. She was wearing a hot pink tank top and black Capri pants, and was short and slim. Our eyes locked and I could see her expression of recognition, having just seen several photos of me. "I'll be damned, it *is* ya!" she exclaimed.

I stayed near the door, slowly smiling at her. "Thank you, Margo, for trusting me. I won't run, so why don't we sit down and decide what to do?"

Her face revealed much confusion. "How do I know that? Ya could get me, Alvin and Sam all killed if we break our promise to Mr. White."

"I know. That's why we need to make a plan…something that will work for all of us."

"Lady, ya may be in a bind, but I can't risk our lives for it," she said, now crying. "I've worked hard all my life and have *nothin'* to show for it. We work like slaves on this island, and all ya Americans pay us like crap! This is me and Alvin's *only* chance to build a new life and I don't want to screw it up!" she said, the gun still pointed towards me. I doubted she would use it even if I did run for the door.

"I know, Margo, and I understand, but *please* try to understand my situation. I was abducted and forced to marry Richard White. He had the only other person who tried to help me killed, so I *know* what he's capable of. I don't want to risk your life, or Alvin's or Sam's, but I need to get away before he captures me again. I can't go on living as his wife. I need to get back to my fiancé and my family, to the people I love!" I said with passion. "And I swear, if you help me, I *will* make sure you get the reward money…the $500,000 mentioned in that article will be yours."

Margo lowered the gun, walked over to the couch, sat down and gestured for me to come over. There was a box of tissues on the wicker coffee table, and she grabbed one to wipe her eyes and runny nose. I walked over and sat in the wicker chair that was beside the sofa. Its old, worn cushion had the same pastel-colored seashell pattern as the sofa. I reached for a tissue as well, and we sat there staring at each other as we wiped away our tears.

"Thanks for trusting me, Margo," I said quietly, giving her a small smile of gratitude.

She smiled back. "Alvin *won't* like this, but tis' his fault for leavin' me here. I knew this wouldn't go smoothly. I had a bad feelin' about it all along. But when does life ever go smoothly?" she asked, shaking her head and smiling cynically. I noticed she had smooth, flawless skin the color of milk chocolate. Her eyes were framed with long, black lashes and she had perfectly shaped full lips.

"Not very often," I said, noticing the clock on the wall read eleven o'clock. It was later than I'd thought and I felt a great urgency to make my escape. "Listen, I *really* need to get away from here before Richard finds me. I also need to call for help and warn my fiancé…Richard threatened to kill him if I ever left," I quickly explained. "And I need to warn my family as well."

"Okay, but you can't use this phone," she said. "If Alvin calls and it's busy he'll…"

"Okay, I understand. But I *need* to get away from here and call for help. It needs to look like I escaped on my own. Does Richard know someone is guarding me?" I asked.

"No, he only requested that ya be locked up and the key left outside. Alvin didn't promise anyone would stay to guard ya.

"So it needs to look like I escaped. I need to break down the door and make it look real, and then I need to get away from here. How far are we from the nearest town?"

"This place is a twenty minute drive from the next town. It would be a long walk and this ain't a tourist area…it wouldn't be safe for a white woman on her own," said Margo.

"Would you drive me and drop me off near a police station?" I pleaded.

"I *can't* leave yet! If Alvin calls and I'm not here he'll panic! Look, I wanna help ya but I can't risk our safety!" she said, clearly feeling caught in the middle. "But ya *can* come with me when I leave, once Alvin calls," she said. "I can let ya out anywhere along the way, so long as nobody sees," she said. "And you'll need to swear you'll *never* mention this to anyone. Shit, I'm so stupid! Why am I riskin' my future for a rich American lady I don't even know?" she said, finally putting the gun down beside her and shaking her head.

"Because you're a *kind* human being, Margo," I said. "And I'll be forever grateful to you. If you ever need *anything*, I will do everything in my power to help you."

"I may be *kind*, but I'm also very *stupid*," she said.

"I *promise* that I'll *never* utter a word to anyone that you helped me. I'll have a story ready that involves me escaping and hitchhiking to wherever you drop me off. Now I really should break down the door so Richard thinks I escaped," I said, feeling my anxiety rise as midnight drew closer.

Margo then locked me in the room so I could break down the door. I stood at the back of the tiny room and ran for a couple of steps, throwing myself at the door. It didn't break. I kicked it as hard as I could, and the wood began to splinter. I threw myself at it sideways multiple times, unleashing my fury and visualizing the door being Richard. Finally, after a few minutes, I was able to crack the wood substantially. After a few more minutes the weak lock finally gave way and I came crashing out, landing on the floor in pain, but a joyful pain. "YES!" I said, quickly forgetting about my many new cuts and bruises.

I thought of writing a note to Richard, telling him not to try to find me and that I could never love him, but decided there was no point as it wouldn't stop him. At this point I doubted if there was a rational cell left in his body.

Margo and I chatted nervously as midnight approached. I told Margo what it had been like being abducted and forced to marry Richard. She explained how she didn't like the idea of holding me for ransom, but how Alvin convinced her by painting a much brighter picture of their future, and assuring her that nobody would get hurt in the process.

When midnight came we were both extremely nervous, and kept staring at the phone and clock. Every minute felt like an hour. 12:10 came and Margo began to panic. "Why hasn't he called? He should be on the road by now! All they had to do was load a few boxes! What if he's hurt?"

"Margo, I hope and pray he isn't, but if there's no call by 12:15 we *have* to do as he said and get the hell out of here!"

"I'm *so* scared," she said, now sobbing. I hugged her and my own state of fear eased from comforting another human being.

"I'm scared, too," I said, flinching as the phone finally rang at 12:13.

Margo grabbed it. "Alvin?"

"No, it's *not* Alvin, Margo," said the deep, assured voice, which I could clearly hear as I leaned near the phone. We both froze in terror.

# Chapter Thirty

MARGO GRABBED MY HAND AND squeezed it tightly, and I felt her shaking. Her dark, chocolaty skin seemed to become several shades paler, and her eyes were wide with terror. "Who's this and where's Alvin?" she demanded.

"This is Richard White. I have Alvin and Sam…they've confirmed where you are and we're on our way. My wife *better* be there when we arrive or I will ensure that you are killed, too," he said calmly, but with certainty.

"Wh…what d'ya mean? Did ya kill Alvin?" she asked, her eyes filling with tears and her body shaking uncontrollably.

"We're keeping him alive until we're sure his directions are accurate. In the meantime, I suggest you stay put because we *will* find you if you run," he said, "and we *will* kill you. If you stay there and guard my wife I'll let you go unharmed," he explained. I shook my head as I knew this was a blatant lie.

I made eye contact with Margo and silently pleaded with her to hang up. She nodded back at me, tears now streaming down her face. Suddenly her look of grief transformed into sheer rage, and then she took a deep breath and said, "I'm *not* stayin' here to be killed by ya, ya rotten bastard, but I'll leave yer wife locked up!" Then she hung up. I was glad she didn't say we were both be leaving, as I still thought the staged escape was safer for her. Whether I left with her or escaped on my own, my loved ones were still at risk and I needed to get to the police as soon as possible.

I hugged her tightly as she sobbed. "I'm *so* sorry this is happening, Margo. Thank you for covering for me. Now we need to get out of here," I exclaimed, and we ran for the door. I looked over my shoulder one last time at the broken door, then ran out to the car. Margo started it immediately, and we sped down the road. We were both terrified, and were constantly expecting another vehicle to appear and chase us. Margo turned from the side road onto what looked like a main road and accelerated.

"You're a brave woman, Margo," I said, gently touching her arm.

Her eyes then spilled over with tears again and she began sobbing. "I don't want my Alvin to die! We've gotta get to the police!"

"Do you have a cell phone?" I asked, thinking we needed to be in touch with the police sooner than the drive would take.

"Yes, there's one in the glove compartment," said Margo. I immediately realized that I could have called the police on it earlier had I known. I quickly located the small, black phone and tried to turn it on, but it didn't light up.

"Shit! That's right, the battery's dead! The charger broke so I can't charge it through the lighter. I have a plug-in charger and totally forgot to charge it in the cabin…too much on my mind. Shit, shit, shit! I'm so stupid!"

"No, you're not, Margo," I said, trying to remain calm.

"I'm sorry, I didn't mean to—"

"How far is the nearest police station?" I interrupted, not wanting to take any more time discussing what was already done.

"The next town is quite small, so it doesn't have one. The town after that is about a fifteen minute drive and I know where the police station is. My brother was in the drunk tank there last year," she said, driving faster and faster down the dark stretch of road.

"As soon as we get there I need you to explain what's happening, while I call my fiancé and family to warn them. The police need to know that Richard, and whoever else is helping him, are armed and dangerous, and we *need* to be hidden immediately. I think Richard would fight or pay off the police to get to me, he's *that* crazy. You need to park the car around back or somewhere out of sight," I quickly explained, articulating each idea as it formed in my panicked mind.

"Okay, and they need to find Alvin before it's too late! Lord, I hope they can help us! I don't wanna die," she said quietly, tears continuing to roll down her soft, dark cheeks.

"You *won't* die, Margo. We'll be safe *very* soon," I said, trying to ward off the doubts that kept creeping into my head.

All of a sudden, as Margo sped around a curve, there was the dark figure of a man walking across the road. It was too late to slow down, and she turned sharply to avoid hitting him. We both screamed and then our car veered off the road and rolled over into the ditch. The sound of breaking glass was my last memory before I lapsed into unconsciousness.

* * * * *

Tony had Joe guarding Alvin at gunpoint in a van parked near the Sunshine Hotel. Sam was already dead; he tried to escape after he'd told them the information they wanted, but Frank pulled a knife and slit his throat.

Tony had carefully planned how they would intercept Alvin and Sam when they were collecting the boxes at midnight. It had been much easier than they'd anticipated to sneak up on Sam from behind as he held a gun, while Alvin carried each box to their vehicle. These guys were as novice as they came, Tony said mockingly, after they had both of them held separately at gunpoint.

It took not only threats but physical force to make Sam break, and even more to get anything out of Alvin. After assaulting Alvin repeatedly, coupled with constant threats, he finally broke down and begged them not to hurt his girlfriend. He explained that she hadn't been part of their plan and was only guarding Mrs. White. "Please, if ya need to kill someone, kill *me* instead!" Alvin had bravely begged. Badly bruised and bleeding, he was sure his nose and a few ribs were broken, and he could feel that some teeth were missing. His body was throbbing in pain, almost to the point of forcing him into unconsciousness.

"We'll see, Alvin. If she does what we say and my wife is safely locked up, I might consider sparing her life," responded Richard coldly. "Although, I must admit that I have run out of patience given that someone I hired and *trusted* stole my wife away from our island *and* from our honeymoon! OUR HONEYMOON! HOW DARE YOU

THINK YOU CAN TAKE AWAY MY WIFE!" he roared, punching Alvin in the gut repeatedly until he fell to the ground in agony.

Richard had been in a state of rage ever since he found out Cadence was missing, and his anger continued to intensify with every passing hour. Tony had to stop him from killing Sam and Alvin with his bare hands on the beach in front of the Sunshine Hotel. "Richard, be rational," Tony said. "If these guys are dead, finding your wife will be like finding a needle in a haystack on this island!" This thought made Richard hold off on his impulse to kill, as he couldn't bear another day without Cadence. He felt as though he would explode if his rage built up any more…he needed to keep it in check.

Now this nightmare was finally coming to an end, Richard thought, as they screeched to a halt in front of the cabin. He and Tony jumped out of the Jeep and ran towards the door. The directions weren't perfect, but the two small wrong turns only ate up about ten minutes. Tony had a gun and was ready to blow off the doorknob if it was locked, but it wasn't. Their jaws both dropped at the sight of the broken door. Richard's instincts told him immediately that she wasn't there, as he ran into the small room. He could smell her perfume, and knew this was where she'd been kept. "AGGHHH!" he roared. "Where are you, Cadence?"

Tony examined the door while Richard stood beside him, breathing quickly and deeply, beads of sweat forming all over his red face. Richard then started pacing around the living room, violently kicking and punching walls and furniture. Tony felt Richard had become a wild animal and was making an already dangerous situation substantially worse. He stood anxiously in the back of the kitchen, clutching his gun nervously. Tony was usually tough and confident, but at this moment he realized that he was dealing with a man who was losing it.

Richard walked towards the kitchen after a few minutes and stared furiously at Tony. "Why has this happened? I'M PAYING YOU TO FIND MY WIFE, YET SHE'S STILL MISSING!"

Tony swallowed hard, still gripping the gun tightly for reassurance. "Boss, *please* calm down, I'm doing my best. We *will* find her, we just need a bit more time," he explained.

"She could be anywhere by now! She could be at the police station, or even on her way to the airport! If she's gone, you and your men will be sorry!" he roared, his fists clenched tightly as he stood a few feet away from Tony.

Tony felt his own anger begin to boil. "Don't threaten me or my men! This is *not* our fault. Your wife left on her own accord and that makes this even more complicated. We're not only dealing with an abduction, but with a runaway too," he said angrily.

"I don't care how or why she left, I need her back! I'm paying you to find her, so get back to work! Whether my wife is a runaway or has been abducted is none of your business, getting her back *is!*" Richard roared, pounding his fist forcefully on the kitchen table.

Tony almost pointed his gun at Richard as he backed out of the cabin. Richard was a dangerous man to be working for; he had immense resources and could come after Tony and his men if they screwed up or quit on him now. Plus, Tony knew they would be richly rewarded when Cadence was found. After that, they could stop working for Richard White. With that thought, he said, "Okay, let's go and I'll call my guys from the cell in the Jeep to tell them our next move. I also have Frank stationed at the airport, keeping an eye out for both women. And, I also have some contacts between here and the airport, so I'll try to get some roadblocks set up."

"Good, let's go!" said Richard, and they ran out to the Jeep.

Tony was on his cell immediately, quickly spelling out detailed directions to both of his men. Richard tuned him out, stared ahead at the dark road, and let his thoughts turn once again to his wife. Why had she escaped from the cabin? Didn't she know he would be able to find her, that there was no escaping him? He had warned her that he would have Christian killed if she ever tried to leave him, which she now had. She had betrayed him once again, he thought bitterly.

He remembered back to the day of his mother's funeral, when Cadence had come over to visit him. He had begged for her love and to give him another chance, yet she walked away from him when he was suffering the most. She had walked out of his life that unbearable day ten years ago, and was now doing so again. His anger intensified into fury, and he decided that now was the time to follow through on his threat. If she was going to get away, he would *not* let her go back to her life as she knew it. He fished his phone from his pocket and dialed the number he knew so well.

Ring...ring...ring..."Hello?" said a sleepy voice, as it was the middle of the night in New York City.

"Dominic?"

"Yep. Is that you, Mr. White?"

"Yes, I have some work for you that I need done *immediately.*"

"Okay, tell me."

"Christian Davidson...I want him killed before morning, but you'll have to be very careful as he's being guarded," Richard ordered.

"Any particular method?" asked Dominic.

"How about..." but suddenly he stopped speaking as they rounded a corner and saw the scene of an accident ahead. A car was upside down in the ditch. Tony was forced to stop rapidly as the area was barricaded with pylons, as well as police cars and an ambulance. Two paramedics were carrying a stretcher towards the ambulance. Richard immediately noticed the long, auburn hair spilling over the side of the stretcher, and froze in terror. He threw down the phone and scrambled out of the Jeep, sprinting towards the stretcher. He immediately recognized that the injured woman was Cadence.

"That's my wife!" he yelled, through protests from the ambulance workers. He took her hand while they tried to load her into the ambulance. "Cadence!" he said, in a panicked voice, while kissing and clasping her hand. She seemed to be unconscious.

"Okay sir, just let us load her as she needs to get to the hospital... she's badly hurt. You can ride with her," explained one of the paramedics. Richard looked panic stricken and moved out of the way so the ambulance workers could load Cadence into the ambulance. He then climbed inside and sat beside her, clasping one of her hands in both of his.

Tony ran to the back of the ambulance and caught Richard's attention. "I'll be in touch shortly. I'm sorry about this," he said, looking awkwardly towards Cadence who was wrapped in a bloodstained blanket. Richard ignored him, focusing all of his attention on his wife.

"I've found you, my love," he said, as the ambulance sped off into the night, while she lay where she belonged, at his side.

# Chapter Thirty-One

I FELT A SHARP PAIN in my leg as I tried to move into a more comfortable position. The pain was intense and I felt myself fighting to stay asleep, yet consciousness took over and I slowly opened my eyes. I saw the white walls and for a moment thought I might be in the same room in which I had awakened at Richard's house. Then I noticed the intravenous tube leading into my hand and heard the faint beeping of a machine. I was in a hospital! My memories were foggy and I tried to piece together what had happened, but the pain in my leg was throbbing and I cried out in reaction.

Suddenly I heard Richard's voice, "Cadence? Are you awake?" he asked. I could hear him from behind, and at once he was beside me, looking down at me anxiously. He looked as if he had just woken up.

"It...it hurts so much," I whispered.

"I'll get the nurse," Richard said, gently squeezing my hand then running out of the room.

Then it slowly came back to me...the cabin...Margo...the broken door...and the car ride. We'd crashed...I couldn't recall how, but I was certain we'd been in a car accident. And...Richard had found me! I shuddered, ripples of fear beginning to wash away the feelings of intense physical pain I was experiencing.

A nurse entered my room, followed by Richard. "Is yer leg hurtin', ma'am?" she asked, in a thick Jamaican accent.

"Badly, very badly," I said, wincing in pain.

"I'm goin' to give ya another shot of morphine to ease the pain. Yer leg is broken and badly cut, but it's healin'. And ya have a concussion and a few broken ribs, but yer gonna be just fine, Mrs. White, just fine," she said reassuringly, as she worked on the IV from behind me. Then she brought a glass of water to my lips. "Sip some of this, Mrs. White," she said gently. I sipped the cool water, which felt refreshing.

"What...happened?" I asked.

"Ya was in a bad car accident last night," she said. "You're lucky to be alive, ma'am. Now ya just rest, there'll be plenty of time to talk about it once yer feelin' better," she explained. She was a plump, black woman with a calm demeanor and kind smile. "Yer husband hasn't left yer side since ya got here. You're a lucky woman, Mrs. White, a *very* lucky woman," she said. "Now get some rest."

When the nurse left, Richard pulled a chair beside my bed and held one of my hands while stroking my hair with his other hand. "I'm *so* glad you're alive, my love. *So glad,*" he said tenderly, relief clear in his deep voice.

I looked up at him, into his deep green eyes that were staring intently at me. I sensed that he was very sad and saw the pain in his eyes, as I felt my own eyelids getting heavy with the effects of the morphine.

"Just one question, Cadence...why did you leave me again?" he asked hesitantly. He sounded as though he didn't really want to know, yet couldn't resist asking.

"I didn't..." I whispered, finally succumbing to sleep.

I woke up again to find Richard asleep, his head resting beside my arm. I could still feel the pain in my leg, but this time it wasn't nearly as intense, more like a dull ache. I was careful not to move, but just lay there and tried to think. I needed some time to process this mess. My first thought was that Richard knew I had escaped. My second thought was that I had not been able to warn Christian or my family as planned. A feeling of dread filled me and I needed some excuse to convince Richard that I had not broken my promise, that I hadn't tried to purposely escape from him, but instead had been terrified and wanted to find him. Would he believe me? I had to try.

"Richard," I said, touching his head. "Please wake up."

He stirred and then lifted his head. "Cadence?"

"Yes, I'm here. Richard, I need to explain..."

"What?" he asked, dazed.

"Richard, I *wasn't* trying to escape. I was so terrified alone in that room that I had to get out and try to find you," I said, as my heart raced.

"I broke out and I thought Margo had left but she was still there. She was leaving and said she wanted to get away and would drop me off at the nearest town. I didn't want to stay in that cabin *alone*. I didn't know if you would ever find me and I was sooo scared," I explained.

Richard stared at me. "Go on," he said calmly, now fully awake.

"I thought that if I got to a town I could call you and…"

"You don't even have my cell number," he said, matter-of-factly, his eyes scrutinizing mine.

"Yes, I had it memorized, Margo gave it to me. I was going to call you as soon as I got to a payphone."

"You didn't have any money, Cadence. I think you were trying to leave me," he said, his voice cracking as though he were about to cry. He stared off into the distance, his green eyes filled with pain.

"I was going to call collect, Richard!" I said frantically.

"Cadence, you *broke* your promise, that's all there is to it. You tried to escape from me and by doing so reneged on our deal," he carefully explained.

"Richard, I…I realized when we were apart that I *do* care about you. I really *do* want to be with you," I said, trying to make my lie sound as honest as possible. I squeezed his hand.

"You *do*?" he asked cautiously, his eyes displaying a look of confusion and surprise.

"Yes, I *do*. Please believe me. I was scared and needed to find you. I couldn't wait at that cabin, Richard, I was just too afraid. I know now that I should have waited, but…*please* believe me."

He looked worried. "But I thought you had…"

"No, I *wouldn't* break my promise!" I said emphatically. "And I hope you wouldn't break yours before at least talking to me. I could never, *ever*, forgive you if you did," I added, looking at him with pleading eyes. Surely he hadn't had Christian hurt before I was even able to explain myself?

He sat in silence for a second, then responded, "No, of course not, my love."

"Thank you, Richard," I said, exhaling a long breath of relief. I felt utterly exhausted from the conversation.

"I *love* you, Cadence. I'm just so glad you're alive. I'm sorry you had to go through all of this. The men who did this to you got what

they deserved. They are both dead and can burn in hell for all I care…
nobody tries to steal my wife," he declared.

Suddenly Margo entered my mind again. "Was Margo hurt?" I
asked.

"She was killed in the accident. That bitch got what she deserved,"
he said coldly.

My eyes welled with tears. Poor Margo! "That's terrible. She wasn't
a bitch, she was just trying to make a better life for Alvin and herself,"
I said weakly.

"She was a good for nothing bitch who deserved *exactly* what she
got. And don't mention Alvin ever again…he was scum of the earth
and I only wish I had more time to make him suffer for his crime," he
said, his voice lacking even a trace of emotion. His extremes of speaking
of intense love to pure hatred were overwhelming my drugged brain.

"Richard, please…please don't…" but I couldn't finish my sentence
as exhaustion once again overtook my weak body and mind.

\* \* \* \* \*

Richard walked briskly to the hospital stairwell, and once cloaked in
its privacy dialed Dominic's number. He hoped like hell that it was not
too late, but knew that it probably was. As much as he wanted Christian
dead, once and for all, he also wanted his wife's love and trust, both
of which would be shattered if Dominic had successfully followed his
orders and Cadence ever found out about it.

"Dominic here," said the gruff voice on the other end.

"Dominic, it's Richard White. Has it been done?" he asked, his
heart racing.

"Yep, boss, it's a done deal. Finished him off two hours ago," he
said, pleased with himself.

"Are you sure?" Richard whispered.

"Shot him a few times in the chest, then one in the head for good
measure," he said. "You know you can count on me. I was surprised
there wasn't more security."

"Thanks Dominic, I've got to go," Richard said, at a loss for what
to do next. There was no turning back…he had broken his promise to
Cadence. But up until a few minutes ago he had been certain she had
broken her promise to him! Maybe she had and her alibi was all a lie,
but he couldn't be sure. All he knew for certain was that she would

never forgive him if she found out. So he had to make certain that she never learned the truth. She would continue to have no contact with the outside world – no Internet, television, newspapers, magazines – *nothing*! He had hoped to gradually increase her freedom as she fell in love with him, but now he knew this could never happen, not for a *very* long time, if ever. Cadence would be his and his alone. Her life would be completely in his world, and he would do everything in his power to make sure she never found out that Christian was dead.

# Chapter Thirty-Two

I STAYED IN THE HOSPITAL for a few days. Richard was with me most of the time and when he was not, he had one of his men, Frank or Joe, guard my door. The hospital staff agreed to this arrangement due to my recent kidnapping and the fear of another attempt. Richard seemed to have accepted my alibi, but I sensed that he still didn't trust me completely. And he was correct in this regard, for if there was any way to escape I would not have hesitated to try it. But being constantly guarded, plus not being able to walk without crutches, put me at an extreme disadvantage.

I felt myself sinking into a depression. I had been so hopeful that I was getting away from Richard, only to be back under his full control. I promised myself that once I recovered I would begin plotting another escape, this one more carefully planned and executed than the last. I *would* get away, I had to. But the anticipation was difficult to build up, since escape seemed so distant. I knew I would have to spend more nights in Richard's bed and continue to pretend to care about him... both thoughts revolted and terrified me.

During my last morning in the hospital I broke into tears alone in my room and sobbed uncontrollably. I heard the door open and in walked Frank. I saw his blurry image through my tears.

"You okay, ma'am?" he asked awkwardly.

"No, I'm not," I said hoarsely, continuing to cry.

"I'll get the nurse," he said, turning to leave.

"No, I don't need anything. I just miss my family," I said quietly.

"I guess you must," he said, once again awkwardly, as he avoided making eye contact. I had a sudden burst of energy. Maybe I could get some information out of him? Perhaps he knew something about Christian or my family? I believed that Richard hadn't done anything to them because I couldn't bear to believe otherwise, but if this wasn't the case I needed to know. I knew that Richard didn't fully trust me and I felt exactly the same way about him. Surely his hired help would know the truth of what was happening with my loved ones.

"And I'm very upset about what Richard did," I said, in a weak voice. Maybe, just maybe, I could get this guy to share what he knew by pretending I already knew something.

"Huh?" asked Frank, nervously.

"You know what I'm talking about! I found out and I am sick about it," I said, my tears continuing. "I know there's nothing I can do now that my life's with Richard, but how *cruel* of him," I said.

Frank looked surprised that I knew what happened, but his surprise soon turned into sympathy. "At least it was fast so it would've been painless, ma'am," he said, trying to give me a bit of comfort. I shuddered…there *was* something! Part of me didn't want the conversation to continue, but the other part of me needed to know the truth.

"Do you know if he died instantly or in the hospital?" I asked cautiously, almost in a whisper.

"Probably at the site, but it would've been quick. He wouldn't have even heard the gun shot."

"Did you know he was my *fiancé*?" I asked, as my crying grew more intense.

"Yes, ma'am, I'm sorry," he said quietly. "I can't talk no more, though, the boss wouldn't like it," he whispered, stepping out and gently closing the door.

I sobbed for a long time after that, eventually hyperventilating from the lack of oxygen. At some point the nurse brought me a sedative, but my grief was so intense that it had little effect. Richard had ordered the murder of the love of my life! There was no way I was leaving this hospital with Richard…I would end my own life before becoming part of his.

* * * * *

"Hello," Richard said into his cell phone as he sat in the Jeep outside the hospital. He had been making some business calls and had a brief meeting with Tony about planning a secure trip home. He felt good about things...there was *no way* he would lose her again.

"Boss, it's Dominic here," said a nervous voice.

"Yes?" asked Richard, his brows furrowing into a frown, not having expected to hear from Dominic again on this trip.

"You're not gonna like this, but you need to know," he said, anxiously.

"What is it?" Richard demanded.

"I got the wrong guy," Dominic responded.

"WHAT?" Richard exclaimed.

"He looked exactly the same...I was certain it was him!"

"How COULD you screw up this badly?" roared Richard.

"These things happen, boss. People make mistakes, even professionals," he explained. For once, Richard was speechless.

"I can finish the job, but it won't be possible for a while as the cops have increased their guard. They know the attempt was on Christian since it was right outside of his apartment and because they looked alike.

Richard thought about it...maybe this wasn't so bad. He hated mistakes made by his staff, as he expected no less than *perfection*; however, he'd sworn to Cadence that he had not harmed her loved ones and this would at least make his part of the deal truthful.

"Dominic, forget about it, I've changed my mind. I don't want him killed, but I'll warn you now to *never* screw up like that again."

A surprised silence was all the response he received, and then, "Okay, boss. I promise I won't let you down again."

"Good-bye," said Richard, his blood still boiling from hearing about such a mistake. He would have to find another hitman, as he knew this was the last conversation he'd ever have with Dominic.

\* \* \* \* \*

"Get the nurse right now!" I screamed, as I pushed open the door, nearly knocking down Frank who was standing directly outside of my room. "I have an emergency!" I yelled.

"Okay, ma'am, just stay here," said a confused and panicked Frank. He ran down the hall towards the nurses' station. When he was out of sight I hobbled on my crutches in the other direction, as quickly as my damaged body would take me. This was *it*, I thought. I would put up the fight of my life in order to escape from Richard. Four doors down I saw a door that said "Staff Only" and was relieved to find it open. I stumbled inside and flipped on the light. I noticed that the door had a lock, so immediately turned the deadbolt. Not much good *that* will do, I thought, but at least it would buy me a bit more time. It appeared to be a small office and filing room with a desk and a couple of chairs.

A phone sat beckoning to me on the desk, and I immediately lurched towards it. I had to call for help right away. Should I call the police or my parents? I was in shock about Christian's death, yet the surge of adrenalin was helping me continue. My head spun with the confusion of telling my story in mere seconds and the fear of not being believed. I decided to call my parents first and then they could call the police. From having travelled in other countries I had some experience with the hassles of placing international long-distance calls. Luckily, I was able to get the operator to help me place a collect call. "It's an emergency, I need to get through as soon as possible," I said, reciting my parents' phone number and hoping they were home.

One ring...two rings...three...

\* \* \* \* \*

Richard's eyes widened as the elevator doors opened and he saw Frank speaking anxiously with the nurse. She quickly came out from behind the desk and they both ran towards Cadence's room. Richard caught up in seconds. "What's going on?" he demanded, as all three entered her empty room.

"She's not here!" exclaimed the nurse.

"What? FRANK!" Richard barked.

"I only left for a minute to get the nurse. Mrs. White said that she needed her right away!" answered Frank defensively.

"Where is she?" Richard demanded. The nurse was the calmest of the three of them and had the sense to check the bathroom, which was also empty.

"Calm down, sir," she said. "She must've been lookin' for help. I'll get the staff to search the floor immediately. She can't have gone far on crutches."

"She has a mental condition, nurse, and may be trying to escape… she's probably having delusions again! Call security and get as many people as possible searching this hospital NOW!" he demanded, rushing out of the room after the nurse. "Frank, you look down that hall and I'll search this one!" he ordered.

Richard began running down the same hall in which Cadence was hiding. He threw doors open at random, yelling her name. He could *not* lose her…it was *not* an option. His emotions had taken control of his body, as a combination of adrenalin, fear and anger brewed and boiled over inside his mind. He came to a door marked "Staff Only" and yanked on the knob, which refused to turn. He was immediately suspicious, as this was the only locked door and he had a feeling she might be inside. "Cadence, are you in there?" he barked, now using his full force to try and open the door. He threw his weight against it, all of his fury unleashed against the wood.

"Sir, *stop* that!" demanded the nurse, who was now behind him.

"NO!" he shouted, throwing his large body against the door yet again.

"I have a key, sir!" she yelled, quickly inserting it into the lock as he prepared to throw himself at the door again.

\* \* \* \* \*

While listening to the phone ring, I was startled to hear Richard shouting and then banging loudly on the door. What little time I had was almost gone. *Please answer!* I prayed, shaking with fear and anticipation. Then something crashed heavily against the door, and I thought it might break, but it held. Three rings…four rings…then "Hello?" said my mom's voice.

The door suddenly opened. "Mom, I'm alive!" I yelled into the receiver, as Richard stormed into the room and yanked the phone away from me, before I had the chance to say anything else. In a fit of rage he not only took the phone away but yanked the cord out of the wall and threw the phone at the wall. "NOOOOO!" I screamed, followed by, "HELP ME!" I tried to reach for my crutches beside the desk to use as a weapon, but he grabbed me from behind and held on tightly as I struggled.

"Nurse, she's having an episode, please sedate her!" Richard ordered.

"NOOOOO! He kidnapped me and drugged me!" I yelled, knowing as I said the words that I sounded like a schizophrenic. Just the same, I stared pleadingly into the confused nurse's eyes, desperately willing her to believe me. Having to act like I cared for Richard in the past few days obviously didn't help build my case, but I pressed on. "I need to talk to the police! Please let me tell them what happened!" I begged, and then felt Richard's large hand cover my mouth. The nurse still looked a bit undecided, but I could tell she was leaning towards siding with Richard from the way her eyebrows rose slightly as she glanced his way.

I continued screaming into the palm of his hand, but to no avail. My words had been cut off and once again he held the position of power. Desperately, I bit down hard on the pad of his thumb. He howled in pain as he snatched his hand away. I could taste his blood on my lips as I begged the nurse to get the police.

"That's it!" she snapped. "I'll be back in a minute and we'll get her calmed down," she said, moving purposefully out of the room. Frank then appeared in the doorway, looking very anxious.

"GET OUT YOU BASTARD!" commanded Richard, seething with rage. His wounded hand formed a fist while the other firmly held me around the waist.

"But, I can explain!" he said, looking even more worried.

"There is no explaining to do, Frank. You failed miserably at your simple job, and almost lost Cadence. He lowered his voice to a whisper so that the nurse wouldn't hear. *"Get out of here before I kill you."*

Frank had turned beet red and suddenly his anxiety switched to anger. He spoke quickly and furiously, "What do you expect, that you'll always be able to keep her trapped like an animal? You even told her you had her fiancé killed…man, you're heartless! I'm glad I never have to work for a piece of shit like you again. GO TO HELL!" he shouted over his shoulder, as he walked briskly away.

"YOU'LL BE SORRY!" retorted Richard, who was breathing heavily. It was now just the two of us and I sobbed in his arms, not bothering to struggle as there was no escape from this room. He slowly released his grip on me.

"Just let me *go*!" I begged, between sobs. "I can't stay with you after what you did to Christian. How could you? You're a monster!" I wept, feeling his heavy breathing on the back of my neck.

"You are *not* going anywhere, Cadence, you are *mine*," he said firmly, his voice still trembling with rage. "And I did *not* have Christian killed," he added.

"You *liar*, Frank said that you had him *shot!*" I said bitterly, hot tears running down my face.

"That was the plan when I found out you left me," he explained. "But my man got the wrong guy, *unfortunately*," he stated coldly, as if explaining a simple, everyday type of clerical error as opposed to a botched murder.

"You're lying, you horrible *bastard!*" My voice rose hysterically.

"I wish I were and that the son-of-a-bitch was long gone, but I'm *not*," he said. "But since I *love* you, I told my guy not to try again…at least for now," he explained. "Unless you try to escape or tell anyone else you are being held against your will," he said threateningly.

"I don't believe you," I said. Richard was very convincing, but how could I possibly trust him after everything that had happened?

"Suit yourself, but be warned that I will have him killed if you try *anything* else, like that call you just made to your mother. I should have him finished off for that one! I've had *enough*," he said with finality, as the nurse and an assistant entered the room with a needle to sedate me. Before I could say anything, he firmly clasped his hand over my mouth. I wondered if I should continue to fight and struggle. I didn't believe Richard, but if Christian was still alive I simply couldn't risk his life again. I shook my head in defeat as I looked at the ominous needle in the nurse's hand.

"Administer it NOW," ordered Richard, and the nurse obliged as I fought the urge to struggle. I felt the hot sting of the needle and then Richard scooped me up into his arms and carried me back to my hospital bed. He stood looking down at me protectively as I succumbed to the sedative and closed my eyes, surrendering to the solace of sleep.

# Chapter Thirty-Three

WHEN I FINALLY OPENED MY eyes again, I was startled to find that I was no longer in my hospital room. Instead, I was inside Richard's private jet, lying down across a soft, white leather sofa. Richard was sitting in an armchair across from me reading a newspaper. I felt very groggy and a wave of sadness swept over me. I had been so close to escaping or at least to letting my mom know who had abducted me. I wondered fleetingly if she had been able to trace the call. *It probably doesn't matter anyway*, I thought despondently. *We're probably a thousand miles away from that place by now.* Maybe I should just give up and accept this new life, I thought. What was the point of continuing to try when all I faced were dead ends and risking those I loved? A feeling of depression once again enveloped me.

"You're awake, my love," said Richard, folding the newspaper and putting it on the table beside him. "How are you feeling?"

"I wish I never woke up. I'd rather be dead than here."

"Cadence, how can you say that? Please don't *ever* say those words again," chastised Richard.

"Where are we going?" I asked coldly, ignoring his statement.

"Back home, sweetheart. Unfortunately, I couldn't risk going back to White Island to finish our honeymoon. I can't believe we had to cut our time short; instead you had to be in the hospital while we should have been making love every day on the beach," he said nostalgically. "And I've been working so much this week tying up so many loose ends following this huge mess, like having Bob, that idiot security guard, killed for screwing up the night you were taken. Plus I've paid Tony enough to finish off Frank, I hope his corpse rots in hell," he vented.

I felt distant and detached as I listened to him rant about the lives he had taken as if they were merely pawns in a game of chess. I felt my feelings of depression being replaced by extreme revulsion at his lack of humanity. He concluded his rant with, "So instead of our romantic island we'll now have to settle for the comforts of our home to finish our honeymoon."

"*Your* home," I corrected. "*My* prison."

He looked hurt and slowly shook his head as he tried to make eye contact with me, but I turned my head away.

"Cadence, do *not* make comments like that. We made a deal and if—"

"The deal is over" I snapped. "The *deal* was that I wouldn't try to escape or tell anyone you are holding me against my will!" My voice was rising, and even though it was against my better judgment, I couldn't help but speak my mind as cold fury took over. It felt impossible to continue the façade of caring about him, and the drugs seemed to make me unable to keep my mouth shut.

"Well, deals can be expanded upon. What kind of life is it if you treat me poorly? I spared Christian's life, but I'd be more than happy to finish him off, so don't give me the motivation to do so," he said menacingly.

"So you expect me to be able to act like a normal wife, even though you're holding me captive? Richard, I'm not a good actress!"

"Well you sure as hell better try!" he snapped.

"I'll try to be civil, but I *can't* act like I love you. People aren't puppets that you can make into what you want, Richard. I, too, have my limits, and if you keep threatening my fiancé I won't be able to even look at you, let alone pretend we have a relationship."

He stared at me for what seemed like forever, then walked over and sat at my feet, lifting and placing them on his lap. He began rubbing one foot and I tried to pull it away, as his touch made me cringe. "All I want is to be loved by you, so however long it takes I'm willing to wait. I'm not a patient man and I'm used to getting *what* I want, *when* I want, but for you I'll continue to be patient. I won't mention that man again if you don't give me any reason to do so," he said, always needing to have the final word. Yet another business contract, I thought angrily, with me as his commodity.

I was tired and didn't want to keep talking, so closed my eyes. Suddenly he was maneuvering to lie beside me and next he was kissing my neck.

"No, Richard, I'm exhausted and sore," I said, but to deaf ears.

"I'll be gentle. God I've missed being with you!" he said, sucking gently on my earlobe and delicately cupping my breast.

"Not *here*, please," I begged, as he pulled off my top and then frantically undressed himself.

I continued to fight him off, but to no avail. My body was still in a lot of pain and I cringed as he had his way with me. I closed my eyes and pretended I was somewhere else. I pictured myself in the orchestra, creating music. I imagined each note and tried to picture the black notes climbing up each staff…anything to take my mind off of being with Richard, high in the sky and utterly helpless.

\* \* \* \* \*

"I am sorry, my love, but you need to be blindfolded for the rest of our journey," Richard explained, as the jet touched down sometime later.

"That's ridiculous, but I suppose I don't have a choice," I said.

"Darling, you *will* have choices, just not until I can trust you," he said, as if to a child.

I didn't respond, and turned away, not wanting to make eye contact. Soon the blindfold was secured, and I couldn't see a thing. Richard carried me in his arms off of the jet. The air was warm, with a slight breeze. He helped me into a vehicle, which felt like a limo.

"I thoroughly enjoyed our lovemaking on the flight," he commented, clasping my hand in his bandaged one. I ignored him as I thought, with great satisfaction, of how hard I had bitten him.

"You're a beautiful woman, Cadence, and I know you will make a wonderful mother to our child," he said as I flinched.

"Richard, you know I'm not ready for a child, I told you that before. Please let me have birth control pills, at least for a while," I begged, the world still black through my blindfold.

"No, Cadence. I think a child is just what we need. I've always wanted a family, and there's no other mother in the world who I want for my son or daughter," he explained with confidence, excitement pulsing in his voice. "The combination of our genes will make a beautiful and intelligent child."

"I'd rather get settled and get to know you again before bringing someone else into the equation, Richard. Forcing this is just plain wrong…it has to be a mutual decision!" I said. *Would there ever be a pleasant moment with this monster?* I thought with sinking spirits.

"Even if you're already pregnant, which would be *fantastic,* we'd still have nine months for you to settle in and get to know me again," he said in a logical tone.

"My body has been through a *lot* lately, and the last thing I need is to get pregnant. *Please,* Richard, let's wait," I pleaded.

"It will happen when it's meant to be. It's not in our hands, but in the hands of fate," he said. "Now let's talk about tonight's dinner."

"I don't *want* to talk. My opinion doesn't matter, anyway," I said, trying to pull my hand out of his grasp.

"Cadence, don't act that way. I very much value your opinion, but on certain topics I know what's best for *us* and that's just the way it is," he said firmly, clasping my hand tightly.

I couldn't imagine being pregnant with his child. Christian and I had often talked about having a family and I remembered one of our last conversations in his apartment after making love. We were laying together and talking about our future.

"Let's brainstorm some musical names for our kids," Christian said, playing with a piece of my hair.

"Nothing too strange, though," I laughed. "People these days are going so overboard with odd names. I mean, my name was unique at the time and some people mispronounce it or call me Candace, but I like that it has musical significance."

"I agree. I've always loved your name. How about Legato? It's a nice smooth name and could be either gender," he joked.

"No way," I giggled. "That's almost as bad as naming our child Staccato. Can you imagine the poor kid trying to explain why their parents chose such a bizarre name?"

"Or we could go with the famous composer route, like Mozart or Chopin," he mused.

"Ah the last name as first name trick, no way!" I laughed.

"I love your laugh, Cadence," he said, planting a passionate kiss on my lips. I ran my fingers through his soft, dark curls and before we knew it we were all over each other again.

\* \* \* \* \*

My daydream was suddenly interrupted by Richard. "What are you thinking about, Cadence? You seem so peaceful," he observed.

"Nothing, Richard," I replied. It was beyond my comprehension to think a baby would ever be forced upon me. And there was nothing I could do to stop it, unless I could find another way to escape. Once I recovered and could walk without crutches, I could somehow flee from the mansion. The thought offered me a glimmer of hope, which I so desperately needed to get through the coming days. It was either that or slip into a deep pit of depression, which I may never find my way out of.

The vehicle came to a halt and Richard helped me out and carried me inside. He then removed the blindfold. We were back in his mansion, my grandiose white prison. He brought me up to the large master bedroom and proceeded to force himself on me again. How was I going to endure any more days here? I said a silent prayer as I lay on the bed that perhaps the call I made from the hospital was traced, and that the police were able to get a good description of Richard, and were now on their way here to rescue me. But I sadly thought that the chances of me being found here were miniscule; Richard was too crafty for that.

Richard had a nap while I lay beside him examining the large master bedroom. It was opulent with gleaming hardwood floors, white walls and a huge ensuite with white marble throughout. I could see the large tub with unlit candles all around it. I could also see a balcony, but had no desire to explore as I was still weak from my injuries and the emotional storm of the past number of days.

Richard treated our first week back in the mansion like a honeymoon. He told me he wanted to make love in every room and he was true to his promise. After each incident I said a silent prayer hoping that I wasn't pregnant. Richard wasn't rough or kinky when it came to sex, which I was grateful for.

Days passed by, turning maliciously into weeks. My leg healed and I was finally able to walk without crutches. My ribs were very sore for a couple of weeks, but also healed nicely. My days consisted of having three meals a day with Richard, including a fancy dinner every evening for which he insisted I wear an evening gown. I walked a fine line between ignoring him and trying to be civil, as I was still wary of his threats against Christian.

Richard spent time each morning working out and running, followed by several hours working in his office. Occasionally he left early in the morning on his private helicopter for meetings so he would be home in time for dinner together, which was easily accomplished with a personal pilot on standby. When he was working I would sit by the pool. He kept insisting I play my flute in the elaborate music room, but I refused. I simply had no drive to play even a single note in this jail. I could tell he was getting increasingly frustrated with my lack of enthusiasm and absence of any affection towards him. Yet despite my obvious lack of attraction or interest in him, not a day would go by where he didn't force himself on me. It became a grueling part of every day that I dreaded. To disassociate myself from these terrible daily violations of my body, I thought of Christian and my family, or tried to imagine performing with my orchestra to a packed auditorium. I worried constantly about becoming pregnant, and was tremendously relieved the day I found out that I wasn't. Richard didn't share my feelings, and when he found out he looked grief-stricken. "Cadence, this is *terrible*! I thought we'd definitely have conceived a child by now! Maybe if we make love more often..."

*Make love? More like sexually assaulting an unwilling victim!* I thought with disgust.

"I'm not a *machine*, Richard! I'm a person and I should have a say about my own body!" I pleaded, resisting the urge to slap him.

"Don't raise your voice at me, Cadence! You *will* have our baby and soon!" he said, storming out of the room before I could utter another word of protest.

\* \* \* \* \*

I tried every day to think of a plan to escape. My plan had to involve getting to a phone to warn Christian and my parents, before Richard knew I was gone. This was my biggest hurdle, and if I could find another way to warn them I might have a chance of getting away *and* seeing my family and Christian alive.

Richard seldom left the mansion. He explained to me that he rarely needed to meet face-to-face with anyone to run his business; he had other people managing his empire, while he saw to the major decisions and the buying and selling of companies from the comfort of his home office.

"Cadence, I have set up a brilliant system…I earn more money than I could have ever imagined possible, and let other people handle all the day-to-day issues and operations. I'm like God, watching over things from a distance yet maintaining ultimate control…it *couldn't* be better. And this way I can spend more time with my beautiful wife."

I thought of trying to sneak into his office at night to try and access the Internet, but he kept our bedroom door locked with a keypad so I couldn't get out. He had thought of everything. I also noticed there were more video cameras installed throughout the mansion than I remembered previously. Since the abduction on White Island, he had increased his security system ten-fold, I realized bitterly.

Another possibility for sending a message was the mail, but that was quite risky. And from what I could tell, Richard did all communications online so probably rarely sent things out through regular mail. Again, this would involve breaking into his office, which was impossible as it was locked at all times.

One day as I was walking by the music room an idea popped into my mind. I came to a halt and walked into the room that I usually avoided. The gleaming hardwood felt smooth under my bare feet. My eyes fixated on my flute case sitting on the shelf. I carefully took the case and sat down on the white leather sofa, slowly opening it. The gold of my flute shone brilliantly as the sun from the skylights caressed its fine surface. I took out one of the three pieces, the mouth piece, and slowly smiled as I thought of what a perfect place it would be to transport a message. A note could be conspicuously rolled up inside of it in such a way that when the technician tried to play it, the muffled sound would clearly indicate that something was inside. The risk was if Richard examined the inside of the flute, which was possible but unlikely.

My mind raced as I formulated the details of my plan. I would convince Richard that my flute was in need of repair, and that I really wanted to play again. Surely he would agree to send it to a technician! For the first time in weeks I felt the excitement and anticipation of finding a way out of this nightmare. But I'd have to act carefully and not stray too far out of character, or Richard would suspect something was amiss. But if there was *anything* I could outsmart him on, it was music. I smiled again as I pictured my flute being my golden key to escape.

# Chapter Thirty-Four

ALTHOUGH I WAS TEMPTED TO initiate my plan immediately, I took another day to flesh out the details in my mind. I knew that Richard was very detail-oriented and had taken his time to think through every avenue of escape I might choose. If I was to outsmart him, I needed to be extremely organized, cautious and creative in my planning.

The next morning I entered the music room and quickly assembled my flute. I knew Richard was in his office, which was nearby. I took a deep breath and blew a note. I then played a scale, the room giving the notes a full, rich tone. What great acoustics, I thought, as I continued to play. I was suddenly aware of Richard's tall form standing at the entrance of the room. As I played some higher notes I purposely changed the position of my lips so that the notes cracked, sounding horrible. My expression was one of surprise, as I repeated the same notes, ensuring that they came out poorly. I lowered the flute from my mouth, examining the keys and trying to look genuinely perplexed.

"Cadence, I'm happily surprised to find you in here!" exclaimed Richard.

"I've missed playing and want to get back into it," I said, making brief eye contact with him and then fiddling with the keys again. "But something's wrong with my flute. It won't play some of the higher notes. I think it must have been damaged in the move," I explained, trying to sound genuinely disappointed. I had acted out these words dozens of times in my head over the past twenty-four hours.

"I thought it sounded off. Can you fix it?"

"I'll try," I said, continuing to examine the keys and mechanisms, and looking closely at the various parts. "But I can't see anything obviously wrong. This happened once before and it had to be repaired by a flute technician. It's a pretty complex instrument and I'm not trained to take it apart....I guess I'll just forget it," I said, looking sadly at my flute.

"No you won't! You love playing, Cadence, and there's nothing more I want than for you to play for me every day. I'll never forget the day we met, hearing your beautiful music. I can order you a new one right now...is there any particular kind you want?"

"Richard, this flute was *custom made*...it is one of a kind and nothing else would compare. The man who made it passed away and I'd never be able to get one made exactly like it...he was the best," I explained, sounding melancholy. "I'll just forget it. It's no big deal." It was actually true that the man who made my flute passed away only months after finishing it. I was lucky to own such a fine instrument, which to me was priceless.

"Okay, I can tell how much this instrument means to you; I'll get it fixed as soon as possible."

"Okay, but it has to be a *really* skilled technician, not just anyone."

"Well, I can't have it sent to anyone who would be able to trace it to you, but I'm sure I can find someone who is great. Don't worry, I'll get it done as soon as possible for you, my love. Give it to me." I had anticipated this might happen and had my reply ready.

"Let me try playing it some more, just so I can get a better idea of what might be wrong; maybe it's something minor I can fix and if not you can send it away soon."

"Okay, whatever you want, darling. I have to go back to my videoconference now." He smiled, enjoying the first normal conversation we'd had in many weeks.

"Do you mind if I play it outside?" I asked, knowing that he loved having the power to give me what I wanted. Rarely did I ask him for anything, but I had learned that he liked granting me permission, as it made him feel powerful.

"I don't mind...whatever makes you happy. I'll come join you after my meeting." With that he walked up and kissed me gently, then left. I heaved a sigh of relief, my heart thumping wildly. I looked up at the video cameras mounted on each side of the room, tracking my every movement. I had also learned that the only safe places that were out of surveillance were in parts of the backyard garden. That is where I would plant the note, which I had carefully crafted the evening before in the bathroom, another place where I was out of sight.

Getting the pen and paper had been difficult. I supposed that Richard had thought I would try to write a note, perhaps to sneak out with one of his staff. He had therefore not given me access to pens or paper. But there *was* a pencil in my flute case, which I had used to mark my music during practices. As for paper, I used the back of the instruction sheet that was included in a box of tampons, something Richard had also not thought about. I had sat on the toilet, trembling, as I wrote the note the evening before:

> *Help me! Today is July 17. I have been kidnapped by Richard White. PLEASE call Christian Davidson (212-444-3451) and Shirley and Dan Weaverly (406-235-2211). Warn them that Richard has threatened to kill them if he finds out about this note. They need to be under police protection as Richard is VERY dangerous and has had others killed. I was abducted from San Francisco on May 4. PLEASE do not tell Richard about this note, as he will kill my family! Give this to the police right away! Thank you! Cadence Weaverly*
>
> *PS – I'm a flautist in the San Francisco Symphony – this flute is not broken. Please tell Richard it will take a month to fix to give the police time to find me.*

That was all the space I had on the back of the instruction sheet, plus I couldn't risk taking any more time. I flipped it over and wrote, "HELP (read other side)," then folded it and placed it in my pocket, hurrying out of the bathroom as Richard might become suspicious if I was in there for too long. I couldn't imagine what he would do if he found this little note. I had tucked it into the pocket of my khaki pants, feeling hope that I hadn't felt in many weeks.

\* \* \* \* \*

I arrived in the elaborate backyard garden, which consisted of trees, large hedges and flowers with winding pathways throughout, contained by a high and insurmountable wall. Nestled within the garden were a fish pond and waterfall, and a few different stone benches. I knew my way around quite well since Richard often insisted we take an evening stroll through the garden after our "romantic" dinners. I had not seen a single camera in the garden, and had once commented on this to Richard, as he was kissing me and insisting we make love on one of the benches.

"Richard, please not here! What if someone comes by and sees us?"

"Cadence, nobody will see us...the staff were told *never* to follow us here. This is our private time, and there are no cameras here either, so don't worry."

At the time that was certainly not the answer I wanted, but knowing that fact now allowed for the final step in my plan. I sat on one of the benches in the very back of the garden. It was a sunny day and already hot in the late morning. I hadn't seen the gardener, Fritz, and had observed that he only worked every second day, with today being his day off. Although the garden was large, I wanted to do this on a day when he wasn't around, just in case.

I knew time was limited and quickly removed my flute head joint and placed it beside the other part of the flute on the bench. Next, I took the note from my pocket, unfolded it and rolled it into a size slightly smaller than the tube of the head joint. I made sure the "HELP (read other side)" message was clearly showing and slid it carefully into the head joint, but not far enough that it would be apparent through the blow hole. I then stuffed a cotton ball inside, which I had done just to make sure the sound would be muffled when played, so the technician would know to look inside. Plus the cotton ball fitted snugly and would ensure that the note didn't fall out. Luckily, I had been able to take a cotton ball from the supply of toiletries under the bathroom sink.

As I pulled my fingers out of the head piece and breathed a sigh of relief, I jumped in shock as I looked up and Richard was walking quickly towards me. He was supposed to be on a conference call, I thought anxiously. What if he saw? I had only taken a minute to complete the entire process, and even that may have been too much time. I shuddered but tried to remain calm.

"I ended my call early so I could come and hear you play...*if* your flute is working, that is," he said merrily, as he stood in front of me. He bent down to kiss me on the head. "But I see your instrument is in pieces, my love. Any luck fixing it?"

"No, I tried everything," I explained. With great effort I willed my hands not to shake as I picked up the other piece of the flute and joined it with the head joint. I then gently tapped the keys so I didn't have to make eye contact with Richard. "I think an expert's needed as I don't want to risk trying to do anything more myself."

"Okay, sweetheart, I'll have one of my assistants send it to the best technician in Europe. She's looking into who that is right now."

My heart skipped a beat. Europe! Well, I guessed the note would have the same effect, so long as the technician could speak English. "Richard, there are great technicians here, why send it all that way?"

"Because I am *not* risking it being linked to you, my dear. My assistant will make sure the technician we choose has absolutely no contact with any American musicians. But the technician *will* be the very best we can find, I promise you." His tone indicated that his decision was final, so I knew there was no point in arguing.

"Okay, but I hope he knows what he's doing. I love this flute, Richard."

"When have I ever given you a reason to doubt me, Cadence? I have more money than I know what to do with...I can certainly pay for the very best and get it back quickly."

"Richard, don't rush it, as a rushed job could lead to poor tone quality. These guys like to do a thorough, diligent job, which normally takes several weeks."

"Okay, my love, I won't rush it, but I *am* anxious to hear you play again. Maybe," he said, a smile forming on his face, "I'll buy you another flute to tide you over until yours is fixed. How would you like that?"

"I'd love that!" I said, trying my best to sound enthusiastic. Actually, I was excited since this would buy some time during which Richard wouldn't hurry the technician. The more time that note had to be acted upon, the better. "I'm thirsty, Richard," I said, standing up with my flute in hand.

"Okay, let's go get some of that freshly squeezed lemonade our chef made for us." And with that he took my hand and we walked into the mansion, as I thought sadly of dear Yamoto, who was now just another name on Richard's long list of victims. I explained that I needed to put my flute away, and he accompanied me to the music room while I carefully took apart the three pieces and placed them in the case, then clicked it closed.

"Safe and sound, ready for the trip overseas," I said, placing its outer leather case around the hard inner case and zipping it up. He watched each step carefully, always on the lookout for details. He must constantly be on alert for any suspicious moves on my part, I thought. But he seemed to be comfortable with this series of events; at least he appeared that way. I handed the case to him. "Please get it boxed securely, Richard. Travel is never very safe for instruments and it has already been through a lot," I said, in as sweet a voice as I could muster.

"Of course, darling. Don't you worry, I'll treat it just as precious as I would our child," he said, then stood and took the flute to his office as I followed, my hands clasped in a silent prayer for the safe journey of my potential ticket to freedom.

# Chapter Thirty-Five

EVERY DAY THAT PASSED SEEMED like an eternity as I awaited the outcome of my note. I wondered if the technician would believe my note and tried to put myself in his or her shoes. How bizarre and far-fetched such a plea would sound. A continuous prayer silently ran in my mind as I tried my best to get through each day without losing my sanity. One week passed and then two. Was I ever going to get out of here?

"Darling," said Richard, interrupting my thoughts as I sat by the pool silently thinking about my note's fate. "You look so concerned. What's bothering you, my love?" he asked, kneeling down beside my white-cushioned lounge chair.

"I was just thinking about my parents," I said, wondering why I said something that could stir the pot.

He gazed at me intently, his brow furrowing. "Cadence, one day you will be able to call them again and keep in touch. I know you must miss them terribly," he said calmly, sounding rehearsed and not genuinely sympathetic.

I felt tears well in my eyes, the sadness quickly followed by anger. *Cadence, contain yourself!* I thought. I wanted to punch him in the face. For a split second I thought I could push him hard enough to send him over the edge and into the pool. Maybe even knock him over the head with something so he'd be unconscious and drown. Although tempting, my chance of success was almost nil, I concluded bitterly. "Yes, I do miss them *every* moment of *every* day," I said, in as calm a voice as I could muster.

His expression of contrived sympathy quickly turned to anger, and his face became red. "Cadence, will there ever be *any* moments when you can forget about your past life and focus on *me?*" he asked, his voice rising with agitation and frustration.

I thought for a moment. I wanted to say "absolutely not," but instead tried to appease him by saying, "Of course, Richard, I know you're doing your best to make me happy here." An image of the note inside the flute continued to flash in my mind…surely it wouldn't be much longer!

"And I know you are *not* happy here," he said quietly, almost in a whisper.

I was silent, for I could not find any words to respond. If I agreed with him, it would escalate the situation. If I disagreed, it would be a blatantly obvious lie.

"Well, maybe one day I will make you as happy as you make me," he said, sounding very subdued. "I would give everything I have for that, Cadence. *Everything*," he said with certainty, then stood and walked back inside.

\* \* \* \* \*

Later that afternoon I decided to play the new flute Richard had bought me in the hopes that it would distract me from incessantly worrying about the whereabouts of my note. I went into the music room and began warming up with scales. I could only play minor ones, as the sadness that enveloped my life wouldn't enable me to play joyful music. I closed my eyes as the notes sang through the beautiful instrument, which rivalled the quality of my own. Evidently Richard had spared no expense.

Suddenly I felt hands clasp my waist. I continued to play on, willing him to move away from my personal space. His lips began to kiss my neck. "Ahh," he sighed. "This is a fantasy I've dreamed of for ten years. Making love to you while you play. Please, *please* continue," he whispered urgently. I knew I didn't have a choice as this was going to happen regardless of whether or not I stopped.

I continued to play, trying to imagine that the hands and lips were Christian's. The music was a nice distraction and I tried to focus on different parts of Christian. His lovely long, strong fingers. His dark, soft hair. The warmth of his lips.

Hands crept around and worked to smoothly undue the button of my Capri pants, fluidly sliding them down, along with my panties. Next, I felt my bra being unclasped and hands slowly cupping my breasts. I was now only wearing a shirt and hoped nobody would hear or see us.

I continued to imagine this was Christian, and coupled with the music from my flute I felt myself moving with Richard's strokes. "My God, you're enjoying this," he whispered lustily into my ear. Hearing his voice instead of Christian's immediately turned off my imagination, as well as any feeling of responsiveness. I opened my eyes and stopped playing. "I need you *now*, brace yourself against the wall!" And with that my flute was down and he took me quickly from behind, with a roughness and urgency I hadn't yet experienced.

\* \* \* \* \*

Another couple of weeks passed and I was giving up hope of being rescued. I'd have to plan a more aggressive approach to escape. I was sitting in the music room, contemplating other possibilities, when Richard walked in.

"Darling, the technician said he'll be shipping your flute back this week, and that it's as good as new!"

I froze, feeling a myriad of different emotions. "Did he say what was wrong with it?" I asked cautiously, trying to appear happy about the news.

"His English isn't great, so I didn't bother to waste much time on the phone, but the bottom line is that you will have your instrument back very soon. I can't wait to hear you play it again."

"Well, I'm excited about it," I lied, turning away so he wouldn't see my confused look.

"Cadence, look at me. I have a gift for you," he said, handing me a small white bag with a red bow attached near the top.

Over the past weeks he'd regularly given me gifts, ranging from lingerie to expensive jewelry to books. I dreaded receiving each as it was tough to act thankful, and I detested wearing any of the lingerie.

"Well, what are you waiting for? Open it!"

"Okay," I said, carefully pulling the top open. I reached inside and felt a box. I pulled it out slowly, and then my jaw dropped as my mind registered what it was...a pregnancy test. I shook my head, then dropped it back into the bag. "Richard, I *don't* need this," I said, trying to keep the revulsion out of my voice.

"Well, you *are* almost a week late, my love. I need to know if I am going to be a father!" he said, squeezing my knee lovingly.

I flinched, then cradled my head in my hands as the tears began to flow. I knew he was right. I hadn't even thought about it lately as my main focus was on escape. Perhaps I had blocked it out of my mind subconsciously. My God, I thought, *please* don't let this happen.

His arm circled around my back, and he gently rubbed it up and down. "Darling, I know you're still adjusting, but this will make things better for you, and for *us*. Now let's go do the test," he said, trying to grab my hand as he stood up excitedly.

"No," I said quietly, but with certainty.

"What did you say?"

"NO!" I said more forcefully, refusing to budge.

"Cadence, this *isn't* your choice," he spat.

"What part of peeing on a stick *isn't* my choice?" I retorted.

"Okay, fine. If you are going to be like this again you will force me to resort to measures I do *not* like taking," he said irately.

I sat silently, still crying and shaking with anger and fear…fear about the potential result that I did *not* want to know.

"Cadence, I'll give you one more chance to behave like a normal wife and come with me to do this test, otherwise I will make sure your parents *do not* live to be grandparents," he said in that authoritative tone that I had come to detest.

My crying turned into sobs, but a small voice in my mind said, *Cadence, regain control of yourself! This guy is a lunatic and he will do what he threatens.* I tried to breathe deeply. My two choices flashed in my head: I could continue to fight or I could give in and appease him. When it came to my parents' lives, there wasn't any other option but to stand up and oblige Richard. "Okay, let's do it," I whispered mournfully, walking out of the room like a robot as he followed.

\* \* \* \* \*

Okay, the positive symbol should come up if you are pregnant," he said excitedly, holding the test in his hands as we both sat on the edge of the bed. Suddenly we heard loud knocking on the bedroom door. Richard was startled, his whole body tensing with rage. "WE'RE BUSY!" he roared, still carefully holding the plastic stick with the viewing window facing us.

"But sir, it's *urgent!*" replied Maria.

Richard handed me the test and walked rapidly to the door, throwing it open. "What would make you interrupt me in my *bedroom?*" he asked furiously.

Maria looked petrified as she stared up at Richard. "Sir, I need to tell you privately," she explained.

He stepped forward and slammed the door shut behind him. Curiosity made me run to the door, pressing my ear against it.

"...police...search warrant...Plan Z," were the words I caught. Before I had a chance to move out of the way the door flung open and knocked me to the floor.

"Cadence!" exclaimed Richard, looking down to see me sprawled on the floor. He reached for my arm and quickly pulled me up. "We've got to get out of here *right now,*" he declared, running out the door and down the hall, pulling me behind him.

"What's going on?" I yelled, trying to be as loud as possible. My heart was racing and I felt immense hope since hearing the word 'police.'

"I'll explain later," he said, pulling me forcefully as he quickly ran down the stairs and out the patio door.

I tried to think quickly. It was obvious he was in escape mode, but if the police were here, the last thing I wanted to do was escape! I purposely tripped and fell down on the patio. "I think I sprained my ankle, I can't run Richard," I lied.

He didn't say a word, but instead bent down and lifted me into his arms.

"I'm *hurt!* Put me down!" I screamed at the top of my lungs, as his large, sweaty hand covered my mouth. I prayed that the police had heard my voice.

"Don't say another word, Cadence, or Christian is a *dead man!*" Richard snarled viciously, as he sprinted towards the landing pad with the helicopter ready to lift off.

I tried to scream through his hand. I was able to bite his palm, but this time he barely flinched. I fought as hard as I could, but was once again no match for Richard and found myself inside the helicopter in seconds. Maria climbed in directly behind us.

Richard held me down firmly on his lap, so I couldn't see out of the window as we quickly lifted off from the ground and flew away from the mansion.

A minute later Richard removed his hand from my mouth. "What's going on?" I asked, but before he could answer there was a giant explosion, so large that it made the helicopter shake in the sky. It was the loudest sound I'd ever heard and I was temporarily deafened. I was able to sit up and look out the window to see in the distance that the mansion had blown up and flames were shooting into the sky.

"Damn cops can go straight to hell for meddling in my business," Richard raged.

I was speechless and could not focus on anything else but the huge fiery inferno that was becoming smaller and smaller in the distance.

Maria was seated on the other side of me. "Sir, what have you *done?*" she asked, her voice quivering in fear. "Many people must've died in the explosion, many of them your staff!" she said, clearly confused and terrified. I immediately understood that Richard had only given her part of the escape plan, conveniently leaving out the part about blowing up the mansion and killing people.

"Maria, *this is* Plan Z. I couldn't risk the police finding evidence or any of the staff giving them information that could lead to our whereabouts. I'd hoped to never have to enact Plan Z, but *somehow…*" he said, slowing down and emphasizing that word then repeating it, "…*somehow* the police found a reason to locate me."

"I never agreed to be part of *this plan*," Maria whispered. Her dark eyes looked terrified, as well as very angry.

"Well, you *are* part of *this plan*, Maria. You have no choice, unless you want us to turn around and drop you back at the mansion…from the air of course," he said menacingly.

She shook her head and turned away, tears falling down her cheeks. I reached across and took her hand, hoping Richard would not try to stop me. Finally, after all this time, I knew I had an ally in Maria. But I couldn't get my mind off of the fact that several innocent people had just been blown up; it was surreal, almost like a movie that looked real but in fact was merely special effects.

"Richard, you are truly evil," I said quietly, not able to stop myself.

He turned to me and looked down into my eyes. His green eyes were piercing as he stared me down and then slowly shook his head. He was choosing his words carefully. "Well, my dear Cadence, I wouldn't have had to enact this plan had our whereabouts not been leaked to the police...and the only one who would be motivated to do that would be *you*," he said, in a calm, calculated voice.

"I've been your *prisoner*, Richard! How on earth could I have ever gotten a message to *anyone*?" I asked. "You don't let me use the phone, the computer, the mail...nothing! I've been completely cut off from the world!"

"At this point, I truly don't know, but let me tell you *this*," he said coldly, "I will have one of the best investigators in the world looking into how the police were tipped off to go to our home," he promised. "Plus, I do of course have some connections at the police department, guys who will tell me anything for the right price. I *will* understand how this all transpired and very soon," he said.

"Well, you won't find that I was involved," I said assuredly, but underneath I was more terrified than I had ever been.

"We'll see. Now I need to blindfold you both, as you cannot know where we're going," he explained, quickly placing dark blindfolds over our eyes. Maria sobbed as I silently prayed that the helicopter was being tracked.

# Chapter Thirty-Six

WE FLEW IN DARKNESS FOR what felt like hours, stopping once to refuel, and then landing on a secluded concrete pad situated in a heavily forested area. Richard removed both of our blindfolds. In the distance sat a magnificent log home, nestled in the trees. Maria and I were helped out of the helicopter and waited beside a nearby Jeep as Richard exchanged a few words with the pilot. Our eyes were locked together in panic, two terrified women wondering how on earth they would escape from this lunatic.

"We've got to get out of here or he'll kill us both," I said softly.

"I know, but how? We're in the middle of nowhere," she whispered.

"BANG!" went a loud shot. We both gave an involuntary shriek and turned around quickly to see Richard pointing a gun at the pilot's head. The poor man lay slumped over his controls, blood pouring down his face.

"RICHARD!" I screamed, as he lowered the gun and walked towards us.

"It had to be done…this guy could have leaked our whereabouts and it's important that only a few very trusted people know where we are," he assured. All part of the ominous Plan Z, I thought, feeling sick to my stomach.

"You are *so* horrible," I said. "That poor, innocent man…"

"Well, Cadence, I repeat that it wouldn't have been necessary if our whereabouts hadn't been leaked. So I refuse to take the blame for this little necessity. Now, let's get settled into our new home," he said, swinging his long legs into the Jeep as I shakily climbed in beside him.

Maria started to get into the back seat, but her knees gave way and she collapsed. Richard snorted impatiently and jumped back out to help her into the Jeep. "Thank you, Mr. White," she mumbled, looking at the floor, her hands nervously working at the fabric of her skirt.

"I need you to be strong, Maria," said Richard. "You need to take care of Cadence…she may be expecting our child," he added with a merry grin. He turned the ignition and stepped on the accelerator, guiding the vehicle up a narrow trail into the forest. I held on to the door handle as the Jeep bounced up the dirt track. In a few minutes, we slowed to a stop outside the enormous oak doors of the main entrance to the large log home.

He led us up the steps and into a huge entranceway. The home looked to be quite new, made of beautiful logs, with high ceilings and a lot of open space. In any normal circumstance I would have shown my appreciation for its lovely craftsmanship, but all I felt like doing was vomiting. I cringed as I saw an oil painting of myself on prom night, sitting above the large stone fireplace. *This gets sicker and more twisted every second,* I thought with fading hope.

"This is our home in the woods, Cadence. I had it built three years ago. Your room is down the hall by the kitchen, Maria," he explained happily, his psychopathic personality evident as he displayed no remorse over the souls he had murdered on this dark, hopeless day.

"How long will you make me stay here?" asked Maria, avoiding eye contact with Richard.

"I don't know…it depends on many factors," he responded. "Your role here will be broader, including cooking all the meals and keeping the place clean," he explained. "There are some clothes for you in the closet and dresser that should fit, so make yourself comfortable." He paused as he looked from Maria to me. "And you should both know there are NO phones here; in fact, there is nobody around for miles. This place is fully wired with a state of the art security system, so if either of you leave the premises I will know immediately. My security team will be stationed nearby and there is no way either of you ladies are going *anywhere,* so don't even bother *thinking* about it. If I catch you doing so, Maria will meet the same fate as her coworkers."

Maria and I looked at each other, panic clearly etched on our faces. He took my hand in his like that of a child. "Now, come along, Cadence, our suite is upstairs. Maria, please have dinner ready in two hours; there are plenty of meals in the freezer to select from," he commanded, acting as if he hadn't just threatened the poor woman's life. Maria's face was pale, and her beautiful brown eyes were brimming with tears. She, like I, had never done anything to deserve this unimaginable treatment.

*******

I couldn't believe what was happening. Was there even a point in thinking I might someday get away? What if Richard found out about the note? Would he have Christian killed as a lesson to me? Was Christian still even alive? Would Richard harm my family as further revenge? Maybe I should just give in, have this man's children and live out my life in isolation? At least then my loved ones would be safe forever, but it was likely too late for that. I was almost in a trance as I followed Richard up the large, wooden staircase.

Our bedroom was grandiose, of course; it had high ceilings and massive windows looking onto the dense, dark green forest. I headed for the bathroom and was sick in the toilet. When I came back into the room Richard was laying on the bed looking towards me. "Cadence, I need to know the *truth*," he said slowly. "Please come lay with me and let's talk."

"I already told you the truth, Richard," I said, still standing near the bathroom.

"Cadence, how *stupid* do you think I am? The police wouldn't have been able to locate me without a tip and a *lot* of investigation, and to arrive with a search warrant meant they were fairly confident I had something to do with your disappearance," he said, his voice becoming harsh and agitated.

"I don't *know*, Richard, maybe one of your staff tipped them off. I certainly didn't have anything to do with it," I said, with as much confidence as I could muster.

"Well, like I said, I'll get to the bottom of it soon enough. I would like to believe you, but I have a *bad* feeling about this," he said calmly. "But until I have the facts I want to enjoy my beautiful wife and give her the benefit of the doubt. All of this adrenalin turns me on, so come to bed and join me," he ordered, lust taking over his suspicion and agitation.

Then his expression suddenly changed. "The pregnancy test...I forgot it! Damn it, and I don't have one here. I'll have to get one flown in by my security team tomorrow. I can't believe the timing of this curveball. Now we'll have to wait a day to know for certain," he vented, shaking his head.

I felt helpless and decided I needed to put my energy into thinking about escape rather than arguing with Richard, so I walked back over to the bed and sat down passively as Richard began to nuzzle my neck. My hope was almost lost, except for the fact that he said *flown in by my security team tomorrow*. Our best chance of escape, I thought to myself, was to do so before his security team arrived. If Maria and I could somehow outsmart Richard tonight, maybe we stood a chance, even a small chance, of getting away.

I continued to think through various escape plans as Richard had sex with me. The helicopter kept entering my mind. Maybe, just maybe, there was a radio that Richard had not removed. But how would we know where we were, if we did in fact reach another human being over the radio? Maybe the police could somehow track it. There were two of us against one, which was the best odds I'd had since being abducted, I thought with a hint of optimism.

"I love you, Cadence. I'm exhausted and I'm going to have a nap before dinner, and you should too…you need your rest as I'm *sure* you are carrying our baby," he whispered, as he lay beside me and closed his eyes.

Once I was sure Richard was asleep, I crept to the door of the bedroom, and quietly opened it. I *had* to talk to Maria, even though it would be risky. She must have read my mind as she was pacing down the hall, and a relieved expression came over her face when she saw me approach. We embraced…*finally* she knew I wasn't insane. "Maria, we're taking a major risk by talking like this. He threatened your life and I understand if you don't want to talk with me," I quickly explained.

"What choice do I have?" answered Maria. "I must try to escape, but I'm sooo scared. He's such an *evil* man…may God help us," Maria whispered back, making the sign of the cross while reaching over to grip my hand. Hers was cold and shaking. "Oh, Mrs. White, I just don't know how we'll ever get away!"

"Please, just call me Cadence," I said gently. "I was married by force, as you now know and believe."

"I believe you, Cadence, and I'm sorry I ever doubted your story, but what are we going to do? We're in the middle of nowhere and he warned us of the security system. If we can escape, we can keep running, but where to? And unless we hurt him, he'll follow us and catch-up quickly," she whispered, sounding defeated as she calculated our chances of success.

"I know it seems impossible, but I think tonight is our best chance of escape because his security team doesn't arrive until tomorrow. We need to think quickly, as I bet he'll wake up soon," I whispered. "What if we could somehow lock him in a room, set the house on fire and then run? It would hopefully catch the forest on fire and alert help. What do you think?"

"It's a possibility. Let me see if I can even find matches or a lighter, and whether there is a room that locks from the outside. You should go back before he wakes up," she said.

"Okay. I'll explore the master bedroom while he sleeps and see if there is anything there that might help. We can connect sometime this evening or if not, then in the middle of the night once he's asleep again." I gave her a hug and she held me tightly for a moment before scurrying off.

I quietly walked back into the bedroom and closed the door behind me. He looked so peaceful…it was hard to reconcile the man before me with the monster he had become. As he slept, I explored the room, carefully opening drawers and looking at the door to test if it locked; unfortunately, it only locked from the inside.

"There is no point in trying to devise an escape plan, Cadence," Richard said sharply from the bed, startling me. "If you don't want to have the guilt of knowing you contributed to Maria's death, then you need to stop this *immediately*. I know you were just in the hallway talking with her. I know *everything*, Cadence…the way your mind works, the calculating look in your eyes, the fact that you still love *him*…" his voice trailed off, anger mixed with sadness.

"Richard, I…"

"No more excuses, *please*. I am just warning you that there is *no way* for you two to escape. You know the rules…any more plotting with Maria will lead to me having her killed, and this time I'll make you watch," he said coldly. "And more importantly, this would mean you broke our deal, and I will happily have Christian killed, which will probably happen when I get to the bottom of this whole mess anyway," he said, scowling at me from across the room.

"I'll keep my promise, but don't you EVER harm another person again. So many people have lost their lives because of your need to possess me, and it *can't* keep happening, it just *can't*," I said, tears streaming down my face, as I walked to an armchair and sat down.

"Well then, I suggest you start acting like a *wife*...a wife who *wants* to be with her husband," he said firmly.

"Okay, you win," I said softly. "But no more murders, no more innocent lives lost...I *beg* you, Richard." I stared at him intensely, finally realizing as our eyes remained locked that I had lost. I had to give up fighting because I couldn't risk losing Maria or anyone else.

Richard stood up from the bed and walked over to me, bending down to kiss me gently on the lips. "I knew you'd come to your senses. Now let's get ready for dinner," he said, heading to the shower and gesturing for me to follow.

*******

Maria's dinner was a simple one of lasagna. Richard and I sat in the dining room at a large wooden table, with thick log legs. Large picture windows provided a view of the dense forest. Midway through dinner Richard received a call on his cell phone and excused himself to the deck, where there was better reception. Instantly Maria was beside me, checking in on our plan under the guise of pouring me water. "I found some matches and..." she whispered eagerly.

"Maria, we don't stand a chance. He'll *kill* you if he sees us talking, and I don't think it's worth it to even try. I cannot risk another person being killed, so I have to give up," I said quietly, the words sounding final and heartbreaking to my ears.

"We can't give up!" whispered Maria urgently. "There has to be a way!"

"Maria, if you want to try, go ahead, but I can't be part of it. Too many people have already died because of me. I'm sorry," I said, bowing my head in defeat.

"But..."

"No, I refuse to discuss it further. I'm sorry," I said, standing and walking out to the deck to join Richard so he wouldn't be suspicious. I didn't look back to see her expression, as I was already feeling torn and terrible for letting her down. But wasn't saving her life doing her more of a favor than risking it?

"Thanks, Tony…the sooner, the better. Okay, bye," he said, looking startled as he saw me standing beside him.

"Darling, you've come to see the view?" he asked, taking my hand and walking towards the edge of the huge wooden deck.

"Yes, Richard," I said, feeling alone, isolated and utterly defeated. He pulled me in front of him, so we were both looking out at the magnificent vista of sprawling forest, his arms tightly holding me. I could feel his heart beating, and despite his immense warmth and tight hug, I couldn't remember ever feeling so cold, empty and alone.

# Chapter Thirty-Seven

WHEN IT HAPPENED, IT HAPPENED fast. A loud bang sounded behind me, and I was jolted forward and nearly lost my balance as Richard crumpled to the deck behind me. I shrieked in panic as I turned around to see Maria brandishing a kitchen mallet in one hand and a large carving knife in the other. Her initial blow to the back of Richard's head had knocked him out cold. Before I could say anything, she brought the mallet down on his head again, hard.

"Maria!" I screamed, torn between helping her and telling her to stop. Richard was clearly unconscious, and for the first moment in this whole ordeal I actually had the opportunity to kill him. Terror gripped me like a bolt of icy panic as I somehow got to my feet and grabbed Maria's arm.

"Don't stop me, Cadence! This man is evil and we need to kill him!" she exclaimed, switching the knife to her right hand once she was certain he wasn't going to move.

My impulse was to run, rather than to kill him. Despite all he had done to me, I was surprised at my hesitation to put an end to his life. "Let's just tie him up and run, Maria," I suggested urgently.

"And risk him finding us, Cadence? You of all people know what he's capable of!" Maria said, still standing over Richard's limp form with the large knife pointed down towards his chest.

My moment of empathy switched to anger, as I thought about his latest threats to kill Christian and Maria. "Then at least let *me* end it," I said, grabbing the knife from her and thrusting it towards his chest. As the blade touched his shirt my hand froze; I couldn't bring myself to push the sharp, silvery point into his warm flesh. Flash backs of the college boy in the pasture, his love and neediness so genuine, entered my mind, diluting my anger with feelings of sorrow. Before I could retreat, Maria forcefully brought both of her hands onto the handle around mine and forced it down into Richard's vulnerable chest. "Nooooo!" I screamed, utterly torn between so many emotions and surprised at my confusing reaction. Everything seemed to happen in only a few seconds.

"It had to be done!" she yelled at me, as she ran back into the dining room.

I was on my knees beside Richard, the blood gushing from his wound as I wondered why I didn't have the courage to stab him repeatedly. "Good-bye, Richard," I said softly. His cell phone had fallen to the ground and I grabbed it.

"Come on, Cadence!" yelled Maria, gesturing wildly for me to come into the dining room. I walked inside and inhaled the strong scent of gasoline. "I'm going to light this place on fire and we need to *run!*" she ordered, grabbing my arm and leading me towards the front door.

"Okay, Maria," I gasped, as I ran quickly behind her. Once we were at the doorway, she lit a magazine on fire and threw it towards the area rug, which was soaked in gasoline. We both ran down the front steps as fast as we could, and turned to see the flames.

"I have his cell so we can call for help, but let's get as far away as we can before this whole place explodes," I urged.

We ran into the forest and came to a barbed wire fence; he had truly built a prison out here. Fortunately, we were able to help each other over, with only some minor cuts and scrapes along the way. I thanked God the fence wasn't electric; I suspected it probably was, but had not yet been activated by his security team. Richard would have never made it so easy to get over otherwise.

We ran for about twenty minutes, hearing loud noises and explosions coming from the distant house as it burned. I dialed Christian's cell number.

Ring....ring.... "Hello?" said his deep, calm voice.

"Christian! It's me, Cadence!" I choked, feeling utter relief.

"Cadence! My God! Are you alright? Where are you?"

"I'm okay, but we *need* help. We don't know where we are…we're in a heavily forested area. I've been held captive by Richard White and we killed him and set his log home on fire…" I rambled almost incoherently. Tears spilled from my eyes as I relayed my far-fetched story. "I love you!"

"Cadence, stay where you are. I'm calling the FBI and they'll trace your signal!"

"Don't hang up…don't leave me!" I begged, clutching the cell phone tightly to my ear with both hands. Beside me, Maria wrapped a protective arm around my shoulder and squeezed firmly. Christian's voice caught with emotion as he said, "I love you too! Hold on." His voice became faint as he spoke with the FBI on another phone. "Cadence," he said urgently, as he came back on the line, "I gave the agent the number showing up on my call display and he's going to call you right now so they can trace your location!"

"Christian, I love you! I'm so scared," I sobbed, hearing the sounds of the fire in the distance and not fully believing that Richard wasn't right behind me. The smell of smoke was thick in the air, making both Maria and I cough.

"I don't want to let you go, but you *have* to hang up, Cadence," Christian urged. "The FBI need to talk to you. Call me as soon as you can and I'll let your family know what's happening. I love you *so much.*"

"Okay!" I cried, my panic rising. Tears spilled down my cheeks as his voice rose to a near shout, "Hang up *now*, Cadence! I need you to HANG UP!" His urgency jolted me into action and I ended the call with badly shaking fingers.

Maria kept her arm around my shoulder as we collapsed on a nearby log, both breathing heavily from our run and the adrenalin pumping through our systems.

Just then we heard the sound of a distant helicopter, while simultaneously the phone rang. My hands fumbled as I answered. Thank God the agent got through so quickly, I thought.

"Hello," I answered quickly.

"Where's Richard?" asked a gruff voice.

"Who's this?" I demanded.

"It's Tony. What the hell's going on down there?" he asked.

"Hang up!" Maria whispered urgently. "The helicopter must be carrying Richard's security team," she continued. I pressed the Call

End button, my heart racing. "We've got to keep running, Cadence," Maria said. We scrambled to our feet and continued running through the forest to get as far away as we could from the house and the sound of the swiftly descending helicopter. As we ran, the cell phone rang again. I was afraid to answer it but had to in case it was the FBI.

"Hello!"

"This is Agent Kent, is this Cadence Weaverly?"

"Yes, it is. A helicopter's almost here with Richard White's security team, and we're running for our lives through this forest!" I said, in a panic-stricken voice.

"Okay, Ms. Weaverly, just stay on the line for me as it will take some time to get a good trace. You say you're in a forested area; tell me everything that you see and how you got there," he asked calmly, his voice reassuring.

"We were taken here by helicopter after he blew-up the mansion he was holding me in. I have no idea where we were, but Maria is with me and she knows," I suddenly realized. "Hang on!" I said, handing the phone to her so she could speak to Agent Kent while we continued to walk briskly through the forest.

"This is Maria. I worked for Mr. White in his home outside of San Jose," she explained. "The trip here by helicopter was probably three hours, maybe longer with refueling, and we were blindfolded so we couldn't see where we were heading."

"Thanks, Maria. Now can you describe the forest? Are there any landmarks?"

"There are fir trees, very tall, thousands of them, and large hills, not really huge mountains."

"Okay, thanks. I think I've got a trace. Can you pass the phone back to Cadence please?" Maria handed me the phone.

"Yes?"

"I think we have a trace, but stay on the line so we can be sure. I need both of you to stay in close vicinity so we know your approximate location. Try and get to an area with enough of an opening for us to land a helicopter."

"I don't see anything like that yet. And what if Richard's security team follows us?" I asked. "How long will it take for you to get here?"

"It looks like you're in Oregon. They launched two helicopters and I estimate about fifteen minutes to get to you. Just try to stay calm," he added gently. "We're all so happy you're okay and rest assured we'll keep it that way!" he promised.

It sounded as though the helicopter landed, but we continued to make progress moving through the woods. "We have to run, Cadence, in case they follow us we need as much of a lead as possible," Maria said.

I spoke into the cell phone. "They've landed and we're going to run now," I explained. "We'll keep the phone on speaker."

We ran as quickly as we could through the darkening forest. Maria tripped on a log but quickly scrambled to her feet. We kept looking at the sky over the large canopy of fir trees, hoping to see a rescue helicopter or hear the sound of one approaching. After a few more minutes, we came to a clearing that looked large enough to land a helicopter in. Beyond that, the dense forest continued in all directions. We slowed our pace to a walk so I could explain this to Agent Kent.

"We're in a clearing that should work for the landing," I explained. "Are they almost here?" I asked anxiously.

"They say about ten minutes. Both choppers should arrive a couple of minutes apart. You'll need to stay put so they can get a fix on your exact location."

I noticed the other line was showing an incoming call, for which I clicked ignore. "Looks like another call is coming in, I think it's the same number as before, Richard's security guys," I said.

Just then Maria and I heard a man's voice in the distance shouting, "Cadence? Cadence?"

"We need to hide!" whispered Maria, pulling my arm towards the thick forest at the side of the clearing. "Now!"

"Agent Kent, we can hear someone coming, they're calling my name," I whispered. "We're going to hide in the trees."

"Okay, but stay as close to the clearing as you can, help is *almost* there," he said.

"Cadence, where are you?" The man's voice was getting closer. Maria and I hid behind a large bush nestled between the tall trees. We knelt down, arms around each other, trembling with fear.

"I hear the helicopter," whispered Maria, looking up at the sky through the dark green canopy above.

"Thank God!" I whispered back, as the noise above became louder.

"She must be around here, as that chopper's heading this way," said the man's voice, which was now much closer.

Why couldn't this all just end peacefully? Richard's dead and his security team should be getting out of here as fast as they can rather than trying to follow me, I thought bitterly.

The men were now so close that we could hear them talking clearly, punctuated by yelling my name. "Cadence, if you come with us you'll live. If not, we'll have to kill you both!" someone shouted. I shuddered and Maria gripped my hand.

Just then the helicopter came into view, making its descent into the clearing. "Agent Kent," I whispered into the cell phone, "the guys threatened to shoot us if I don't go with them, what should I do?"

No response.

"Agent Kent?" Nothing.

I looked at the cell and it was dead; it had run out of battery power from the looks of it. Could our luck get *any* worse? "Maria, the phone's dead!" I whispered in her ear.

"Oh, no...we need them to see us," she whispered back, in a panicked voice.

"But those guys will shoot us!"

As we sat frozen in panic, the helicopter landed and two agents quickly climbed out. We watched through a small opening in the brush and trees.

"Cadence, are you here?" they yelled, both holding guns.

BANG! BANG! Shots were being fired towards them from the woods. One agent was down and the other was firing back. A third man was firing shots towards the woods from a window in the helicopter.

"*Oh my God!*" I whispered, trembling, tightly gripping Maria's hand. Multiple shots continued to be fired in both directions. We couldn't get a clear view of what was happening, but felt relief at the sound of another helicopter overhead. It seemed to be firing shots below as it circled over the meadow. This was unbelievable, like an action scene out of a movie.

Maria and I tightly held hands, making ourselves as small as possible in the dense sanctuary of the bushes. It felt like the shots went on for an eternity, but in reality was probably only a few minutes. Finally, the other helicopter landed in the clearing. A man's voice yelled, "Cadence and Maria, it's safe to come out now."

"What if that's Richard's guy trying to trick us?" I whispered, as Maria tugged at my arm to help me stand because the trees were obscuring our view of him.

"We can approach slowly and try to see him through the trees without him seeing us," whispered Maria.

"Agent Kent told us you are somewhere near the perimeter of the clearing. White's men are dead. There's no threat to you. I repeat, there's no threat!" his voice boomed, leading Maria and I to heave a collective sigh of relief.

"We're here!" I exclaimed, as we stepped out of the trees and into the clearing where the last rays of sunlight played a symphony of colors across the shiny helicopters.

Two agents ran towards us as soon as we were spotted. In the distance, near the first helicopter, lay two agents who had been shot. About one hundred yards away, near the opposite perimeter of the clearing, we could see the bodies of two men who were not in uniform.

"Are you ladies alright?" asked one of the agents.

"Yes, thank God you're here," I said, my voice cracking with emotion. He put his arm around my back and the other agent did the same to Maria, comforting us and promising to get us home safely.

"You two are amazingly brave to escape like you did. These guys were *crazy* and willing to do *anything* to stop you," the agent beside me explained. "Two of our men were killed and one is injured. Seems there were two of them, and we got them both," he explained. "But we want to get out of here right away, just in case. Another team is on its way to investigate the burning house."

"I can't thank you enough and I'm so sorry about the two agents being killed in this..." my voice trailed off.

"Everyone knows about your case, it made national press, but most people didn't expect to hear you were still alive, as most abductions end on a more negative note."

"This wasn't just any abduction," I said.

"I second that," said Maria, shaking her head and smiling weakly at me as she reached for my hand and squeezed it before we climbed into the helicopter.

"*Thank you* Maria, for making this happen as I'd given up hope," I said to her tearfully, as we were buckled in.

"It's the least I could do after not believing your story and helping hold you prisoner," she whispered back.

As we ascended into the dark sky I could see the smoke and the remainder of the house in the distance, small flames still licking hungrily at the remaining wooden frame. I closed my eyes to block everything out as we flew towards safety. I knew my life would never be the same, but still ached for the comforts of Christian and my family and friends.

'Good-bye, Richard,' I silently mouthed.

# Chapter Thirty-Eight

WE LANDED IN PORTLAND AND went directly to the police station. I asked immediately to speak with Christian and my family. I was to be flown to Montana the next day. Christian was just boarding a flight to meet me there, but I needed desperately to hear his voice again.

"My sweet Cadence, I thought I'd *never* see you again. You must be so shaken up after all this," said Christian soothingly, airport announcements playing in the background.

"Yes, and I was *so* scared for you too, Christian," I said, tears welling in my eyes once again. "I honestly thought I'd *never* see you again either." My tears now flowed freely, as I cried with relief and for the pain we had all suffered.

"That crazy son of a bitch...I hope he burns in hell! The agents said you two lit his place on fire?"

"Yes, it's all over," I said, hardly believing it myself.

"I can't wait to see you! I'm glad the agents can continue their questioning from your folks' place...it'll be much more relaxing for you and we can all take care of you. I'm still in shock that you're safe...I love you so much," he said.

"I wish I could go there right now and see them and you," I said.

"You need a good night's sleep, honey. It's late and the FBI want to make sure your parents' place is secure, even though he's dead. They want to make sure none of his thugs can get to you," he said. "You'll be safe there."

"Do you have security with you right now?" I asked, suddenly feeling my heart beat more quickly, realizing this may not be entirely over. Could Richard continue his insane pursuit of my life and loved ones even in death? Anything was possible, I thought angrily.

"Yes, after what's already happened they are being very cautious. I have a great security guard with me twenty-four seven since they tried to kill me the first time."

"Thank God! I am *so* sorry, Christian," I muttered.

"Don't apologize, Cadence. None of this is your fault. We'll get through this together. I've got to board my flight, but I'll call the station and check in when I land. I love you," he said.

"I love you too, more than you could *ever* know," I smiled into the phone, wiping my tears with a tissue.

The next call was to my parents. My mom cried, saying that her prayers were answered. Dad just said, "We love you honey," over and over, as I tried not to cry, but his voice cracked. They wanted to be with me, but the agents wanted to send me to their home instead of them flying to me. She reiterated that security on both ends was everyone's top priority. She said that my brother and sister were flying in as well, and that my rescue was making national headlines, as had the abduction and ongoing search.

The FBI needed to ask some important questions before Maria and I were taken to a hotel for the evening. "We know you're exhausted, but we need to hear the general story so we can continue our investigation knowing some inside details. This case has been extremely perplexing and we've been working around the clock to find you. We're so very sorry for what you've endured."

"Where should I start?" I asked.

"Well, we know some details about the night you were abducted, but what do *you* remember?"

I explained that I didn't remember much as I was drugged and woke up in Richard's mansion. Maria reiterated where it was located, and how Richard had trained his staff for months in advance to prepare for the arrival of his mentally ill fiancé. She explained the large salaries and extreme measures of confidentiality he put in place, along with the subtle threats if anyone questioned anything. I relayed information about the death of Yamato with tears in Maria's and my eyes.

I cried as I explained the trip to White Island, the forced wedding, the short honeymoon, and the abduction to Jamaica. I left out the rapes as I wasn't ready to talk about that yet, not in a roomful of strangers.

"You have been through an unbelievable ordeal, Ms. Weaverly", said the captain, his face showing empathy and shock at the extent of what Richard had put me through.

I then explained my attempted escape, the car accident and my hospitalization in Jamaica.

"We tried everything to trace that call you made," said the agent on speakerphone from San Francisco. "It was just too short, and tore us all apart knowing you were out there but nobody knew exactly where."

"Right after the call he flew me back to his mansion in California, and it took weeks for me to figure out a way to get word out about my captivity."

"The note in your flute was ingenious. The technician in Italy found it and his English wasn't great, but his wife happened to be fluent and persuaded him to notify the authorities right away. The FBI was already involved and did some incredible investigating to zero in on White's location."

"I feel so terrible for the rescue team that faced that explosion," I said, looking down and shaking my head.

"It was tragic and made us all realize the level of risk we were dealing with. We couldn't have imagined the extent of Mr. White's wealth and criminal connections. It's an unbelievable case, like nothing we've ever seen."

I went on to explain the final chapter of Maria and I being flown to his isolated log home and what transpired there. "Without Maria, I would've given up hope," I said, squeezing her hand once again. "I wasn't willing to risk anyone else's life ever again," I added.

"I just got an update from the scene of the fire," said one of the agents on the speakerphone. "They have been unable to locate Mr. White's body, but are still trying. And there was no helicopter there when the team arrived."

My jaw dropped and my eyes widened. "Could he still be...*alive?*" I asked weakly.

"We don't know. It's tough doing the search at night and it could very well be that his body is just buried in the rubble. We'll know for sure in the morning. Given this new information, we'd advise extreme security measures around you two ladies, as well as your families, until we sort this out."

"But I stabbed him right in the heart!" exclaimed Maria, her eyes filling with frightened tears. "And with the fire...how could he be alive?" she asked.

"Ma'am, whoever was in that chopper could have taken his body away, so we cannot be sure whether he's dead or alive. I'm sorry."

"Ladies, we will have a security team watching over you and your loved ones tonight and until we find Mr. White, dead or alive," assured Agent Kent.

"If he *is* alive, he'll try everything to find me and kill anyone in his way," I said.

"We know...this is one of the worst cases of stalking and abduction we've ever seen, which is why we put in place the best investigative team possible to understand Mr. White's life, finances and connections. Trust me, you won't be his property *ever again*," assured Agent Kent.

But despite reassurances from those in the room and on the phone, Maria and I were gripped with fear and struggled to get through the night. What little sleep we had was punctuated by vivid nightmares.

"Nooooo!" I screamed. "Leave me alone!" I ran down the stairs and out the massive doors, looking over my shoulder to see Richard coming after me with a knife protruding from his chest and blood spurting from his wound.

"You're never leaving me, Cadence!" he roared, gaining on me as I ran as fast as I could into the woods. I felt him close in on me and suddenly woke up screaming. I was in a cold sweat and my heart was pounding wildly. The dream felt so real I could hardly believe I was actually safe and away from Richard. It took me almost the rest of the night to fall back asleep.

# Chapter Thirty-Nine

THE NEXT MORNING MARIA WAS interviewed further and then flown to be reunited with her family in Mexico. It had been tough saying our good-byes, but we promised to keep in close touch. We were both afraid that Richard was still alive, but tried to remain optimistic. I could never thank her enough for helping me escape.

When I stepped off the small plane at Mountain View Airport and saw Christian and my family, tears of joy sprang to my eyes and I ran directly into Christian's arms. He kissed me passionately then hugged me tightly. Next, I was pulled into a giant group hug with my mom, dad, sister and brother. There were tears of joy from everyone, and everything seemed surreal after months of captivity. It had been over three months since the abduction, but felt like much longer.

Security surrounded us and escorted us back to my parents' place, where a 'welcome home' lunch and celebration awaited. There were balloons and music from my orchestra's last CD playing in the background. My family avoided asking questions about Richard, knowing that I was very tired and there would be plenty of time to tell my story when I felt ready.

Agent Kent came into the house after about an hour saying that the investigative team would like to continue questioning me that afternoon. "Sure, okay. But I really want an update on whether his body's been located," I said, needing to know the level of risk we still faced. "Let's talk over here," I added, gesturing towards an unoccupied end of my parents' large deck. We made our way over to the railing and stood facing each other.

"They have done quite a thorough search of the area and still no body. But it could be that his thugs took away his body in a helicopter, or that he wasn't dead but has since died…it's tough to say."

"But worst case…he's *alive* and recovering?" I asked weakly, feeling Christian come to my side and squeeze my hand.

"Yes, ma'am, that would be the worst case. But rest assured we are on an international search for this guy and working around the clock to find answers and rein in these criminals."

"Thanks. I just hope this ends soon. I'll live in fear for my family and myself until I know he's dead."

"I know…we'll have security measures in place that will be unbreakable. We promise, Ms. Weaverly."

"Just call me Cadence," I smiled. "Can I have a few minutes with my fiancé and then I'll continue the interview?"

"Sure, take as long as you need."

I kissed Christian then hugged him tightly. I then led him upstairs to my old bedroom, which hadn't changed since I was a teenager. We sat on the bed and Christian held both of my hands, staring at me with his soft brown, twinkling eyes. I ran my fingers through his curly brown hair, which was longer than I remembered. He pulled me close to him and kissed me tenderly. He smelled fresh and musky, but looked exhausted.

"You must be so tired after all of this," I said.

"Me? You're the one who went through the *worst* of it. I can hardly complain compared to what you must've endured," he said, sadness etched in his deep, calm voice.

"It was hard on everyone, and I only wish I could have escaped sooner. By the end I thought I would *never* be able to get away…he made so many threats," I said, trembling but trying not to cry again.

"Oh, sweetie, I'm *so sorry*. I wish I could've killed him myself," he said, his fists clenching. My gentle musician fiancé being consumed with rage and hatred wasn't something I had ever experienced.

"I pray he's dead," I said firmly. "I should go finish answering their questions…the more information they have, the better chance of them finding his accomplices and hopefully dead body," I said, kissing him once more.

"Okay sweetie, I suppose I can spare being away from you for a little while, but not for long," he smiled and hugged me tightly.

\*\*\*\*\*

I spent another two hours answering detailed questions from the agents, both in person and on speakerphone. The toughest part was explaining that Richard had raped me repeatedly. Even though everyone must have assumed that, stating it for the record was extremely difficult and emotional, and worse than I had imagined. It was particularly tough as it brought the possibility of pregnancy back into my mind, and when I was finished with the interview I immediately found my mom and asked for a few private moments with her.

"Darling, I can't begin to imagine what it was like…not in a million years would I have ever imagined Richard White abducting you! I know he cared for you all those years ago, and was a little over the top with his commitment to you then, but who could have predicted *this*?" she shook her head and embraced me tightly.

"I know, Mom, but there's something I need to tell you. I…he… there's a chance I'm pregnant with his child," I stuttered, unable to look her in the eye as tears welled in mine.

"Oh, darling, I…I'm *so sorry*." I had clearly shocked her but she continued to hug me as tears trickled down both our cheeks.

"I'd like to do a pregnancy test as soon as possible…I *need* to know," I said.

"Does Christian know about this?"

"No, and if it's negative then I don't even want to bring it up. But if it's positive, I have to tell him. And…and schedule an abortion for as soon as I can," I said, the word *abortion* sounding odd to my own ears…something I could never have fathomed until now. I had thought a lot about it and realized that no matter how pro-life a woman was, her actions when impregnated from a rape could entirely reshape her opinions on the matter.

"Darling, I will be with you and support you every step of the way. I can go to the pharmacy and pick up a pregnancy test before dinner," she offered.

"That would be great, mom, as long as security is with you. I'm really worried still…he's capable of *anything*," I said softly.

"Absolutely, security at all times until they catch those crazy… bastards." My mom never swore so her language surprised me.

\*\*\*\*\*

That evening my mom and I sat in her master bathroom and awaited the test results. We held hands anxiously as a blue cross began to form…a positive result. I burst into tears and she held me for several minutes as I sobbed. I felt that Richard was continuing to control me and resented him bitterly. She said she would call the nearest abortion clinic, as there wasn't one in Mountain View, and book me in quickly, and that soon this would all be behind me. I wondered briefly if I should keep this from Christian, but felt that he should know the full truth of what I had been through and was continuing to deal with. I got up and went to go find him. He was sitting with my dad talking about the new security measures the FBI had briefed us all on.

"Christian, can we talk in my room?" I asked. He nodded and we climbed the stairs and when we were in my childhood room I closed the door and motioned for him to sit on the bed. I clasped both of his hands and looked him in the eye. He looked nervous in anticipation of what I was about to say. I took a deep breath. "I have something to tell you," I said in a sad, weak voice.

"What is it?" he looked alarmed, as he put an arm around me. He gently squeezed my shoulder, holding me close to him on my bed and clasping my hand even tighter.

"I'm…pregnant…with *his* child," I said, feeling oddly ashamed. "He *raped* me, Christian…many times," I whispered, tears springing to my eyes.

"Oh *sweetheart*, I'm so sorry," he paused, rubbing my back lovingly. "If you…want to keep it…I understand," he said, surprising me with his offer.

"No! No, Christian, I want to have a baby with *you*! I don't want to bring a child of *his* into the world," I said.

"Okay, I just wanted you to know that either way I will love you and your decision. But truthfully…I'm glad you don't want it as it would be a constant reminder of all he put you through." And with that, Christian's voice cracked and he began sobbing as he held me tightly. I cried bitterly too, as the stress from many weeks of worry and threats had taken their toll. I ran my fingers through his soft hair and we lay down together and eventually fell asleep from the emotional exhaustion of the day.

# Chapter Forty

THE FOLLOWING DAYS ALL BLURRED together. Between the comforts of my family and visits from close friends, I spent many more hours with the investigative team on the case. One breakthrough that brought all of us some relief four days later was the arrest of Tony, who was Richard's main security guard, if you could use such a formal title for such a lowlife thug. There had been an international manhunt, which led to Tony Marcato being arrested at Heathrow Airport. Tony was interrogated and admitted to being on the helicopter the day Maria and I escaped, and to being employed by Richard White as a security guard. He said there were three of them on the helicopter: the pilot, Peter Presecco, as well as Joe Vietto, another security guard.

Tony said that Joe was shot, which had been confirmed at the scene when the agents faced off with Richard's men while Maria and I hid in the trees. He explained that the pilot was told to find Richard's body but the fire was out of control, and when Tony got back to the scene they both elected to take off without risking themselves in the flames and debris. They were sure Richard had died in the fire. Apparently the FBI tried all angles to determine if this was a cover-up, but even a thorough search of the helicopter and a lie detector test indicated that it was the truth. Tony plea bargained for a shorter sentence in return for assisting the FBI in locating the helicopter pilot, as well as Dominic Smith, the hitman who had made the attempt on Christian's life. Tony also agreed to answer extensive questions about all of his dealings with Richard and his associates, and to lead the agents to White Island so they could obtain more information from there.

It turned out that Richard also had luxury properties in Aspen, as well as the Bahamas, Spain, France, Greece and New Zealand. Dozens of interviews were conducted with anyone who had any type of dealings with Richard White, including staff at all of his properties, and business associates. What Richard lacked were any family or friends – his life was centered on his business, including the business of owning me. The agents were amazed at the elaborate information he had collected on me over the past ten years, as well as the massive collection of art, photos and mementos he had stolen over these years – an extreme obsession unlike anything they had ever seen before. "This is beyond anything Hollywood could've dreamed up," Agent Kent stated.

Despite the strong efforts of the agents, Richard's body remained missing, with absolutely no sign of any remains at the site of the fire. Maybe he was all ashes, we wondered, but the lack of even dental remains or any DNA made the team certain that Richard was taken from the scene. But Tony's story was solid and the only other option was that somebody else took the body, dead or alive, from the scene in the short time before the FBI had arrived. Maria and I had been certain that Richard was dead when we ran from that fire, so this loose end was extremely frustrating and stressful for us both. I wondered how we would ever live normal lives until his body was found.

Throughout it all - the investigation, the comings and goings of friends and law enforcement officials, and the small day-to-day tasks that were helping to restore some semblance of normalcy to my life - a voice in the back of my mind kept whispering: *You're pregnant with his child, and if he's alive, he'll want to see it.* I shuddered at these thoughts, and focused instead on my fast-approaching appointment at the abortion clinic.

*****

Not surprisingly, my story attracted widespread attention from the media. I was not at all ready for interviews, even for the opportunity to appear on various talk shows that were offering large sums of money to have the exclusive rights to my first interview. Those early days were fraught with emotion, and the last thing I wanted to do was discuss my bizarre captivity and traumatic escape in front of millions of strangers. And not knowing whether Richard was dead, the last thing I wanted to do was draw attention to myself.

I suffered from high levels of anxiety and was often looking over my shoulder, despite knowing that I was always surrounded by security personnel. My nightmares were vivid and horrifying, including the recurring one of running away from Richard, who chased me while he burned and screamed in pain. When he caught up to me in that dream, and landed on top of me, I would always wake up before the fire burned me, and would be sweating, shaking and sobbing uncontrollably.

The therapist who came to the acreage to work with me recommended that I take several months off work to recover from the trauma. She used the term post-traumatic stress to describe what I was experiencing. Christian was able to take a one-month leave of absence from work and we agreed to spend this time at the acreage, where we would have the comforts of my family plus a full security team.

\*\*\*\*\*

The abortion had been scheduled for two weeks after my return, as I wanted to get it over with as soon as possible. Both Christian and my mom came with me to the clinic early one morning. I had been so very certain about the abortion until two days before, when I surprisingly started to panic about the idea. I had somehow drawn a picture in my mind of this baby, and felt sorry that it would lose its life for reasons beyond its control. I knew my thoughts were all very irrational, yet in my heart I began to struggle with the decision. How could I end the life of this tiny, helpless being who was part of me? Sure, his or her father was crazy, yet I was the other half of the equation, and although I didn't feel it lately, I was usually relatively normal. And for all the terrible attributes Richard had, there was no denying that he had been extremely intelligent and physically healthy. Could the baby take on his positive attributes and the negative genes might not necessarily be transferred to him or her?

I didn't share these confusing feelings with anyone, even Christian. I thought about calling my therapist the day before the abortion for an emergency appointment, but felt foolish. Why wouldn't I get an abortion and start a fresh life and family with Christian? We had already talked about getting married within the next six months, and the idea of becoming pregnant in the next year made sense to us both. I repeatedly kept stating in my mind: *Cadence, you need to get this abortion…there's no turning back.*

The day finally arrived. Christian and my mom both hugged me in the waiting room, as I was whisked away to be prepped for the procedure. The doctor was a kind, dark haired man in his late-forties, and explained the procedure as a simple one that wouldn't take long. "You'll feel back to normal, Ms. Weaverly, in a couple of days."

As I lay on the table in the minutes before the abortion was to take place I couldn't control the images of the baby in my mind. Flashes of holding it, feeding it, watching it grow. For all of Richard's horrendous actions and obsessions, my mind kept reverting to the young man I'd known as a teenager, who was kind and compassionate and cared so deeply for me. I kept forcing my mind to focus on his strange behavior, even back then. But just as soon as I would picture my evil version of Richard, my mind would revert back to him sobbing over his mother's death, to him begging for my hand in marriage, to him trying desperately to be loved by a woman who could never return his feelings.

"We're ready to begin, Ms. Weaverly," said the doctor, his nurse standing beside me and smiling warmly.

"No…no…I've changed my mind!" I exclaimed, as their faces relayed their shock. "I can't do this…I just *can't*," I said in a hysterical voice.

The doctor and nurse exchanged confused glances. Then the doctor looked me in the eye. "Ms. Weaverly, this occasionally happens, so if you need more time to think it through, by all means, you can always reschedule," he said kindly.

"I'm sorry, I thought I could do it but I don't think it's right for me or this baby," I said, the words sounding odd to my own ears. "Can I speak with my fiancé and mother?" I asked, needing to explain and see if maybe they could talk me out of this seemingly irrational decision.

"Sure, I'll get them in right away. You can chat with them in the room where you signed your paperwork," the nurse said, as the doctor helped me off the table and walked me to the meeting room where I took one of the four chairs.

My mom entered the room moments later, followed by Christian, and then the nurse closed the door saying to take as much time as we needed. They both stared at me with bewildered looks on their faces. I cried as I pieced together my explanation. "Mom, Christian… I just *can't* do this…it doesn't feel right. This baby…it's part of me and…not its fault. I know it was conceived against my will, but it's an innocent life and I just have a feeling that this is wrong...for me and for the baby," I said, not able to look at either of them directly and bowing my head in shame as the tears fell onto my pale blue medical gown.

Christian knelt in front of me and hugged me tightly. "Sweetheart, I support your decision...I love you and will be a father to this baby and love it like my own," he gently said.

"Thank you! I love you *so much*," I said, hugging him tightly as I cried.

"Darling, we respect you and you know what's best...nobody can decide this for you," comforted my mom. "If this is our first grandchild, he or she will be welcomed with open arms."

"Oh, mom..." I stood and we embraced. "I am just *so* confused. I thought this abortion was the right thing to do...I was so sure until a couple of days ago. I feel like I'm going insane and am not being logical. I want to have a baby with Christian and maybe that should be my first child, not this one. Maybe I should just go for this abortion NOW and not look back." I looked from Christian to my mom, almost pleading for them to convince me.

"Cadence, you and I can still have babies. No matter what decision you make, we'll make it work. I can't tell you what to do...you need to decide," said Christian, lovingly.

"Christian's right...we can't talk you into or out of this, Cadence. Why don't you take another week to think it through and you can always come back if that's what you decide. But for now I think you need to come home and relax," said my Mom.

"Okay, let's get out of here," I agreed, knowing in my heart that there wouldn't be a second appointment.

# Chapter Forty-One

THE MONTH AT THE ACREAGE passed quickly. I didn't doubt my decision to keep the baby and Christian was wonderfully supportive of this difficult choice. The investigation still hadn't turned up Richard, which was extremely frustrating and nerve-racking. Although they continued working on the case in the coming months, they advised me that it was time to move forward and plan for my life without expecting a conclusion.

"We may never have conclusive evidence that Richard White is dead or alive, but we have exhausted all of our leads at this point. We will provide continued security wherever you decide to settle, Ms. Weaverly, and are very sorry we weren't been able to close this case over the last month," explained Agent Kent.

"From everything you've heard and learned in this case, what do you think the chances are that Richard is alive?" I asked the question that was constantly on my mind.

"Well, it really did sound like the stab wound inflicted by Maria was fatal and it's most likely that he either died in the fire or while being transported from the scene. His body could have been disposed of anywhere. Likely he had issued orders for what to do in the case of his death. He was one of the most methodical and organized criminals that we've ever encountered. If he were still alive, chances are he would have tried to make contact with you. So to answer your question simply, Ms. Weaverly, I think there is a ninety percent chance he's dead and that you can expect to live your life without any further interference from him."

I pondered his explanation. Ninety percent would normally give a person great confidence, but when it came to my life, and to Christian's and my family's lives, that ten percent error margin would keep me up in the night and looking over my shoulder for many years to come.

"Thanks for all you've done. Hopefully there'll be new leads to confirm his death. I'm planning to move to New York with my fiancé for a change of scenery and a fresh start. And with security in place I would be able to lead a somewhat normal life."

Although Christian would never stand in the way of my career, he preferred us to be together and in the same city after all that had happened. I was still not ready to return to work, and figured I would wait until after the baby came and take this time as a stress and maternity leave, and time to plan our wedding. My plans and values had truly shifted after all I'd been through, and my strong career ambitions were no longer a top priority.

"I think that's a great idea. Our team will work at securing your property in New York. A security guard will be with you twenty-four seven, and we'll stay in close contact as we continue working towards a resolution. To be honest, this case is a very unique and challenging one that has baffled my whole team...none of us will give up until we find an answer for you," he assured me.

It was tough saying good-bye to my parents, but I knew that they would visit us frequently in New York City, and we would be back to the acreage often, especially with the first grandchild on the way in six months. Christian and I debated whether to have our wedding quickly, before I got too large with the baby, or to wait until after he or she was born. We opted to wait and take our time planning the wedding we wanted and had dreamed of. And I needed to focus on recovering from my ordeal.

I wanted to start teaching flute, so that would fill some of my time, along with practicing as I was used to a regimen of several hours a day before my abduction. I needed to keep up my skills in case an orchestral position came up in the New York Philharmonic with Christian, but I knew I needed other focuses as well. Preparing for the baby would be a huge focus, my mom kept reminding me. We would be selling Christian's apartment and moving into our own place well before the baby arrived. Despite the fears I had, I was also able to get excited about our new lives, the baby, and living in a new city. As we drove from the acreage, accompanied by security as always, I shed tears of joy for having escaped a situation that could have consumed my entire life. I was finally starting anew with the true love of my life.

*****

Only a few days after our arrival in New York, Christian had to return to his orchestral practices and performances. I was busier than I'd imagined with listing the apartment, hunting for a new place, and practicing. I opted to put off the idea of teaching, as I was hesitant to explain why a security guard sat outside my door at all times. I couldn't risk putting any students in jeopardy until Richard was found, dead or alive. My security guard, Josh O'Brian, was a muscular, Irish man who was calm yet alert. On his time off he was replaced by Gordon Brown, a native New Yorker who was more talkative, but also made me feel safe and protected. When I went out one of them was always with me, so we got to know one another.

My pregnancy began showing and I started to feel the baby kick when I was about five months along. I felt a bond with this little being and was constantly relieved that I had made the decision to go through with this. It was as if Christian was the true father, as he was genuinely excited as well. We opted not to find out the gender, as we sat having breakfast in bed one day.

"Should we find out what it is?" I asked. Christian's hand was on my stomach trying to feel the baby kick.

"I like the idea of a surprise," he said, then added with a smile, "but we can still come up with a really unique gender neutral name...like one of our musical terms, maybe Legato?" he joked.

"Very funny. I agree, a surprise is good. I mean, not the type of surprises we've been through this year, but a nice, sweet, newborn baby surprise. I can't wait!" I said, squeezing his hand and feeling so grateful to be together on this relaxing Sunday morning.

*****

My parents, sister and close friends all came out for visits. We found a lovely three bedroom apartment, with a cozy living room complete with a practice area, as well as a small office and a dining room. We moved there when I was six months pregnant. It had beautiful hardwood floors and it was fun to furnish and decorate, especially the baby's room, which we painted a pale yellow.

The anxiety never fully left, but I noticed myself begin to relax and put Richard out of my mind for longer chunks of time. The FBI had been calling weekly to update me on what little progress they'd made; each call left me feeling paranoid and was like reopening a wound that had somewhat healed. I told them I appreciated their hard work and updates, but asked them to only report significant developments. After that I rarely heard anything.

Christian and I were deeply in love and now that we were back together we spent every moment we could with each other. We went on long walks through Central Park, talking about the past but also the future dreams and plans we had for our family. We would cuddle as often as we could, his hand resting on my belly to feel the baby kick. It took me some time to feel comfortable sexually, and I attended trauma counseling weekly as well as a support group for people with post-traumatic stress disorder. As bad as my abduction was, hearing some of the other women's survival stories helped me put my life in better perspective.

We planned our wedding for the fall, when the baby would be about eight months old. That would give us time to adjust to being parents, and me time to hopefully get my figure back. I felt as big as a house, having gained almost forty pounds.

*****

My water broke in the middle of the night two days before I was due. "Christian, I'm soaking wet. I think this baby's coming!" I exclaimed. He was awake immediately, excitedly timing the contractions and then rushing me to the hospital. He never left my side, and although the labor was agonizing it luckily only lasted a few hours. I screamed as I made the final push.

"It's a girl!" said the doctor. When he brought her to my chest I was consumed with love and joy. Her head had soft, reddish blond hair and her skin was as smooth as velvet. It was too early to tell if she had any resemblance, besides the light hair, to Richard, but it was clear she had my nose and lips.

"She's so lovely," Christian whispered, with tears in his eyes. He was ecstatic and bonded immediately with his little sweetheart. We named her Sophie Maria and in those moments my ordeal was completely forgotten, as was the security guard stationed outside of the delivery room.

Sophie was healthy, weighing in at seven pounds, twelve ounces. We were only in the hospital for a little over a day and were overjoyed to have Sophie home with us. Flowers and gifts started arriving in droves and it was great having my mom stay with us to help out in those early days. Our security guard, Josh, would greet all the deliveries, and loved seeing our new little girl. He had two children of his own and it was funny seeing such a large, tough guy cooing and making baby noises to a tiny newborn.

"Wow, this is a large one!" he said, struggling through the door with a gift basket wrapped in cellophane that must have been three feet tall. My mom and I pulled off the light pink cellophane and inside was a large assortment of beautiful baby toys as well an 18 karat gold child's bracelet and an envelope that, to our shock, contained ten crisp one thousand dollar bills. I froze and held my breath.

"My goodness, this is unusual," commented my mom, while flipping through the bills that I had dropped back into the basket with trembling hands.

"Mom, it's from *him*," I whispered, my heart racing, fear gripping my entire body.

"Oh darling," she said, putting her arm around my back, "that isn't for certain. What if..."

"Mom, there's no card."

"Yes, there is, right here," said my mom, pulling a small pink envelope from the lower part of the basket. I closed my eyes, not wanting to see if I was correct. Again I held my breath. "It says: *To my little girl, Sophie. I love you very much and our family will be reunited one day. Love, Daddy.*" My mom hugged me tightly as I burst into sobs and could barely catch my breath. Christian rushed over to see what was going on.

"Oh my God," he said, dropping the note to the floor to embrace me tenderly, as Sophie started crying from her nearby bassinet.

The FBI came and took the basket, analyzing its contents and investigating the order and delivery process thoroughly. But, as usual, Richard had covered all of his tracks, as there wasn't a loose end to be found. Agent Kent said that we couldn't be one hundred percent sure that this meant he was alive, as Richard could have delegated this task in his will, but that it did point to increased odds that he was in hiding and we needed to ramp-up security and continue being vigilant. "Had the note been in his writing, we would be certain, but we cannot trace who typed it," said Agent Kent, with frustration.

*****

We went on with our lives as best we could in the following weeks and months. Sophie was an easy baby and we loved being parents. Her eyes turned into a combination of green and blue that seemed to change color depending on the lighting and her outfits. She loved listening to our music, both to the high tones of my flute and the lower, rich tones of Christian's cello. No matter how she was conceived, I knew that this child was meant to be part of our lives. When she was three months old, we took Sophie on a lovely spring picnic in Central Park, now flanked with two security guards who stationed themselves inconspicuously near the trees around us.

"Cadence, we have *so much* to be grateful for. We're together, we have this beautiful baby girl and we're getting married in less than five months," Christian said, as we nibbled on cheese and grapes as our daughter slept peacefully on a blanket between us. He leaned forward and planted a soft kiss on my lips and did the same to Sophie's fuzzy, strawberry blond head.

"We do...we certainly do," I said, smiling warmly at him. I turned to glance at the security guards, as it was now an ingrained habit to always know where they were. As my eyes scanned the beautiful park and fell on the walking path, I tensed as I noticed a tall figure in the distance. He stood next to an ice cream cart that was far enough away that I could only make out his distant image, but close enough that I could recognize the signs...his tall form, his perfect posture, a black hat and sunglasses masking further recognition. But I knew. I froze, torn between screaming and keeping quiet as I knew he would get away in an instant.

"Cadence, what is it?" Christian asked anxiously, trying to locate what I was staring at. Just then the tall form walked quickly away, turned around a bend and was out of sight almost immediately.

"Josh!" I screamed, knowing he was the closest security guard and that only one of them could leave us. "Richard was just there beside the ice cream cart…black hat and sunglasses…he just walked around the bend!" Josh sprinted away as Gordon hurried over to us. He called the police immediately. Josh and the police searched Central Park but to no avail. That spring afternoon erased any doubt in my mind that Richard White was alive and well. He'd somehow miraculously survived, and was back to his old habits of stalking me and now little Sophie too.

"We could relocate you both with new identities if you'd feel safer that way," offered Agent Kent, as we spoke with him on speakerphone the next day. "We fear that this will continue to be a game of cat and mouse. He's successfully disappeared altogether from society and is dead on paper as far as any records are concerned, yet continues to elude the nation's top agents. Even with the significant rewards for any leads, we are hitting constant dead ends."

"No, he would find us regardless," I said, shaking my head. "We have great opportunities here and can't live our lives hiding and running," I said, squeezing Christian's hand as I protectively gripped the handle of Sophie's sleeper seat beside me.

"I totally agree with Cadence. As long as you can keep providing security we would much rather live our lives here," added Christian. We had discussed these options at length in the fear-filled hours following the incident in Central Park.

"Absolutely, we'll continue with two guards for the foreseeable future as we continue the investigation."

*****

When I thought about Richard in the weeks that followed, my feelings of anger were also complimented by feeling sadness for him. I knew that seeing what he believed was *his* family with another man must constantly torment him. Yet he was not making any bold moves to try and get past our security. Given his means, I knew, deep inside, that if he wanted to snatch Sophie and me that he had the power to get through any level of security. Maybe, I thought (and prayed), he'd finally given up and other than occasional sightings we'd have little to worry about.

Richard had taken a lot from me, the most important of which was my freedom. The freedom to walk my baby to the park, just the two of us, was not an option. The freedom to have time with Christian, Sophie and I that didn't involve two security guards in the vicinity, witnessing our private family moments, was also not an option. But rather than let bitterness consume me, I also had to think about what Richard had given me…a beautiful, healthy baby daughter. He also taught me that I was a survivor and that I was resilient beyond what I thought possible during my captivity.

I sat in the nursery after having fed Sophie and put her back in her crib. I was now wide awake and decided to read a few pieces of mail in the soft glow of the nursery lamp. I sat in the gliding chair, my feet on the ottoman, flipping through the mail: a letter from a musicians' association, an unsolicited application for a new credit card and a pale pink envelope. This was odd because now that Sophie was almost four months old the baby cards had tapered off. The envelope was addressed to me, another anomaly as most were addressed to both Christian and I. I opened the envelope and pulled out a pale pink sheet of paper…a letter from *him*.

My breathing and heart rate sped up immediately as I read the words:

*Dear Cadence,*

*It has taken me this long to put into words what I have been feeling. Your betrayal hurt more than the stab wound and burns that I endured that day. I would rather have died knowing you loved me, than lived on knowing you left me to die. As fate would have it, I survived and am trying to forgive you for the sake of our daughter. Sophie is beautiful and I cannot thank you enough for bringing her into this world.*

*I can see that you are happy – that he has taken the role of loving husband and father. I would give anything to have you and Sophie as my own. But I know taking you would lead to the same outcome – you constantly trying to escape from me. I have decided that until Sophie is old enough to understand that I am her real father, I will keep my distance. But when that time comes, she will know who I am and how much I love her.*

*I will look in on you two from time to time to make sure
you are doing well, and I will put money aside in an
account for Sophie so she never has to worry about money
for the rest of her life.*

*Cadence, despite what you did to me, I cannot stop loving
you and our daughter. I hope before I meet Sophie one
day that you will explain to her who I am and the fact
that I wanted her more than anything and would never
hurt her. Please don't portray me as a monster but as a
husband and father who deeply loves his two ladies.*

*Love Always to you both,*
*Richard*

I sat and re-read the letter many times, my emotions switching between fear and sadness, tears silently trickling down my cheeks as Sophie slept soundly. I thought about waking up Christian or calling Agent Kent to pass on this information, but instead I folded the letter and replaced it in the envelope and placed it in Sophie's small chest of keepsakes kept in the top shelf of her closet. There would be no way to trace it, I knew that for sure. And the letter implied that Richard would leave us alone, at least for many years to come. Could I really ask for more from this strange and troubled man? My life would never be completely my own, but I was grateful to be where I was, surrounded by the love of my family.

"Good-bye, Richard," I whispered, as I locked the keepsake box, placed it in the closet and walked to the crib to stare once more at my sleeping daughter. Unbeknownst to me, a small micro-camera installed very carefully in the nursery wall decor enabled Richard to watch us and say his own good night.

## The End

CPSIA information can be obtained
at www.ICGtesting.com
Printed in the USA
LVOW10s1510211216

518286LV00002B/225/P